AN
ANTHOLOGY
OF
SHORT
STORIES

May 18 2021

To my good friend Susan
with best wishes
and love.

George Katsikis

AN ANTHOLOGY OF SHORT STORIES

George Karnikis

Author Publisher
Eastsound Washington State

This book is dedicated to my maternal

Grandfather Nikitas Papanikitas

My hero

Contents

THE TREASURES OF PARTHENON

A Mystery Story

Without a doubt this was one of the best retirement parties Gregoris had attended and this one was for him. There were many friends and relatives at his party along with several of his customers all wishing him good luck with his new life as a retiree. But that was a bitter pill for Gregoris to swallow; he loved his job and he had mixed feelings about retiring. On the way home Martha said, "Now we can travel overseas and not worry about coming home on time." "I guess so."

Gregoris was a good driver, but on that fateful night, as they were driving through an intersection, a drunk driver hit them. Their car was totaled and both of them ended up in the hospital; Martha's injuries were not very serious and after a few days she was able to go home, but Gregoris went into a coma.

"Why are you up so early, you don't have to go to work today, remember? You are now officially retired." "I know, but I can't stay in bed any longer." Martha knew her man; he was a workaholic and seldom missed a day at the office. Gregoris Takanakos was the first one at his desk and the last one to leave. Real Estate was his business and he was good at it. Left to his own devices he would have kept working until he dropped dead, but his wife Martha, and the children, convinced him that it was time to quit working and spend more time with the family and grandchildren.

It's not that he really needed the money; he had sold enough real estate in Athens and made enough to last him two lifetimes.

For the last thirty years he worked for one of the biggest real estate companies in Athens and loved his work. His office was on the top floor of a large building and from his vantage point Gregoris could see the Parthenon in all its glory, and he never ceased to admire its splendid architecture. He knew he would miss the familiar faces and places, associated with his employment; but most of all the beautiful view of the Parthenon. That's why, before he quit his job, he purchased an older but well kept house in the Keramikos area overlooking the Acropolis and the Parthenon. The house came with a large backyard with enough room to plant a garden.

Martha liked the house too; it came with all the modern conveniences, and she also added another large guestroom for friends and especially for her grandchildren. Gregoris wasn't much of a sports fan but loved gardening. It was quite a switch for him from office work, to being retired, but to be so close to the Parthenon, it was like working in his office. As he was preparing the ground; in his mind he was already planning a list of different flowers and vegetables to be planted in his new garden.

The Find

One early morning as Gregoris worked the ground, the blade of his shovel hit something hard—"Not another rock," he thought to himself. But it wasn't a rock; it was a piece of marble and as he dug carefully around it with his trowel, it was getting bigger. It appeared to be an oblong or rectangular piece of marble about four inches thick by four feet wide and so far, five feet long. The right upper corner was broken but covered with hardened clay, he carefully moved the clay and there was a hole large enough to put a flashlight through and see inside.

What he saw in there was unbelievable; there were marble steps leading deep into the darkness. Gregoris was now obsessed with his find; he wanted to know how far down those steps went, and what was at the end of them. He knew that the right thing to do would be to report his find to the proper authorities and have them do the excavation. But he also knew too well he would be dealing with a slow moving bureaucracy and it could take years before they excavated the site. Gregoris decided not to say anything to anybody, including his wife Martha; because she couldn't keep a secret.

Gregoris devised an ingenious way to work on his find without Martha or other people knowing what he was doing; first— he waited for Martha's two week vacation. Every spring Martha and her sister Sophia visited Loutraki, a city about two hours drive from Athens. There they stayed for two weeks at a time at a resort known for its therapeutic water. Martha and Sophia suffered from arthritis and bathing in that water alleviated their pain temporarily; they also caught up with all the happenings in their families.

Soon after Martha left home he covered the hole with a ¼" sheet of metal and then he put top soil on it and planted his first bed with lettuce, onions, mustard, and carrots. Then he dug a ten foot corridor four feet deep by three feet wide and covered it with another ¼" sheet of metal and put more soil on it. At the end of the corridor he dug a deeper hole and put in it a small ladder; then he placed a compost bin on top of the hole. Now any time he wanted to work on his project Gregoris simply moved the bin, stepped down in the hole, and placed the bin above him. Gregoris spread all the excavated top soil all around the garden and since it was a new garden nobody suspected anything unusual.

The last thing he did was to bring underground power into the corridor and now he could see much better without being seen by his neighbors. With a bright light in the corridor Gregoris now could work more easily but although he could not be seen by anybody from above, he could be heard. So he was careful to keep noise at the minimum. He worked carefully with a small trowel until he freed what appeared to be a marble door which was kept in place with two huge hinges mounted one on the very top and the other at the very bottom. Then he used a crowbar to open it; he inserted the tip of the bar in the upper right hole of the marble and slowly pried the door moving the bar up and down until it was wide open.

Discovery

Gregoris wanted to go down the steps right away but he refrained from doing so until he was adequately prepared. He went out of his foxhole and placed the bin over the hole. After his eyes adjusted to the bright light, he looked around him and he was satisfied that his secret was well camouflaged. The vegetables he had planted over the covered hole had started to grow and the rest of the garden looked prepared enough for more planting.

He made a list of items he would need before he went down those steps again; the list consisted of: 2 flashlights with extra batteries, his cell phone with an extra charged battery, a 200' ¼" rope and a few tools, food and water to last him for three days, warm clothing, a camcorder and a first aid kit. Martha was due to come home in two days and he needed to go down there before she arrived.

The next morning he got up early and had a good breakfast and then he took his thermos with hot coffee with him and before long he was in the corridor heading for the steps. Gregoris pulled the power cord as far as he could and then he turned on one of his flashlights and started to descend the steps. He secured his two hundred foot rope on a protruding root and kept going down. He had to be careful because the steps were wet and slippery. He fought his way through many webs with a cane in his hand.

At the end of the steps there was a puddle of water; he checked the depth with the cane, it was safe to step on. Gregoris walked on for a few feet always checking the water with the cane until he came to what appeared to be another door only this one was made either of copper or bronze.

It was a massive door and Gregoris could see that it would take a lot of effort to open it. At the bottom of the door there was about one foot of mud holding the door shut; he used his little shovel to remove it, and when he was done with it the water started to slowly drain from under the door. Then he used his crowbar to pry the door open but it wouldn't budge. He looked around for any locking mechanism and then he noticed a horizontal bar, like a deadbolt which kept the door locked; but there was no locking device anywhere on the door. It was amazing how solid the door was after hundreds of years. Gregoris knew there had to be a secret mechanism somewhere—but where? By now all the water had drained away and all that remained was mud, and lots of it.

Gregoris thought the lock mechanism was either under the floor or in the walls. He excluded the ceiling because it was built with large size marble tiles. He wasn't sure of the floor because it was covered with mud. Could it be somewhere in the walls? That

7

could be possible because the tiles were much smaller. He used the wooden handle of his hammer and tapped several of the tiles closest to the door, and listened for a hollow sound. He tapped first on the right wall and couldn't detect any hollow sound; then he tapped on the left wall with the same results.

Then he tapped on one of the tiles closest to the door and it sounded different; he tapped again and again until he was sure there was a hollow sound. Could there be something hidden behind that tile which could unlock the door? Gregoris was determined to find out and started to move the tile, always being careful not to damage it. He worked until he had used both spare batteries, and now the light of his second flashlight was getting low.

He thought it would be prudent to come back with more batteries and perhaps larger flashlights. He traced his way back to the surface following the rope he had laid down earlier. Outside it was very bright and he found it necessary to cover his eyes with his hand until he went inside the house. He quickly put on a pair of sunglasses to protect his eyes from the intense light that was coming from the two windows in the kitchen.

It was 12:00 o'clock; he had spent four hours down there, but Gregoris was satisfied with what he had found so far. He had a feeling that there was a secret lock or something which would unlock that door. He made a sandwich and had a glass of orange juice, then listened to several messages; one of them was from Martha telling him she would be home tomorrow night. It was a clear day and from the looks of it—it promised to be a hot one.

He stepped out and walked in the garden. It was quiet; he looked at the bin and realized that he was the only one that knew what was under there. He smiled, he liked it that way. At a hardware store he bought two larger flashlights and several more batteries and before long he was down there again trying to dislodge the tile. After working at it for half an hour or so, he managed to remove it undamaged then he put his flashlight in the hole and looked inside. Gregoris had guessed right; inside the hole was a bronze el-shaped bar about an inch in diameter. Now all he had to do was to push the handle-like bar opposite from the door and that should unlock it. Or it should have done so several hundred years ago; but when he pushed the handle it wouldn't budge. Gregoris tried many different ways to push the handle back, but nothing had worked. He decided to use the hammer although he knew he was taking a chance of breaking the bar handle.

He started tapping on it gently until he loosened it a bit, then he tried prying it, success; it opened with a clanging sound. Now the bar was completely pulled away from the latch. Gregoris put the crowbar between the jamb and the door and pried a few times. Finally the door opened with a screeching sound; he stepped inside and looked around. There was another corridor; he could feel fresh air coming from somewhere. He walked to the end of it about fifteen feet or so on the right side. And there above him was a vent that was still working after all this time. On the floor there were drains where all the water from the other side of the door had gone. The corridor was about eight feet wide and the ceiling was very high, about ten feet. The floor was wet but not flooded; now Gregoris walked to the left side of the corridor.

He walked for about thirty feet or so and then there was another stair way; this time going upwards. He counted the steps; there were fifteen, or half of the descending steps. At the top there was another door, but not as heavy as the first one. There was a round handle affixed to it; Gregoris didn't even try to open it by hand. He knew it wouldn't open easily; he put the crowbar through the round handle and pried up and to the left. First gently then harder, after pushing and prying a few times; it slowly yielded and finally opened.

The Underground Temple

There must have been cross ventilation from somewhere because the air wasn't as stifling anymore; it was dry and cool and he felt good being there. Gregoris turned on his second flashlight, and now with more light he looked around him. It was a huge place like a temple with large marble columns almost like the ones in the Parthenon. Gregoris directed his flashlights to something big at the end of the room; as he was approaching it he realized he was looking at a portion of a statue or perhaps a bust but whatever he was looking at, it was huge.

There were other items all of them covered with a thick blanket of dust; it was difficult to distinguish clearly what they were with the inadequate light. Next to the statue, there was a pile of something which looked like a small pyramid, Gregoris went closer and touched it; it felt hard and cool. With his forefinger he cleared a small area and when he directed the light closer; there was a golden glow emanating from it. Gregoris instantly realized he had found gold, and lots of it. He rested his back against a column and thought hard for a moment. He had accidentally discovered an unimaginable treasure which had been kept in there for hundreds or perhaps thousands of years.

At some point in Athens' turbulent history the forefathers of this great city found it necessary to hide their valuables in a safe place like this. Now Gregoris was the only person who knew this place; what was he to do? Should he alert the authorities? And most of all, could he trust this government with the gold and all the artifacts kept safe all these years from Athens' enemies? There was one thing he had to do before he decided what his next move would be; he had to come back with more lights, perhaps with a long power cord and find everything that could be found there. With that in mind Gregoris left his secret place and went up to the surface and into his house. There he made another list of the items he was going to need for the remaining discoveries.

Gregoris installed a proper underground wire, long enough to reach his secret place. Along with a few extra tools, an electric panel, enough light bulbs and a powerful vacuum cleaner, he also brought the latest electronic gear to catalog his finds. He was always careful not to be seen by anybody when he was going into the secret tunnel. Gregoris made sure to bring most of the items he needed for his project inside today, because Martha was due to come tonight and he didn't want her to see any of it.

It took him a couple of hours to install the panel and a few outlets and before long he had, for the first time, enough light to work easily in that dark place. Gregoris could take a better look now at his surroundings; but first before he disturbed anything at all he went over with his video camera and registered everything in detail. He also took hundreds of close-up pictures including his footprints. Now that he had everything registered undisturbed in his camcorder, Gregoris started to vacuum every item small or great; always being careful not to disturb or damage it. He knew for sure no one could hear the noise or see the light, especially with the door closed.

When Gregoris had finished inspecting what he had found, he could not believe his own eyes. Here was a treasure worth billions of dollars kept in this secret place for hundreds or perhaps thousands of years from the intruders who ravaged and damaged most of what was sacred and valuable of this great city of Athens.

But this place had kept its valuable secret until now. Gregoris felt the weight of the responsibility on his shoulders and he took a minute to think what to do next, over a cup of coffee.

He made a list of everything he had discovered in this sacred place; he started first with the description and the dimension of what appeared to be an underground temple. Then he went over each item with his camcorder describing what he was seeing. Gregoris started with the huge bust which he had seen and recognized as the bust of the statue of the Goddess Athena the protector of the city of Athens which was thought to have been destroyed a long time ago. He proceeded with the other parts of the statue which was divided into four different pieces. Gregoris realized the process of cataloging every item could take weeks or even months. But he was prepared to do what needed to be done in order to make sure that nothing was stolen when and if he decided to report his find to the authorities.

Before he started the cataloging process he went over what he had found; in addition to the statue of Athena, there were many other items. There were: four pyramids of gold, each pyramid was ten square feet at the bottom by approximately eight to ten feet high, there were six pyramids of silver of the same dimensions which occupied the area from wall to wall or sixty feet across. The dimensions of the temple were approximately 60'x40' so the rest of the area was occupied by many different sized statues and many other piles stashed carefully above ground; like thousands of scrolls, of which several appeared to be damaged.

Gregoris did not dust those scrolls fearing further damage. There were many ceramic tablets again stashed carefully above the floor; Gregoris carefully cleaned a small part of one of the top tablets and saw the name ΑΙΣΧΥΛΟΣ written in archaic Attic Greek language. Aeschylus was a well-known playwright and soldier. (He was born in Eleusis in 526 BC a city close to Athens and died in Sicily in 456 BC.)

Gregoris thought to himself if all those ceramic tablets, and what remained of the scrolls contained writings of everyday life and plays of those ancient years in Athens they would be more valuable than all the gold and silver found in the temple. He started the arduous process of cataloging everything in detail.

Martha was happy to see the new garden and glad to see Gregoris gardening; however she couldn't understand where all that new soil had come from. Gregoris told her that he had to turn over the soil many times that's why it looked so plentiful to her. Martha wasn't much of a gardener so that was a good enough explanation for her. He stopped going down to his secret place for a few days and concentrated on the garden; he planted the rest of the available area with more vegetables and flowers.

His next chance to resume his cataloging would be when Martha left home for her book reading club. In fact Martha was a very busy woman. In addition to her book club she volunteered a few hours every week at the library and she never missed her bridge game. And that worked well with Gregoris because Martha's busy schedule gave him ample time to work undisturbed in his secret place.

Gregoris worked for many months until he cataloged everything except the scrolls for fear of damaging them; but his guess-estimate was that there were about eight hundred to one thousand scrolls altogether. After he was done cataloging; he very carefully boxed and moved one bar of gold, one bar of silver, two small statues, and most important the little statue the goddess held in her right hand, one golden coin and one silver coin. He then hid them in an apartment in Athens which he had rented especially for this reason. He used an assumed name. He did all that in order to prove at a later time that he indeed had discovered this treasure. Then Gregoris closed both doors but left the wiring in there; at the other end of the wire he removed the fuse and the wire from the panel and hid the rest of the wire in the tunnel. Next he put another piece of 1/4" sheet of metal over the hole and covered it with soil then he planted grass and finally he put the compost bin over it.

Gregoris decided not to go back in there until he had made up his mind whether to report his find or not. In the meantime he downloaded all his cataloging into his computer and put a title over it, "Lost Greco-Roman treasures" A novel of ancient times. And then he gave credit to various museums and encyclopedias for the pictures he had supposedly downloaded. The last thing he did was to upload all the information into DVD discs, and then deleted anything that had to do with his treasure in the computer. Then he deposited three DVDs in the safe deposit of his bank; the remaining two he hid in his office. Gregoris relaxed knowing that his secret was safe underground and above. Now he had to think hard what would be his next move.

For weeks Gregoris was undecided whether he should report his discovery to the authorities or not. Any time he thought of uncovering his secret, he thought of how good a job the Ancient Athenians had done in safeguarding their treasure and culture from their enemies, and he had second thoughts about it. Now it was his responsibility to decide if this would be the right time for the world at large to know. Gregoris tried to think what the ancient Athenians would have done under the present circumstances. It must have been a great need for them to have hidden their treasure so long ago. Perhaps they knew their country was about to be taken over by a more powerful enemy. So they waited for a time when their country would be free again before exposing their secret. But for some reason they died and took their secret to their graves. Now their beloved Athens is free again and she is the Capital of all Greece; wouldn't this be the right time?

Gregoris doubted the honesty of several recent governments; would this new found treasure be safe in their hands? Or would they steal and misuse such an important inheritance? This is what Gregoris was thinking while driving that morning in an area of heavy traffic in Athens. When driving through a green light he barely avoided being hit by another driver. Gregoris was shaken to the point he couldn't drive anymore. He stopped by his favorite coffee house and ordered a cup of coffee. He thought to himself, "That was a close call, one which could have easily taken my life."

He thought of the consequences that would follow should he have been killed. Of course he would be missed by Martha and the children and grandchildren. Then he thought of his underground secret. It would be safe for a while or until Martha sold the house or passed away; then the place would pass to someone else. Sooner or later someone would discover the metal sheets, then the tunnel, and then the temple with all the treasures. Would that person or persons be as honest as himself and be good stewards of this rich inheritance destined for Greece?

Gregoris somehow doubted that, and in a way it propelled him to resolve his predicament sooner than he was prepared to. He thought of the present government which had just replaced a corrupt government that had left the country broke and unable to meet its responsibilities. The present Prime Minister was a good man but unable to fulfill promises he had made to his constituents. Wouldn't this be the appropriate time for Gregoris to help his country? Perhaps now would be the right time, but could he trust the rest of his government? Somehow he didn't think so, and he was struggling to come up with a way to help Greece and at the same time safeguard her treasures.

For many days now Gregoris was working hard to find a solution to his dilemma and slowly but surely came up with an idea which met his goal. A few weeks earlier the office staff had asked Gregoris and Martha if they wanted to join them on a weekend tour to Italy for the coming Easter Holiday; at the time Martha wasn't interested but Gregoris wanted to go, so on Easter he joined his friends and they all went to Venice for the weekend.

It was from Venice Gregoris put his plan in motion. The first thing he did was to make his secret known to the whole world by sending copies of his find to museums and the world media through the Italian post. He sent the first copy by special delivery to the Prime Minister of Greece, Mr. Papaliguris, and waited for his response. He knew he would have to wait a while until his parcel went through a special inspection. He also knew that most recipients would assume it was a hoax and would not bother to reply; but he was almost certain that some of the smaller television channels, hungry for new material, might put it on.

He didn't have to wait long; one of the smaller Greek channels broadcasted it with the title "True or Hoax"? And then it showed the bust of goddess Athena and several other statues and of course the gold and silver. Then it was shown by the larger channels and before long it became big news all over the world. Gregoris addressed a letter to the Prime Minister of Greece and said,

"Dear Prime Minister Papaliguris,

I am sure that by now you have seen or heard about the treasure found somewhere in Greece by the title "True or Hoax"? Let me assure you sir, it is not a hoax! It is a fact; I know the place where this treasure is kept and I am willing to show it to you. The reason I made those DVDs available to the world at large was to make sure that everybody knows in detail what the treasure consists of, so nothing is stolen or misused.

I came to this secret place accidentally and realized that it was kept safe there for hundreds or thousands of years. It became my responsibility to make sure that this Greek inheritance went to the right people. It's not that I don't trust you or your government, but human nature being what it is there may be some unscrupulous people out there who cannot be trusted.

So I have taken a few precautionary measures in order to secure safe delivery of this treasure to you and the appropriate authorities. I have hidden in another place some of the treasure. It is kept in a very safe and air conditioned place. I took this action in order to prove to the rest of the world that I am telling the truth, in case someone decides at a later time to declare it as a hoax and hide the truth from the Greek people. In that case I will call the media and show them the rest of the treasure.

Before I direct you where the rest of the treasure is hidden, there are a few things I expect you to do. I want you and those who are authorized by you, and who will eventually safe guard this treasure, to go inside the place where the treasure is kept and be videotaped beside the statues, the gold and silver and say something about this discovery. Then broadcast the videotape to the Greek people and the world at large. Once this is done I will personally take you to the rest of the treasure. Mr. Prime Minister, I hope you realize that I do all this for the safe-keeping of the inheritance which was meant to go back to the Greek nation and be used accordingly and solely for its security.

Sincerely,

Anonymous

After Gregoris sent all the DVDs to various institutions, the media, and to the Greek Prime Minister, he went back home and had a serious discussion with his wife Martha. He told her about his discovery and that it was under the garden and also that he was the man who sent all those DVDs all over the world. Martha looked at him aghast and said,

"What shall we do now, Gregoris?" "I think we shall go abroad for a while, and tell the Prime Minister where the treasure is hidden." "Why do we have to leave our house?" "Because I don't want us to be found until certain things happen, for our security and for the security of the treasure as well." "Where are we going to go?" "You always wanted to see those cathedrals in England; here is your chance." "How long are we going to be away?" "Until I see the Prime Minister videotaped next to the statue of goddess Athena and the treasure; which I think will happen very quickly."

Right before Gregoris and Martha left the airport Gregoris sent another special delivery letter to the Prime Minister from Athens; in which he said,

"Mr. Papaliguris, if you have received my letter and you are still interested to find the hidden treasure, then find an excuse to have a conference with the media and use the phrase "Greece will always go forward." That will be my cue that you have received my letter and then I will send you information leading you to the treasure.

Sincerely,

Anonymous

Gregoris and Martha were following the Greek news daily on their laptop; by now most people assumed the DVDs were a clever hoax and the media stopped broadcasting them. Three days later there was an announcement through the main television channels in Greece that the Prime Minister would make a statement on the status of the economy of the country at 9:00 p.m. Greek time; Gregoris and Martha were anxiously waiting for the 9:00 o'clock news. The Prime Minister, true to his word, addressed the Greek people. He started by reminding the people how important the coming election was for all Greeks and to go out and vote, or some undesirable people would make policy for them.

Then he spoke briefly about the economy and said they were on the right path to overcome their fiscal difficulties. There was as usual a question and answer period and then he concluded by saying, "Greece will always go forward." That was the cue for Gregoris and Martha. Upon hearing that phrase Gregoris sent another letter to the Prime Minister with directions to the treasure; he put a fictitious return address and that was it.

Gregoris and Martha did their best to make sure the treasure went to the right hands; if everything went well, in a few days they hoped to see another press conference by the Prime Minister; this time announcing that the treasure was not a hoax after all. In the meantime they checked out of their hotel and for a few days they were traveling throughout England and Scotland and living on trains in first class cabins. Gregoris checked his laptop daily hoping to hear the Prime Minister.

A week later one of Gregoris' and Martha's neighbors called their son Michael Takanakos and said, "There is a whole army at your parents' house and some of them are digging in their back yard and are making a mess of it." Michael was at his parents' house within the hour talking to the authorities asking them what they were doing there. First they wouldn't even let him go close to the house but after they were convinced he was indeed Gregoris' and Martha's son they let him talk to the man who was in charge of the operation. Michael said to the man, "What are you doing to my parents' house?" The man said, "My name is Mitsos; do you know where your parents are?

"There traveling somewhere in Europe, why do you ask?" He asked him to wait for a while as he answered an incoming phone call. The man talked to someone for a long time and then he said to Michael,

"I can't tell you right now but you will soon know; but for now go home and say nothing to anybody and if you get in touch with your parents ask them to call me." Then he gave Michael his card. Mitsos Karthakos was in charge of the archaeological department of Greece; Michael was impressed but confused.

Martha was getting tired living on trains for the last seven days, her arthritis had flared up causing extreme pain all over her body and she wanted to go to a hotel and then go home. Gregoris empathized with her but he was afraid they would be arrested the minute they registered in any hotel. So they were both happy to hear the Prime Minister had a very important announcement to make to the Greek people during the news hour. Gregoris and Martha were glued to their laptop watching the leader of their country. As it was agreed, he and his staff were at the place he knew so well; next to the bust of goddess Athena and the gold and silver. The Prime Minister started by saying,

"Ladies and Gentlemen, during the last few years our country has been hit with fires, earthquakes, and lately with a very bad economy. We have navigated successfully through all those misfortunes but inevitably they have left a bad taste in our mouths. Today I am here to announce some good news for a change. Most of you must remember a few days ago the media all over the world was showing all those pictures of gold, silver, and statues, and especially the bust of goddess Athena that were supposedly found somewhere in our country.

Those pictures ran for a few days on most channels and then after a few days they were considered as a good hoax and they were taken off the air. (All this time the camera was zeroed in on the Prime Minister's face but now the cameras started to show the area from where he was talking). Well I am here to tell you that it wasn't a hoax; the treasure, as you can clearly see, is true. The man, who to this day still remains anonymous, has been telling us all along the truth. We don't mind that he made the secret known all over the world, we are proud to show the world the inheritance our ancestors left for us. We will now pay all our bills and start a program to rebuild our infrastructure all over Greece.

We will build a special museum to house the statue of goddess Athena in all her glory, as well as the rest of the new-found statues. I am told from those who specialize in antiquities that the scrolls and ceramics which contain our country's literature far outweigh the gold and silver you see here. We are willing to share once more the new found knowledge of literature and art with the rest of the world and show them again the glory of Greece.

The Prime Minister's speech was aired in Greece and all over the world. The cameras showed over and over the newfound treasure. Outside cameras were showing the police and the army guarding the area. Gregoris and Martha were very happy. Gregoris' plan had gone well and they were making preparations for going back home. Gregoris called Mr. Karthakos at the ministry of archaeology and talked with him for a long time. He said, "Mr. Karthakos, I am Gregoris Takanakos I believe that you have talked to my son and by now you know all about me.

My wife Martha and I are on a train on our way to London as we talk; I am anxious to come home because Martha is not feeling well and also I want to show you the rest of the hidden treasure." Mr. Karthakos was happy to finally get in touch with Gregoris and said, "Mr. Takanakos I am so happy to talk with you and would like to see you as soon as possible in Athens. However it would not be safe or appropriate for you to travel with the usual transportation. Please give me your cell -phone number and I will call you soon and give you directions for a better way to come home." Thirty minutes later Mr. Karthakos called back and said, "Mr. Takanakos when you arrive in London please stay at the arriving and departure area and say nothing to anyone as to who you are; I will send someone from the Greek embassy to get you as soon as you arrive." Martha said to Gregoris, "I am glad we are getting out of here; I am sick and tired living in trains for so many days."

They didn't have to wait long; ten minutes after they arrived, a young lady from the Greek Embassy approached them and said in Greek, "Hello, are you Mr. and Mrs. Takanakos?" Gregoris said, "Yes we are; are you from the Greek Embassy?" "Yes, my name is Tina and I am here to give you a ride to the Embassy; please follow me."

Outside at a ten minute parking area was a fancy black limousine with Greek flags on its front fenders. Gregoris and Martha were whisked into the car which took off right away. They sat in the middle section of the vehicle and the young lady drove the car. It was a comfortable seat and Martha's arthritic body felt relief. After a few minutes driving on the freeway Gregoris realized they were not traveling alone; there were two men sitting in the back seat smiling at them but otherwise serious. Gregoris assumed they were guards and he didn't bother talking to them.

A few minutes later they arrived at the Embassy; they were met by the Greek ambassador who received them with a broad smile and said, "Come in, come in, you must be tired traveling on trains for so many days. Tina will show you to your room and tonight you will dine with us." They both had showers and Martha felt much better after that. At the dinner the ambassador Mr. Davrakis said, "Well I should tell you what your schedule will be for the next few days; tomorrow morning at 9:00 a.m. you will fly to Athens on the Embassy's private plane. Unfortunately you can't go back to your house right away; you could go to a hotel which we can arrange for you, or you could choose to stay with one of your relatives; that's up to you." Martha said, "We would rather stay at our son's place, but we would like to go to our home as soon as possible." "That's something you will have to discuss with Mr. Karthakos."

Next morning Gregoris and Martha were flown to Athens

where they were met by Mr. Karthakos. He drove them to their son's place but on the way he asked Gregoris about his apartment with the rest of the hidden treasure. Gregoris said, "It's very close why we don't go right now." And so they drove to his apartment where Gregoris showed Mr. Karthakos the rest of the treasure. During the next thirty minutes many people arrived along with fifteen policemen with rifles at the ready. Pretty soon everything was moved into special trucks and was taken away. On the way to their son's home, Mr. Karthakos told Gregoris that the Prime Minister wanted to see them and he handed them a special invitation. Martha said, "We want to know when we will be able to go home." "Well this is something I wanted to discuss with you—you see, your place is going to be taken over by the museum, there is going to be a lot of excavation in the area and we wouldn't want any houses in close proximity. But the government will adequately reimburse you." Gregoris said, "I knew this was going to happen as soon as I discovered the hidden treasure; but I hope we could get another place close to the Parthenon." "We will make sure of that Mr. Takanakos."

"Welcome back Mr. Takanakos; how do you feel?" "I don't know; where am I?" "You are in the hospital; after you left your retirement party you were involved in an accident and you have been comatose for a while."

The End

CAVES AND SPACE

An Adventure Story

"Hey, John listen to that—hear anything?" "Yeah, I hear an echo; sounds like there is a hole under here, maybe a cave?" Steve let the long bar fall on the ground, again another sound reverberated from below. "I don't know—but man; anytime I drive over here with my tractor it feels like I am going to sink in; I tell you there is something under here." "Well, Steve why don't we find out what it is; you have a tractor, put it to work." "You mean like—digging a hole?" "Yeah, why not, it won't take long to get an idea as to what's under here; it sounds like the cavity is close to the surface." "I don't know John, this whole area is covered with solid rock; it's bedrock, I tell you, it's bedrock." "But we won't know until we try, right?"

Steve put this whole thing out of his mind for a few weeks; it sounded like too much of a project and he got tired even thinking about it. But on sunny day in April, early in the morning Steve and John decided to finally give it a try and started digging in earnest. Steve carefully scraped the top soil on an area 10'x10' (approximately three and a half square meters). Within a few inches of soil he hit bedrock; then he ran over the rock with the backhoe making deep scratches on it. Within minutes they could see clearly that they were dealing with a huge monolithic rock.

After they swept and moved every bit of soil from the surface of the rock they looked carefully for possible cracks in it but found nothing. The whole thing looked like an impenetrable monolithic mass. Steve pounded on the center of the surface with the backhoe while John looked around for any signs of hair cracks. Finally after a lot of pounding John yelled, "Eureka, eureka, there is a crack here." Of course a hair thin crack on a huge mass like that didn't do much but it was a good place to start splitting it. Now Steve and John thought of different ways of penetrating the stone. Their aim was to dig a manhole so they could see through and possibly go down.

They decided to call Joe and have him use his compressor and jackhammer for the job. Joe was another good friend who was just as excited to take part in their project. Because Joe was busy through the week they decided to start digging during the coming weekend. On Saturday morning after they discussed their schedule over a cup of coffee; they started digging. Actually Joe was the only one able to use the jackhammer; Steve and John were moving the broken rocks away and were there to help Joe with whatever he needed while digging on the site. As he was chipping little by little; he noticed the right side of the hair crack was getting wider indicating that side was larger and was slowly moving away.

It was a slow process but they were gaining on it; they worked throughout the weekend and by the time they finished for the day, the hole had gotten considerably deeper but they were not through the stone yet. Steve used the long bar hitting at the bottom of the hole waiting for the echo which now came faster and stronger; indicating that they were closer to going through but apparently not there yet. The three of them sat down and discussed next weekend's schedule over a beer and decided to resume digging again on Saturday at about 10:00 am.

Next weekend they were back at work bright and early and

continued digging slowly deepening the hole. They kept working all through the weekend and by Sunday afternoon they were five feet down the hole. They were now dangerously close to going through the remaining thin crust of rock and they thought it would be prudent to tie Joe and the jackhammer on a strong rope to make sure that he didn't fall through the hole after breaking it. Joe decided to make a smaller hole about four inches in diameter for the remaining few inches and see inside before he proceeded to finish digging the entire hole.

Breaking Through

Within minutes Joe managed to break through the smaller hole and now they all became excited and could hardly wait to see through the tiny hole. Joe inserted an extension cord with a hundred watt light bulb. He let the cord go down until it touched ground about ten feet below. Then he looked inside. Both Steve and John asked simultaneously, "What do you see in there?" Joe said, "You'll have to see it by yourselves." What they saw ten feet below was a gentle hill formed entirely of obsidian as far down as they could see. The light reflected the shiny brilliance of the glass like diamonds under the sun. This metamorphosed granite was the result of molten lava formed by rapid cooling as it came from a volcano in the distant past.

This is not what Steve hoped to see; he wished for a cave with stalactites and stalagmites with maybe a pond of cool clear water and phosphoric microscopic creatures around it. But that's not what they found. Still, they all thought that what they had discovered was worth their hard labor and perhaps an expedition was now in order. They quickly broke the rest of the bottom rock and now they had a clearer view of four feet in diameter. But even with more natural light they couldn't see much beyond a few feet. There was no doubt in their minds that they clearly had to go down to see more of what was there. They lowered a ladder and Steve was the first one down followed by John and Joe. Steve held the lamp and the three of them walked carefully as far as the cord would go.

They looked around the area and all they could see was a black hill composed of obsidian boulders; it was the same landscape as far down as they could see. They saw that they could walk easily among the huge boulders but how far down should they go; and would it be safe? They all agreed that they needed someone with more experience in underground expeditions. John knew a friend of a friend who was a speleologist and had experience in many caves in different countries of the world. They went up and closed the hole with a piece of plywood, and a heavy rock on top of it. John said, "I will let you know as soon as I get in touch with the speleologist." Before they left for home they decided not to say anything to anybody about their find for now.

Erik Greenstone was an avid spelunker and speleologist and he had lots of pictures and videos to prove it. He had visited "the Sistine Chapel of crystals," Mexico's "Cueva de los Cristales", Majlis al Jinn Cave (Oman) world's second largest cave chamber, Waitomo Glowworm Cave (New Zealand) and other remarkable caves. * Taken from, "A Blog on Oddities."

Erik was by far the best man they could have asked for help and he was happy to do it all for nothing. For Erik being the first spelunker to investigate a newly discovered cave would be a thrilling experience. Two days after John asked Erik to join them on an expedition into the innards of the newly found cave; he was at the site and had already been inside. They had all walked as far as the power cord could reach; but Erik was equipped with a powerful head light and was able to walk a few yards farther.

When he came back; they could see he was visibly excited even in that semi-dark area. He said, "I have never seen obsidian boulders of this size before; this is new to me." Steve and Joe met at John's place almost every night while Erik was staying there for a few days. They were making the necessary preparations for the forthcoming expedition. Fortunately Erik was a member of one of the largest spelunkers' clubs in the U.S. and he could borrow most of the needed equipment and material from the club. So all they had to buy was mostly food and water and their own special clothing.

The next few days were devoted to preparing for the up-coming expedition. Steve's wife Laura volunteered to be the relay between them and the outside world. She was equipped with the latest in communicating gear and that was it. They set a day for going under a week later when they expected to have everything ready. Finally the day arrived and after a hearty breakfast at Steve's house, all four of them; Steve, John, Joe, and Erik, stepped down the ladder and they were on their way. They were all in their thirties and in good health with Joe being the oldest by two years at thirty-five; he was strong because of the kind of work he was doing using the jack hammer and working in construction for most of his life.

Erik was the youngest at thirty-one and was equally as strong; he was capable of climbing all rock formations not only in caves but in open terrain. Erik was an accomplished hiker and spelunker and the most important member of the expedition group. Steve and John were both strong and in good health and added to the group with their "Jack-of-all-trades" abilities.

Erik was unquestionably the leader of the group and everybody looked to him for advice. As they were walking among the gigantic boulders they looked insignificant. It was totally dark and when their head lights hit the obsidian formations they reflected brilliance like millions of tiny diamonds. The ground had sharp knifelike protrusions of obsidian and it was slippery and dangerous to walk on. But they kept on going for three straight hours under Erik's expertise. Finally they stopped to rest and have something to eat; Steve tried to loosen himself from the main line on which they were all hooked but Erik told him that wouldn't be a good idea. So they unloaded their backpacks and sat down in a semicircle to eat their lunches; during their walk they could only see about three feet in front of them. All around the group everything was pitch black. The only things they could clearly see were all the phosphoric markers they had left behind them to find their way back. Erik turned on a flood light making it more comfortable and lifting their spirits at the same time. During their walk they spoke very little but now they were relaxed enough to talk.

Just as they sat down Steve's cell phone rang; Steve said, "Laura is on the phone". They had been only about three and a half hours in the dark cave but with Laura's call they all realized how much they already missed the outside world. Laura said, "How are you doing and where are you?" Steve said, "We are about two kilometers down and so far so good." "Did you find anything interesting down there?" "Well-other than these huge black boulders, there is nothing new to report; how is the weather up there? "Oh it's clear sky and sunny, and I am working in the garden." "I wish you could send some sunshine down here; it would make our lives a lot easier." "Ha-I wish I could; well, next time it's your turn to call; be careful you guys, out for now."

After the call they continued their conversation while eating lunch. It was Erik's trained eye that saw it first—a little white thing that walked over his boot so fast that he barely saw it. Erik didn't say anything to the other guys; after all they had been in this dark environment for hours now and maybe his eyes were playing tricks on him. He just wanted to make sure before he said anything at all. But he kept looking around carefully. It didn't take too long before he saw another one. This time it came within the lighted area and stopped. Perhaps it was the first time it had seen such a bright light and was confused; Erik still didn't utter a word, he kept studying it for a while. It was about five inches long by perhaps half an inch wide, with a pale grayish white color tinged with blue, and translucent.

The other guys were so busy talking, they didn't notice it. Finally Erik couldn't hold it any longer and said, "Guys, don't move! Look where I am pointing; do you see a little lizard-like thing?" They all looked at once where Erik pointed and were amazed to see living things in such a sterile place. Erik said, "If there is life here, somewhere there must be water too." Then he turned off the flood light and when he turned the light on again the lizard had gone. After they were through with lunch they resumed their walk. They walked for four more hours with frequent stops until they were tired and decided to pitch tent for the night.

Erik talked to his club member friends in California through a special link; his talk was specific to terminology often used by spelunkers about environmental and atmospheric conditions, such as oxygen, and ground and air acidity. They built a phosphoric fence around their tent and then they unfolded the prepackaged dinners and settled down while discussing their first day's walk and discoveries. Erik took the first two-hour guard followed by Steve, John, and Joe.

They had prepared for a four day expedition and so far their first day had gone by uneventfully; now as they were finishing their breakfast refreshed and relaxed they looked eagerly forward to the new day. As they went farther down, the landscape changed to being more level with smaller size boulders and it was getting lighter too. In fact it looked like an early dawn; and the more they walked northbound the lighter it became. Finally after four hours walk they came to an area where they could see that the light was coming intensely from a thin break about two hundred feet above their heads. It was approximately five hundred feet long by one foot wide with rocks blocking the incoming light every a few feet making it look like holes rather than a long open line.

Now in that gray light at least they could distinguish each other; and also they could see around them for a few hundred yards. They walked a while longer and then they positioned themselves right under the light and for the first time after so many hours they were in day light. They had lunch directly under that bright spot; Steve was so excited that he called Laura and told her of their discovery. While Erik was giving his regular report to his spelunker friends, John and Joe talked with their families too.

After lunch Erik gathered everybody together and said, "Guys, we could walk a few more hours and finish up the day but we can't go any farther; we have supplies for only two more days for our way back. I think that the fact that we found this skylight opening makes it possible for an even longer expedition by lowering ourselves from up there; but that's for another time. They started walking at the end of the second day and the farther they went the darker it became. Joe looked back and saw the light once more before they were engulfed in pitch darkness again.

What he saw was indescribable; he said, "Look—isn't that something?" The sun must have hit just right over the skylight because there was a strong light coming through the cracks from above, forming a brilliant curtain in the midst of total darkness. It was a panoramic natural phenomenon. They walked for couple of hours more and now they noticed that the ground was getting level and smoother; they were walking on sand and gravel.

Erik said, "I want you to be careful—there maybe quicksand around us; form a single line and hold tight on your rope. They walked for another half an hour making a rhythmic noise with their boots as they stepped on gravel. It was John who noticed something different this time; he said, "I see something like fire down there; what do you think it is?" Erik said, "I keep looking at it for a while now, and I think it's a pond or a lake; but it's water for sure." Steve said, "But why does it look like fire?" Erik said, "It's not fire, it's microorganisms that emit reddish phosphorus. The closer they came the more excited they became and Erik had to constantly remind them to be careful.

It was another panoramic view and the closer they came the more awestricken they were. They looked at each other and laughed; the red reflection made them look red too. Finally they came to a huge ruby red lake which appeared to vibrate. Erik said, "Don't touch the water until I analyze it, and then he took an instrument from his backpack and proceeded to test the water. When he was done he said, "It won't kill us but we shouldn't drink it either; it's sea water. We are at sea level and somehow this body of water is connected to it. They turned on their flood light and pitched their tent once more; but this time by the beach.

It was Steve's turn for the last two hour guard; he had a couple of cups of coffee and kept looking out from the inside of the tent through a plastic window across the ruby colored sea.

Their large tent easily slept a group of four; it had four plastic windows one on each side. The duty of the guard was to check all four sides. Steve spent more time looking through the front window at the flaming sea; mesmerized by its beauty.

He was about to awaken the rest of the guys when he noticed something unusual; he saw patches of water moving toward the land. He directed his flash light at them but all he could see was several hundred of these things about the size of a large dinner plate, about twelve inches in diameter, moving fast in the direction of the tent. Steve urgently woke up all his friends saying, "Get up, guys get up, you have to see this!" They all got up at once and looked at the creatures which were about fifty yards from their tent and still coming in their direction. Erik took a closer look at them with his powerful flash light and said, "They are crabs, but boy, I have never seen them this size before; then he said, put your boots on and gather you gear and get your shovels ready!"

Seconds after they had grabbed their shovels the crabs were on their tent; the first ones easily tore the tent lining and came in followed by dozens. Several of them went straight to their provisions that were lying on the ground and started eating anything that was edible. Others attacked them tearing their trousers and the flesh of their legs with their powerful claws. All four of them were beating and smashing the crabs and for a time they were able to keep them away. But blood was oozing down their legs and they were getting tired. While Erik was frantically hitting the crabs he thought of something that perhaps could save their lives. He ran across the tent and grabbed the flood light and quickly turned it on—the whole area was immediately flooded with intense light and in that instant all the crabs froze miraculously. While Erik had the light on the crabs; Steve, John, and Joe, finished up killing the remaining ones. The rest of the crabs turned back and disappeared in the water.

"Whew, that was a close call," said Erik; "Can you imagine being eaten by crabs?" Joe said, "I have never seen anything like that; we better get the hell out of here before we run out of lights." John said, "That was quick thinking on your part, Erik, thank you for saving our lives." Erik said, "Well, do you remember yesterday the episode with that lizard? It froze when I shone the light on it and I thought if it worked on the lizard it might work on the crabs too, and it worked." Steve said, "My cell phone doesn't work; the battery must be low; can I use one of yours to make a quick call to Laura?" John handed his phone to him but when Steve tried it; it didn't work either. Instinctively the rest of them tried theirs too, but they didn't work. Erik said, "They can't all stop working at the same time; something else is going on here." They tried all the electronic devices they had; no luck. Erick said, "Let's get out of here!" They left the shredded tent where it was pitched the night before and hurried on their way back home avoiding walking close to the water.

They had walked about ten minutes and they were about to leave the water behind them when suddenly John stopped and said, "Do you guys hear a humming noise, I've been hearing it ever since we left the tent site; what do you think it is?" They all stopped and listened intently, now the humming was getting a little louder. Erik said, "If we are close to the surface it could be one of those high voltage power lines above us. "John pointed with his flashlight to something that looked different than the landscape of the immediate area. He said, "I think that's where the noise is coming from." Erik turned on his powerful floodlight once more and directed it towards that strangely shaped object. It was different alright; it had a smooth, round surface but it was hard to make out its color against the black back ground.

They walked closer to it always looking around themselves for any crabs, but it appeared that the strong light had spooked them. Finally they came within ten feet of it and now they could clearly tell what it was, and it was, huge. It looked perfectly round about fifty feet in diameter, and on its center top there was another much smaller addition just as round, about ten feet in diameter. There was no doubt in their minds that the humming was coming from somewhere in there. Erik said, "Do you think, what I think?" John said, "It's a flying saucer, isn't it?" Erik said, "Yeah, that's what it is, and I have a suspicion that somehow it has stopped our cell phones.

Steve said, "From man eating crabs, to flying saucers; what's next?" Erik said, "I don't know guys, but maybe we should get out of here right now and tell someone about it." John said, "I want to have a closer look at it; who knows, by the time we go back and tell someone about it, this thing may go away and then they will never believe us." Joe threw a small rock at the saucer but it bounced off making a cracking noise; then they all started to throw rocks at it as though they were trying to get its attention. Then they stopped and waited for something to happen; for a long moment nothing happened then Erik said, "I think we've played enough with it and I don't want to use our flood lights anymore; I think we'd better get going."

Just as Erik uttered those words, a mixed bright red and yellow color started to flash around the wall of the smaller formation on top; moving continually round and round. The moving light appeared to be more vivid in the dark environment; all four of them were transfixed and not saying a word. Then the lights stopped except on the side facing them and changed into different color combinations. Then they changed into forms resembling musical notes. John who could read music couldn't understand any of it.

After a while the lights turned to one single white light and it didn't move. They were all frozen in place just like the crabs were a little while ago; finally John said, "I think it tries to communicate with us." Then just as he finished saying those words they smelled different fragrances emanating from vessel. There was one particular scent that smelled as if it came from a skunk, only worse, and all four of them held their noses and backed up. Soon after that there were different sweet aromatic smells. Finally there was melodious music playing, and then it was followed by rock music. John said again, "This thing is trying desperately to communicate with us."

Suddenly a bright white light about eight feet in diameter shone near their feet. John started to go into it but Erik grabbed his arm and tried to stop him. He said, "What are you doing are you crazy? Do you trust this thing?" John said, "Look, they want to communicate with us; if they wanted to harm us, they could have done it already, let's all go in and show them that we are not afraid and that we are civilized." Erik let John go, but he, Steve, and Joe, turned the other way and started to leave the area. As they walked away the flood light as well as their head lights went off. As far as there was light coming from the saucer they could see; but it would be impossible to go any farther in the darkness without their headlights. There was nothing else to do but follow John into the light and hope it wouldn't harm them.

A few seconds later they were bathed in a light blue color and were taken away only to find themselves in a room unlike any they'd seen before. It wasn't square or round, it was more like the shape of an egg; there was plenty of light but it wasn't coming from the ceiling or the walls. The light was coming from within the walls; the four of them were in the middle of the room standing just as they were gathered outside before they were beamed in. They looked at each other feeling scared and confused. Steve said, "Now what, do we dare move?" Erik said, "I don't know, this is beyond me I don't know what to say or do." And then they felt the ship moving, Joe said, "Christ, they are taking us away but where?"

Just then a window opened on the wall and they could clearly see outside; the sea was red as they had seen it and the saucer was floating on the water. Pretty soon it dived in and they traveled submerged for a while. The water was dark and they couldn't see much but after a few minutes they felt the ship lifting and seconds later they were flying in space. By now John had lost his enthusiasm and he was just as scared as the rest of them. They looked at him disapprovingly and although they didn't say anything he could see that they were blaming him for being captured. It was well understood by now that they were in a spaceship traveling in space but where and for how long? John was the first one to snap out of that paralyzing state of fear and realize that they couldn't stay in that position for ever. He looked around for something other than the bare room but there was nothing there.

He was examining the texture of the walls; but he couldn't make out the material. It felt like something resembling porcelain but not quite so. He walked the length of the room with his hand on the wall when all of a sudden a picture appeared on the wall right by his hand. In the picture one could see a chair a table, a bed, water, food, and many other necessary things. Joe said, "That looks good, only if it could be real." Erik said, "There must be a reason why it was put there." Then he walked to the picture and touched the chair and to their amazement something looking like a dark colored foggy column was projected from the ceiling and went all the way down to the floor. It started to turn fast like a top and in a few seconds a chair appeared and the fog went away.

Steve said, "Touch the chair in the picture three more times." Erik did as he was told and before long they had three more chairs. Needless to say it didn't take them long to get used to the idea of using the picture to acquire all their basic needs. Pretty soon they had a table and food to eat, and beds to sleep and even a bathroom to wash and for all of their other needs. So far the abductors have been good to them although they hadn't seen them yet.

They pulled their chairs by the window and spent some time looking at the bright stars against the dark background. They were mesmerized by the vastness of space; after a while Erik said, "It's been a hard day for all of us; and we need to get some sleep." John offered to take the first guard and they synchronized their watches just as they did before although they didn't know what good it was going to do since they were helpless against their abductors. Their cell phones were operational too, but that would really be a long distance call for them to make. Still having one of their own keeping an eye on them while they were asleep made them feel a little more secure; and so the three of them went to sleep while John stayed by the window gazing at the stars.

John let his mind go back to the beginning of the day; it started with the crabs' attack, of all weird things, that almost killed them, if it hadn't been for Erik's quick thinking. And then he started blaming himself for being captured. It was he who heard the humming noise coming from the spaceship and then encouraged the others to go closer. And then it occurred to him that the humming had started at the camping area but they were so busy fighting the crabs that they didn't pay attention to it. And then how about their cell phones and all the other electronic gear; they all went out at the same time. So without a doubt the abductors were on them from the beginning; they stopped their communicating gear so they wouldn't ask for help.

Maybe he shouldn't blame himself after all; they would have captured them one way or another. The only encouraging thing he thought was the fact that they let them decide to go on board instead of beaming them into the spaceship. John looked at his watch and realized that his two hours guard was up and woke Erik.

According to their internal clocks this should be the fourth day of their expedition and they should have been nearing home; but instead they were somewhere in deep space. They all got up and gathered around the table. The picture containing their wish list was still on the wall; they pushed the appropriate buttons and removed the beds, then they ordered breakfast according to their liking.

The day before, all of them had sustained injuries when they were attacked by the crabs. They had covered their wounds as best they could, and hoped to be home before their injuries were infected. John had a deep bite on his left forearm and for some reason he wasn't hurting anymore; he was afraid that gangrene might have set in and he pulled up his sleeve to have a look. To his surprise the wound was completely cleared with hardly any sign of the injury. Instinctively the rest of them checked their wounds too; to their surprise they were also clear. But not only that; some of them were cured from chronic diseases; like John's old back injury, and Erik's occasional migraines.

John spoke again, he said, "No doubt we have been abducted for reasons we don't know at this time, but so far they have treated us very well. They have also cured our wounds, so obviously they don't want to harm us. Now judging from our immediate environment we are dealing with an advanced species. The question is, why have they abducted us, how long are they going to keep us here, and are they going to take us back home?" Those were all good questions but no one could come up with a satisfactory answer. They were all discombobulated and they had no idea how long they had been here; they could only guess and their guessing was getting less and less sure as time went on.

In the meantime the lack of communication from the expedition team started to worry several people back home. By now Erik had missed reporting three transmissions to his headquarters back in California and they had already pushed the panic button. Laura was the first one to know that there was something wrong with the team when Steve failed to call her at the appointed time. She called and talked to the other families to learn if they had heard from their loved ones and when they said, "No" she knew that somehow the expedition was in trouble.

Erik's friends were already on the site preparing to go into the cave in search of their friend and his companions. This time six professional spelunkers fully equipped for the search were on the job. The phosphoric markers made their descent much easier and it took them only a day and half to reach to the missing group's last campsite. They needn't be afraid of the crabs because unbeknownst to them the numerous flood lights they were using in the area kept the crabs at bay. After Erik, Steve, Joe and John left their tent with their floodlights and the area was engulfed in darkness, the crabs came back and cannibalized their dead cousins.

So when the second team arrived and found remnants of eaten crabs, they assumed that they had been consumed by Erik and his friends. But they were sickened by the sight of the bloody torn tent. The leader of the expedition, Tom Smithson, alarmed by what they saw, said, "Draw your rifles and be at the ready; it looks like they were attacked by something that slashed its way through the tent and killed them or at least they were badly injured. Larry, another man in the company said, "Look at those bloody shovels on the ground; it appears that they used them to fight the intruder." Tom said, "It's the lower part of the tent that's been ripped all around by many small creatures; because they have not damaged the upper part.

Before they left they picked up the shovels and a few other items that were left behind by the first team and took many pictures in and around the damaged tent; but they couldn't resist taking a few more pictures of the ruby-red sea. Then they spent a few more hours looking around with powerful floodlights trying desperately to get the attention of the first expedition party, but to no avail. They set their tent for the night in another area farther away and used two men at a time guarding the tent with flood lights and their rifles ready to go. They spent the next day searching for signs of the missing spelunkers but had no luck. Finally when the batteries of their lights and electronics were dangerously low they decided to go back. The next group scheduled to go down was much larger; this time in addition to speleologists there was a forensic team, police, geologists, archeologists and selected media.

This was their second day on the space ship and although so far they had been treated well; nevertheless they felt apprehensive about their well-being. They were all looking through the picture window out into space; this was their only entertainment. It was almost hypnotic, but they had said nothing for a long time; each one of them was deep into their own thoughts. It was at that quiet time they heard a melodious chime; it came from behind them. They all turned around at the same time and saw an open door. Erik said, "I guess they want us to go in, shall we?" Steve said, "We might as well; at this point we are at their mercy."

The door led into a narrow white corridor, it was brightly lighted; and as they were walking they noticed two green lights one on each side of the corridors' walls about shoulder high; they were both moving horizontally and fast. They reminded them of neon lights; finally they came to an opening that looked like a little town square with several small and large rooms that had windows one could see through. In those rooms they saw animals that they could easily identify such as apes, cows, horses, cats and dogs, a small whale and couple of dolphins, and many other mammals. There were other different animals from all corners of the earth; and then there were extraterrestrial entities; things and animals they had never seen before. They were all living neatly in their own environments.

After they were through with their tour Joe said, "I have a feeling that we are going to join their community very soon; what do you think, guys?" Erik said, "It looks like it to me too." Steve coined a new phrase and said, "We are going to be residents of an interstellar "Flying saucer zoo." However John thought otherwise he said, "Did you notice that almost all of them had automated feeders and others had robot-like machines attending to them. I saw nowhere a wish list like the one that we used for our needs. That tells me that we are considered more intelligent and therefore we will be treated differently. Erik said skeptically, "I hope you are right, John; for I wouldn't like to live the rest of my life in a zoo."

All of a sudden the floor under their feet started to move like a conveyer belt taking them to another corridor and kept on moving until it came to a much bigger room and stopped in front of it. Then the door opened and they assumed that it was their queue to go inside; which they did. The room looked pretty much like the one they had left earlier, only larger. They could still see space through a picture window but there was also a permanent control panel in the middle of the room. It had an illegible flashing symbol; there were more symbols that looked like hieroglyphics. They looked at each other wondering if they should touch it. John said, "Obviously they brought us here to see it, perhaps this could be a way to communicate with them; they count on our intelligence to do so." They all agreed that John was right and they encouraged him to touch it.

John hesitatingly touched the flashing symbol and immediately a holographic picture appeared in the middle of the room. It felt as though they were in the picture themselves; it showed the middle of a galaxy in three dimensions and somewhere in the center there was a flashing light. Then the galaxy disappeared and in its place there was a star with a group of planets resembling our solar system. Then a grotesque creature appeared right next to them; it looked like a hairless chimpanzee but pale and frail looking, it had big eyes and almost no nose, and a large head. Instinctively they moved away from it but it stayed there as though it didn't see them. Then it started to talk with a synthesized voice; it said, "Do not be frightened, you will not be harmed, we come from the center of your galaxy in search of other living things. Our intention is to gather information of other entities in different solar systems. This vessel has no crew it is controlled by another ship far away. Once we collect our necessary specimens all entities will be taken back to their original places."

Then four clones of Erik, John, Steve, and Joe were shown in suspended animation; and the alien said, "You and all the other living things that we have collected will be studied in our laboratories but we will not harm any of you. Shortly you will be placed back where you were collected." Then the alien and the four clones disappeared. After that episode they were all dumbfounded; Steve said, "How did they do that, we guarded ourselves all the time didn't we?" Erik said, "Maybe they hypnotized the guards before they cloned us." John said, "It appears that they are a technologically advanced superior species; they didn't have to hypnotize us, they probably have the means to fully copy our DNA while we are awake. I am sure that they have been studying our civilization for a long time; they seem to know everything about us, even the kind of food we eat." Joe spoke next, he said, "I have heard that twins have close feelings and when one is hurt the other has a ghostly pain as well; will this happen to us when they start working on our cloned bodies in their labs?" Steve said, "I don't want to even think about it; this whole thing has been too much for me. I want to go back home and forget all about it."

The fact that the alien said they were going to be taken back home unharmed was a big relief for all of them; but the alien didn't specifically say when they would go home. The aliens' time sequence could be different than theirs. Will it be in a few hours, days, months, or years? That was something that worried them. The fear and uncertainty of the last two days on the alien ship had taken a toll on all of them; they were physically and mentally tired. They ordered dinner the usual way from their wish list menu and then sat by the picture window watching the stars, once more deep in their thoughts. Then after a while one by one they went to bed. They didn't bother to keep a guard this time because they thought at this point there was very little they could do to help themselves.

They woke up feeling cold and confused, everything was dark around them; it took them a few seconds to realize that they were back in the cave. They had been dropped unceremoniously on the cold ground but that didn't bother them at all; they were happy to be home. Erik reached for the flashlight in his pocket and looked around; all their belongings were put neatly next to them he found the floodlight and turned it on. They found their hardhats with the head lights and put them on; now they could see their surroundings better.

They tried their cell phones and they were all operational; Joe started to call home but John stopped him, he said, "Hold on a minute, Joe, we all want to call home and talk to our loved ones but we need to decide what to say to the folk up there and we all need to be of the same mind." Erik said, "John is right; do we tell them the truth, that we were abducted by aliens and that we were taken for a ride up into deep space on a flying saucer? And who is going to believe us? They will think that we have lost it; that we are crazy. I think this whole saga should stop here, it should be our experience, our secret; that's what I think."

Steve said, "I think we have been missing for more than two days; they probably have sent people looking for us. What excuse we give them, we can't call and say; we are here safe and sound, we have to say something that makes sense and is believable." They all agreed that they shouldn't say anything to anybody about their abduction including their immediate families. But now they had to fabricate their own story. All three of them looked at Erik for an answer. Erik was already thinking of something that would make sense not only to the common folk but especially to his more inquisitive spelunker buddies.

Erik said, "Do you remember during the second day of our arriving here right before we saw the sea; I said, 'be careful of quicksand;' the reason I said that is because low flat land next to a big body of water can sometimes be wet and muddy and if it's deep enough those who step in it often perish. We need to go back there and look for that muddy place; but we must be careful not to cause our own deaths. If we can find a place like that we could say that we were trapped in it and in our struggle to free ourselves we lost our provisions including our phosphoric markers. Then after the crab episode we ran away from our base and we got lost; and without our markers it took all this time to find our way back." Steve had second thoughts about this elaborate lie, but he couldn't concoct a better one himself so he went along with Erik's idea. Joe said, "What if we don't find quicksand, then what?" Erik said, "Then we'll have to come up with something else; but I refuse to say that we were abducted by aliens." They all agreed with Erik on that.

They were still wearing their shredded trousers as they started their way back; when they came to the low flat land they left the well marked pathway they had marked earlier and walked even lower to the wet lands leaving phosphoric markers behind them. They started to walk on muddy and slippery ground now, Erik said, "Watch it, guys, if there is any quicksand it's going to be somewhere around here." Erik was the first one pushing a stick he had found earlier on the beach into the mud as he lead the way, they all held onto the rope for dear life.

Finally Erik said, "That's it, guys, we don't need to go any farther. This is deep enough to drown a bull." And with that they threw in their markers and a few other important things. On the way back they picked up all the new markers and put them next to the old ones on their way back home. Erik said again, "Now we can say that we fell in the quicksand and lost our markers, and most of our provisions, and damaged our cell phones in our struggle to get out. It's a lie, but if we keep our mouths shut no one is going to know the truth."

John said, "I have a feeling that they will believe this story more easily than if we were to tell them that we were abducted by aliens." Steve said, "That's for sure." Then all four of them held hands and promised that they would not tell anything about their abduction to anyone including their closest relatives, and that was it. Erik made the first call to his club in California, followed by the other three who called their families. Erik told his buddies the story that was decided upon by the four of them and so did the other three; and so it became big news all over the world about the lost spelunkers who found their way back safe and sound. The third expedition to the cave was canceled for the time being but plans were already made by the County and the State of Washington to put this newly found cave under the protection of the Federal Parks and Recreation Department. In the meantime Steve closed the entrance hole in his yard after he was told that an elevator would be installed for transporting scientists and personnel who would be working in the future. The location of the elevator would be about two miles to the north of the entrance and above the long crack that sends light into the cave.

During the last month Erik, Steve, John and Joe; were inundated by the media of this country and internationally to tell their story; there were even offers from Hollywood for a movie about their expedition. A few weeks later the four of them, along with their families and friends, had a potluck party at Johns' place to celebrate their survival. It was the first time after they came back that they had a chance to talk among themselves. They managed to find a quiet place away from the crowd and sat down to talk.

Steve said, "I don't know about you guys but I have been overwhelmed by people and the media who want to hear our story over and over again." John said, "If we were to tell them the real story we would be the laugh of the world by now." They all agreed and thanked Erik for his alternative story. Joe said, "I would happily put this saga behind me if it wasn't for our clones being experimented on in the aliens' laboratories and living in a flying saucer zoo." They all felt a deep pain in their hearts; but they were happy to be back home among their loved ones.

The End

BLACKBIRD LOVE

A Spy Story

Mike looked through the window of the airplane in an hypnotic state. Below was a blanket of white clouds, and at the western horizon the sun was sinking like a huge fire ball. At the end of the middle aisle there was a screen showing the trajectory of the plane with the altitude and the mileage. The dinner had been served and the flight attendants were collecting the trays. There were long lines of people waiting by both restrooms. After a while all the commotion stopped and most people tried to catch up with some sleep.

Mike took a sip of coffee and opened his book, he tried to read but he couldn't concentrate. He closed it and set it in the pouch of the seat in front of him. His mind went once more back to his office and the talk he had had with his manager that morning. "Mike, it's important that we get this contract. A lot depends on it; the survival of our company hangs in the balance. We can't sugar-coat it anymore, at this point this is the best price we can offer. Our competitors are bigger and richer and can offer better deals but we have a better product by far and we rely on you to communicate that to our customers."

"John, you know I always do my best, but this time we are up against Russia and China who have monopolized their factories and they can make better deals with their customers. They also bribe the officials of those countries by depositing huge amounts of money in their Swiss accounts. We are up against the law and if we get caught playing their came we'll be in hot water." "Do your best and I'll take care of the details; you don't need to worry about it, just get that contract."

Mike wasn't new at selling weapons, and missiles were his preferred arsenal. He graduated from Harvard University as one of the best in his class. It hadn't been easy. He grew up in a one parent family with his mother, Hanna and two sisters, Carol and Connie; his father, Jack Woodward, died in a car accident early on when Mike was five or six years old. He barely remembered him. His father drank a lot and after the accident his mother had had enough with men and never married again. Hanna worked in an insurance company as a secretary; she didn't earn much but managed to keep the family together and out of trouble. She made sure her children got a good education but she had a special feeling for Mike; she didn't want him to take to the bottle like his father. She wanted him to be a good person, and unlike his father, be useful in society. Hanna used to say to her children, "I work hard for you so you can have a better life, and that's all I want from you."

Mike had a difficult time growing up poor, but several of his friends were in the same boat, so he had lots of company. As a teenager he got into drugs and alcohol but nothing like his father and when he graduated from college he stopped binge drinking and never used drugs again. He appreciated his mother's sacrifices and wanted to prove to her that he wasn't going to be like his father. He worked hard in college and got good grades which qualified him for a few scholarships that enabled him to get into Harvard University. Mike was an intelligent young man and he did even better at Harvard. Before he even graduated cum laude with an MBA there was a job offer from a defense plant.

Mike was hired not only for his fine education but also for his good looks; he inherited his height from his father and his intelligence from his mother. He was 6'1", lean and muscular with curly black hair, dark brown eyes and an olive complexion. He was in his early twenties and he never failed to get the attention of many young and older women. At the office he had the ability to get along with most people in his immediate area and in a short time he was moved to the sales department because of his good P.R. abilities.

Mike was given a quick course in salesmanship and after he became well acquainted with the plant's weaponry he started selling. He spent a few months negotiating various contracts with the U.S. Armed forces, F.B.I., C.I.A. and other security agencies including some of the biggest police departments in the country. Mike put his heart and soul into the business. He learned a lot and many a time his manager would congratulate him on a job well done. Mike liked his job but unfortunately it didn't pay enough to cover his expenses. By the time he paid his school loans there was little for anything else. He wanted to help his mother with her expenses but he couldn't even do that.

Mike requested and got an appointment with his manager. Mr. John Paterson was a busy man but managed to find time for him, "Well, Mike, I hear that you are catching up with our best in the field; keep it up and soon you will be due for another promotion." "Well, Mr. Paterson, that's the reason I wanted to see you; and I will be frank with you, sir, you see I can't make ends meet with the salary I am getting so far and I thought either I get promoted to a better paying job or perhaps I should move on." "Nonsense, Mike, you are a good man and you belong here with us; let me see what I can do to get you some more money, okay?" "Okay, sir, thank you."

It didn't take long. A week later Mike was promoted to overseas sales; now he was affiliated with the C.I.A. as well. After another quick course in that agency he learned the dos and don'ts of selling weapons to foreign countries. Mike found out that that was an entirely different game. The sales contracts were huge; they involved hundreds of millions of dollars which earned him high commissions. It was a very competitive and dangerous job. In addition it took a long time before he signed a contract, sometime several months; but it was worth it because one sale could give him enough money to last a long time. If he was successful he could be a rich man very soon. Finally Mike got what he had always wanted; a competitive job that made him a lot of money—he was in his element.

A year later Mike was one of the best sales representative in the field; he visited many countries and made presentations about the weapons his company was selling. Mike specialized in high velocity missiles which put him at odds with the Russians and Chinese. In the C.I.A. he learned how to socialize and, if needed, how to protect himself from his competitors. In Greece, Turkey, Italy, and other western affiliated countries he inevitably found himself face to face with other sales representatives at parties given by ministers of foreign affairs, generals, admirals and others. He had an easier time speaking with the Russians but he had to be careful with the Chinese; they smiled a lot but were vicious when it came to making a sale. But Mike wasn't alone, because of his knowledge of the latest weapons he was always guarded by C.I.A. agents.

His flight would be arriving at Roissy-Charles de Gaulle airport in Paris tomorrow at 8:00 a.m. local time. Mike caught up on much needed sleep and in the morning he was relaxed enough to start the new day in the "City of Lights." He knew that agent

SF-Black Bird was to meet him at the airport's cafeteria at a prearranged place but Mike had no idea who the agent was or how he looked, all he had to do was to sit there and wait. He ordered a cup of coffee but he had no time to finish drinking it.

"Hello, I am SF-Black Bird and I will be your date tonight." Mike raised his head and looked at the C.I.A. agent. She was gorgeous—tall, about 5'10", blond long hair, with dark green eyes, and a slim well proportioned body in her early twenties. She smiled at him and said in a stiff way, "Mike, we need to get out of here right now!" "Why, what's going on?" "I can't tell you now; let's get going." And go they did; they got out like a bat out of hell. They walked fast to the nearest parking area where two tall guys dressed in black wearing dark glasses, were waiting for them; they quickly got in and they were off.

The car headed for the American embassy. SF Black Bird said to Mike, "Unofficially I answer to Flora, in fact I like that better." "That simplifies things; I like your name too. So Flora what's going on, is anyone after me?" "Well, Mike, you have information your competitors would love to have, and they'll try to get it any way they can; be careful they are ruthless." "That I know."

Prince Hassan Hussein Nusura of Ducuby (*) was in the Hilton Hotel on a weapon buying spree; and with one of the fattest accounts in a Swiss Bank, he could buy any weapons needed for the security of his little country. Prince Hassan was looking for long velocity missiles and there were three sales representatives from The U.S.A., Russia, and China to fulfill that need. The Russians had the SS Barof 300, (*) one of the most powerful missiles on the market, that had the capability of reaching Ducuby's enemy countries. China had the well known TT-Chu-Tan (*) just as powerful. But the U.S. Punisher SS-300(*) was armored with stealth capacity. That made it the most wanted toy for any General.

Whereas the Russians and the Chinese could sell their missiles at competitive prices with no strings attached; the Americans had certain restrictions that went with the sales. Any missiles sold to any country in the area that could hit countries friendly to U.S. were accompanied by strict rules. That was a dilemma Mike had to overcome if he hoped to make the sale. Then his manager's words came to mind, "Do your best and I'll take care of the details; you don't need to worry about it, just get that contract." Mike knew John was a powerful man who had connections all the way to the White House, but even the President could not change the rules designed to protect America's allies. But Mike was going to try his best any way.

Flora drove Mike to the Hilton Hotel, parked her car in the hotel's parking area, and waited. Her car was a conduit to a more elaborate spying apparatus somewhere in the American Embassy; Mike wasn't alone. At the main lobby he was met by the Prince's body guards who escorted him to his suite.

Prince Hassan Hussein Nusura had met earlier with the Russian agent, Feodor Nebrescky, and with the Chinese agent, Ju Li Nee; Mike was his last appointment for the day. Prince Nusura was a good negotiator and an able diplomat. He had pretty much decided on the powerful Russian missile over the Chinese one. Although he would have preferred the American missile, U.S. Punisher SS 300, with its stealth capabilities but he also knew it would have been difficult to bargain with the American. He was able to convince each agent that he would most likely buy his products over the others.

"Come in, Mr. Woodward, sit down." If the Prince was tired from his other two appointments you wouldn't have known it by the way he was talking to Mike. He was accommodating and sincere with him and willing to go the extra mile to accomplish his goal. "Thank you, thank you so much, Your Highness; I know that you are a busy man so I am going to come right to the point. I am sure you had better offers from our competitors in price and more convenient ways of getting your orders delivered. But I can assure you that no one comes even close to the quality of the U.S. punisher SS 300."

Then Mike opened his notebook and showed the Prince the missile. He explained in detail how superior they were from those of the competitors. Then he finished his presentation by saying, "Your Highness let's not forget that ours has stealth capability; which means that our missiles can penetrate the enemy's territory unnoticed; a feature our competitors cannot offer." "Mr. Woodward, without a doubt you have a powerful weapon which will interest my king; but unfortunately it comes with too many strings attached and that will discourage him. We are not talking about price; we just want to be free to use this weapon against our enemies at our will, not yours. We are a small country and all we want is to protect our people, we don't have any offensive plans."

"If you mean certain restrictions that go with the sale of these weapons, I should tell you that because you will be using them in a defensive mode those restrictions do not apply to you." "In that case I will discuss it with my king and we will let you know shortly, Mr. Woodward. I do hope that you will attend the party at our embassy." "Thank you, my girlfriend and I will be there for sure."

Flora looked intensely at a monitor inside her car; she kept an eye on Mike at all times, she tracked him until he was by the door and she opened it, "Come in, Mike." "I had a good presentation with the Prince. He was very receptive; I just might make the sale." "I know; he is like that with everybody." "Oh yeah, I forgot that you were snooping on me." "Yeah, I sure was." As soon as Mike reached the embassy he had a long discussion with his boss back in the States.

"How did you do with the Prince, Mike?" "Well sir, I understand that you wanted me to go easy on some of the restrictions that go along with these weapons; so I took the liberty to tell him that because our missiles would be used in a defensive mode those restrictions did not apply." "You did well, Mike; we have other ways to protect our friends; I hope you get that contract." "I hope so too, sir."

Mike took a short rest and then he showered and shaved and dressed for the evening's party which was to take place at the embassy of Ducuby. He was checking his latest e-mail before he left for the embassy when he heard a knock on the door. He said, "Come in, the door is open." Flora stepped inside, "Hello, Mike, are you ready for partying?" She was beautiful anyway, but tonight she looked gorgeous and very sexy. Mike was happy to be going out with her but he knew that this was all part of her being a C.I.A. agent—nothing like his previous dates when there was always more than a kiss at the door.

Mike and Flora were driven by two guys dressed in black. Flora held a small purse not large enough to hold a gun, but Mike knew that she had one somewhere; perhaps hidden between her thighs? Mike was certain that he wasn't going to find out any time soon. Flora was a secret agent that's all. The Prince knew how to throw a party—no question about it. He and his sons along with his bodyguards were sipping what appeared to be soft drinks, (Muslims don't use alcohol), but one wouldn't know for sure what was in their drinks.

There were many ambassadors and other V.I.P.s with their

wives or girlfriends; most of Prince's acquaintances had to do with business.

Mike and Flora looked like a loving couple but actually everyone knew who they were. Agent Feodor Nebrescky and agent Ju Li Nee were there with their wives too. There was lots of good food with live music and the alcohol was flowing freely for the guests. Mike and Flora were dancing along with other couples when Flora said to Mike, "Feodor, Ju Li and their wives are gone; I smell a rat, let's get out here." Seconds after Flora and Mike left, a powerful explosion damaged the room killing and injuring many of the guests. Mike said, "Wow, that was a close call, they almost got us." They were both shaken but they felt lucky to be alive. As soon as they arrived at the embassy Mike called his boss and told him what had happened at the Prince's party and how close it came for them to be killed.

As it turned out Prince Hassan Hussein Nusura and his sons survived the explosion but they were injured badly. Several of his guards were killed and others were injured along with many of the visiting participants. The news hit the media like fire. The C.I.A. and K.G.B. were the first to be blamed as usual, but this time other agencies like Mossad, Al-Qaida, or even the Chinese were blamed as well. Needless to say the sale was put off for a while or until they heard from the Ducuby Kingdom; but Mike was asked to stay put in the area for a while.

Flora was at the embassy's cafeteria watching the French news on the T.V. Her French wasn't all that great but she could understand quite a bit. The commentator was assuring the French people that the DGSE, (French Intelligent Service), was not involved in this incident and he was accusing the foreigners who were causing so much trouble lately in their country. The news stopped momentarily and went to commercials; in them there was a woman with an infant, shopping for baby clothes. Flora looked at the woman with envy and wondered if she would ever have that kind of life. Yesterday she had a close call with death. Did she want to push her luck any further? Sure it's a good job and pays well but is it something she would like to do all her life? And who is going to marry a spy, another one in the agency? And what life is that going to be?

Flora had had other close calls in the past and never took them seriously but this one somehow reminded her of her mortality. The glass door reflected her face; she looked at herself for a long moment and wondered if she was wasting her youth on something she didn't like doing anymore. She had finished drinking her coffee and was about to get up when she noticed Mike approaching her.

"Hello, Flora, have you recovered from last night's episode? By the way, thanks for saving my life; if it wasn't for you God knows I would be a goner by now." "I just did my duty; after all I saved my life too." "Thanks anyway; are you going to be around for a while?" "I am assigned to look after you until you leave for the States so I suppose I'll be here as long as you need to be here." Mike told Flora that he had been in Paris before but as a student. At that time he couldn't afford to see enough of this beautiful city. As Mike was talking—Flora noticed what a handsome guy he was and to think that a few hours ago both of them almost perished—what a waste that would have been.

Flora was born in San Francisco Ca. the younger of two sisters by two years; her older sister Debbie became a teacher and taught in a high school. She got married and started raising a family. Her father, Roy Lancaster, became a born-again Christian when he got older. Her mother, Judy, was the steady-as-you-go kind of character and kept things pretty much under control.

Flora, even as a young girl, was an independent person who bothered her father who wanted her to be closer to God.

Flora was adventurous and a daredevil most of her life; she loved to read mysteries and spy novels, and loved outdoors sports. After she graduated from college with a B.A. she worked in a few part time jobs and finally she became a C.I.A. agent. After a few months in a vigorous training program with the agency she became officially, a spy and was given the pseudonym S.F. Black Bird. Flora worked in several embassies as an attaché mostly in Europe. Her ability to speak some French and German helped her in dealing with foreign officials.

Before she joined the agency she had dated several men but as a C.I.A. agent she had to adhere to certain rules of which one was, "Don't trust anyone." Consequently it was hard for her to have any close relationship. Before she was assigned to Mike's case she read his bio and knew enough about him to know that he was an honest man and one she could trust. But was he interested in her? So far she has been unyielding and standoffish with him which had kept him at bay.

"As I said, I haven't had enough time to see Paris in the past, how about you, have you been here before?" "Oh yeah I've been here many times; in fact I've been stationed in Europe for the last two years so I know my way around." "In that case maybe you could show me Paris while we are here." "I would love to; but I have to ask permission from my superior to escort you unofficially, but I will, and let you know if that can be done."

"That sounds great—thanks. Now changing the subject a little; who do you think is involved in last night's explosion?" "Oh it could be any of the neighboring countries, Ducuby has many enemies. "When you spent unlimited amounts of money buying the latest weaponry you are going to make your enemies very nervous." "We can scratch the C.I.A., K.G.B. and the Chinese off the list; they wouldn't kill their prospective buyer, that would be bad business wouldn't you think?" "I agree with that, although with the exception of the two of us they were out of the room like rats leaving a sinking boat; they must have known something." "Yeah, I know that and if it wasn't for your quick thinking we would be history." "Sometimes I wonder if I am in the wrong business."

"Well I am glad you were there for my sake. Anyway there are two more likely parties that could have done it." "And who do you think they might have been"? "Let's not forget Mossad; the Israelis know what's going on in their enemy countries. If one of those countries is buying weapons which could potentially hit their country, they would try to stop such a purchase and blame someone else. The other one could easily be Al Qaida. They hate Shiites; it's like the Protestants and the Catholics killing each other a few decades ago; although the hate still exists even today with some of these people who call themselves Christians."

When Flora asked her superiors about going out with Mike they told her that things were getting dangerous in Europe and the best place for her would be back in the states, but for some reason the agency wanted her here for now. And so playing tourist in Paris was out of the question. Flora and Mike were asked to wait in the Embassy grounds until new orders. Flora didn't mind that at all she was used to that kind of life. But Mike felt trapped and he could hardly wait to get out of there. The upside of that was that both got to know each other better and that was pleasant for both of them.

The order finally came and they not only let them go out; they insisted that Flora and Mike go together. But not in Paris they were asked to go out in another city; apparently the agency had a plan in mind. Mr. Dennis Jackson a man in his fifties had been with the agency for twenty years and was in charge of a several C.I.A. agents working in France. He asked them to his office and said, "Mike, we know that you are not officially one of us, but in your line of work you've been working under the protection of the agency and if you should accept our offer, we would like you to work with Flora and help us catch those who attacked the embassy the other night.

Mike didn't have to think too hard to accept the offer. He said, "Mr. Jackson, I hope this time we are not going to be left alone out there; as you know if it wasn't for Flora we wouldn't be here talking to you." "I know but this time I promise we will be there for you." Then Mr. Jackson went on to explain the plan he had in mind. When they stepped out of the office Mike was both excited and scared. Mike said to Flora, "I hoped you would show me Paris but now we are going to Perpignan; where is this place anyway, have you been there before?" "Yes once; it's a preferred place for illicit sales of drugs and weapons because it's so close to Spain. A lot of drugs are smuggled into Spain from North Africa destine for the rest of Europe through Perpignan. And then weapons from Europe go back the other way."

Mike and Flora looked like tourists to most people but not to those dealers being legal or illegal. They knew who they were and that was the point. What they didn't know was that they were accompanied by many C.I.A. agents inconspicuously keeping an eye on them. Mike was a successful weapons salesman dealing mostly with third world countries and with knowledge of the latest U.S. missiles which was a hot item on the market. Flora was a low C.I.A. agent asset easy to overpower; they were both acting as bait to those who had political reasons to disrupt weapon sales, kill, or even abduct Mike for ransom.

Dennis Jackson was one of the best espionage agents in central Europe and the agency counted on him to find the perpetrators of the recent bombing incident. Dennis excluded the Russians and the Chinese right off hand; it wouldn't make sense for them to kill the Prince who was about to purchase weaponry from them. By default that fell on Mossad or Al Qaida They both had good reasons to stop the sale; Al Qaida hated the Prince and Mossad would do anything to protect their country even if it came to eliminating friends if they were selling weapons to their enemies.

Dennis was not in favor of the sale to begin with but the decision was made by politicians who knew little of the danger that could cause in the field. He sent an e-mail to Ben Brown with a message, "Hi Ben; I bought the stock you suggested, thanks. S-T—That was a coded phrase; I need to see you. There were other phrases they used for the same message. Dennis met Ben almost twenty years ago at a wedding party they were introduced by another C.I.A. agent and they became good friends; Ben was a secret agent with Mossad. Thereafter because America and Israel were close allies they helped each other out in the field.

They met at their usual place outside Paris in a little country café. Dennis looked Ben straight in the eye and said, "Well, Ben; is there anything you can tell me about the bombing?" "I can't help you there sorry; this caught me by surprise too." "Let me put it another way; did you guys do it?" "Dennis, Dennis, my boy— cool down—that's not nice; remember—we are friends, we wouldn't harm the hand that feeds us, now would we?" "All I can say is that if you guys did it; this time the shit is going to hit the fan." Dennis got up and left abruptly without the usual niceties. As he was leaving Ben said, "At least you got out of there unscathed; right?"

Ben's last words were ringing in his mind like a bell; that's right in fact not only did the Americans get out unscathed the Russians and the Chinese did too. One of those "scratch my back and I'll scratch yours kind of thing?" Ben had been helpful in the past but this time he wouldn't come out clearly. That reinforced Dennis' suspicions that Mossad might have been implicated in the embassy's explosions; and if that's true this time they have gone too far. Denny called his superior, Daniel Simpson, at the C.I.A. head quarters, and had a long talk with him. By the time they were through talking, Denny had something to go by.

Perpignan wasn't Paris but Flora knew her way around in this busy place and Mike had the best of times being with such a beautiful girl. In the restaurant Flora was in an unusually good humor and more talkative than she had been during the last few days. He began to feel hopeful perhaps they could have a closer relationship when they went back in the States. Flora said, "Mike, you know—all is not lost, you can still make that sale with the Prince he is injured but not dead; you have a good product and sooner or later he'll call you back." "That's true; let's hope he does." "I wondered how much longer I am going to be attached in this area with you; do you have anything else scheduled in the near future?" Mike thought to himself—I wonder if she is just as anxious as I am about going back to the States; back home days off are days off, we could start a relationship. I couldn't possibly go wrong with Flora. "Yes I do have another appointment at the Jordanian embassy; but for now I don't really know what might come out of it."

Flora excused herself to use the restroom; there she also took the opportunity to use her private cell phone. Mike thought that it was unusual for Flora to leave him alone even for a few minutes, but he also knew that he wasn't really alone with all the secret agents around them. He asked for the bill and by the time Flora came back he was ready to go. She said, "Well Mike I don't know about you but it's been a busy day and tomorrow it will probably be busier yet; so I am ready for bed how about you?" Mike said, "Same here; but next time I hope to take you to a nice restaurant back home." Mike knew he wasn't going to be lucky tonight. Flora said, "Oh I would like that." They both got up and were about to leave the table when four agents appeared out of nowhere guns drawn and directed at Flora; one of them said, "Agent SF Black Bird, put your hands up you are under arrest!"

Flora didn't resist. She knew that sooner or later this was going to happen; it was all part of the game. She looked at Mike and said, "I am sorry."

The End

(*The names of the missiles are fictional.*)

(*The names of some countries as well as the names of people are fictional.*)

PHOENIX

A Sci Fi Story

Elder, Senator Farow Naromi was in charge of the committee for the protection of libraries and museums. The group consisted of librarians, astronauts, exo-physicists, space engineers, astronomers, government representatives, army, police, and sociologists. Naromi was scheduled to meet with his committee this morning. He had worked as a senator in the confederate parliament for most of his adult life and had a successful political career. As a young man he loved literature and arts and his passion was to protect and save the libraries and museums of the world. Now as a retired senator he was going to use his political credit, and savvy, to accomplish his lifelong dream.

"Comrades, I have been entrusted by our government to save our libraries and museums. For the last few months I have been working diligently to put together a group of the most qualified people for this project and here you are. All of you know of the importance to safeguard our libraries and museums or you wouldn't have chosen to accept this offer. People all over the world have been collecting and depositing art and literature in libraries and museums for thousands of years but unfortunately we have seen too many times the fruits of our knowledge being destroyed by fire, earthquakes, and other catastrophes. That's why we need to move copies of all these out there—in space.

Today we are technologically able to digitize most of what has been written and micro size what we have made throughout history and bring them back to their original shape and form at will. I can't overemphasize the fact that for the last one hundred years our planet has been going from one ecological disaster to another. The recent earthquakes in the palaran rim destroyed many cities and killed hundreds of thousands of people; they have caused huge economic damage and it's getting progressively worse.

We can't stop what's happening under our feet but we can salvage our civilization, our history and our way of living before we lose everything that is so dear to us and to the future generations. Our task is going to be difficult but we can do it. We have one year to complete this project; after that things will worsen and we don't want to delay matters any more than necessary. Follow the directions you have been given and don't hesitate to ask me or my associates for anything you might need. May the Source be with us as we are about to start one of the most important projects in our lives, thank you."

Everyone who attended the meeting was aware of the perilous conditions earth had gone through during the last hundred years. Nevertheless Senator Naromi reminded them how much worse it would be in the near future and how important it was for them to start the project without delay. They went back home and started building in earnest the spaceship that would carry the libraries, the museums and the people who would live in it for the long voyage.

As it was predicted the weather became worse with rain, and floods, followed by tsunamis, earthquakes, and volcanic eruptions. The planet earth was going once more through another face of destruction with all the consequences that would occurred;

only this time there will be an advanced civilized human species who would witness at least part of its destruction.

During the last twelve months the scientific world was busy building one of the most complex and multifarious spaceship ever built. It was a floating city capable of supporting thousands of people on a journey into deep space and to unknown territories. Their mission was to find habitable planets and colonize them using the latest technology. Finally they gathered the prefabricated components of the spaceship in Cosmopolis which was the capital of their world. From there all sections were flown in space and were assembled.

When the ship was finished it was a technological miracle that made everybody happy and proud. No one was more proud than Senator Naromi who saw his dream realized. The President of the Confederate States of the World, Elder Philoros and many government representatives, along with the technical staff who built the ship; were all gathered in its main lobby. The President said, "We are gathered here to thank all those who helped to build this wonderful structure. In this ship we can safely guard copies of libraries, museums, and other important documents which represent; our civilization, our way of living, and the inheritance passed to us throughout eons from our ancestors.

"We live in a calamitous world and although we have managed to survive all this time the prognosis of our wellbeing is in doubt. Earthquakes, tsunamis, floods, volcanic eruptions, and other catastrophes, unfortunately have become the norm. For hundreds of years scientists and meteorologists have warned us of the climate deterioration in our planet. But we paid little attention to their warnings and we kept abusing the ecosystem with heavy industries and wars which were often fought with micro nuclear weapons. All these proved to be deleterious for us and for our planet and now we face the consequences.

But all is not lost, even under these conditions life will go on for those of us who are staying behind. We will carry on and live as best we can and in the future many of us will immigrate to other more friendly planets that we hope to discover. That's why this ship is so important for all human beings and the animal world. This ship is our Ark of knowledge and Covenant; it will be saved for us and for future generations. And now it's my pleasure to christen this spaceship, Hope—because we place all our hopes in it."

In the ensuing days and weeks the spaceship Hope was like a beehive with all kinds of people shuttling in and out bringing supplies from Cosmopolis for the long expedition. In the ship were already the specially picked crew who would command it; and a newly elected government to govern the citizens of Hope. The community consisted of men and women up to forty years of age along with infants; they came from all over the world and they were of different races. There were animals specifically picked for the needs of the people. There were also D.N.A. of other animals, trees, and vegetables, collected and kept to be used on other planets. Only ten percent of people and animals were in an animated state the other ninety percent were in a cryonic state to prolong the life of all living beings and to save food and energy. Hope was equipped to operate on antimatter energy for all its needs. For lack of room most of the supplies were micro-sized to be reconstituted in the future as needed.

Finally the rest of the officials arrived on board the ship and now with a full complement of people, crew, and supplies, Hope was ready to start its voyage. President Philoros called from Cosmopolis and said, "On behave of all people of earth I want to wish you good luck with your expedition and may the Source always be with you." And with that, Hope was ready to go.

Governor Flamous and Commander Lacier were at the governor's office along with all the top officials when the Governor spoke to the staff of Hope and the community at large, he said, "Ladies and Gentlemen today we are starting on an one way mission; our destination is to find habitable planets and start a new life for the human species. One of the important things we must do is to build libraries which will contain; our culture, the art and letters, and our technology, for us and for the next generations to come.

In the far future our people will come back to our planet earth to help our people rebuild their lives. But for us Hope is going to be our home for many generations to come until we find habitable planets." Then Commander Flamous gave the order for the spaceship Hope to start the voyage and they were on their way to the near planetary system and beyond.

Citizens of Hope

There was a community of one hundred thousand people occupying the ship and many more animals but only ten percent of them were in an animated state. The rest of them were in cryonic condition; they were all young. They had a zero population system; when a person died he or she would immediately be replaced from the cryonic pool. They also control their birth rate to a prescribed number to avoid overpopulation. The animals were treated much the same way when they died or were used.

They had a type of democratic system with an elected government and opposition parties but they called it Fair Representation. Their constitution of complicated lows, canons, and simple rules; were all run by a master computer and was programmed every five years with the participation of the whole community. There was a police force and a multi service unit which was to protect the ship from outside danger. The Hope community was a microcosm of the planet earth; its people were chosen for their excellent health and education. They were the best representation of the human species for this mission. They were carrying an advance technology and a matured civilization for a genesis to new planets to be discovered some time in the far future.

The spaceship Hope was one of the best ships that was built specifically for this project; it was indeed a floating metropolis. It had its own gravitational system that differed little from that of earth's. There was an artificial sun with days and nights just like back on earth. There was mass transportation that carried people to all places of the ship. It had roads, parks, and huge gardens producing food necessary for a balanced diet. They used credit instead of a monetary system; citizens saved hours of employment in a central bank, and used minutes for purchasing goods. Everybody worked in their own field but they only work four hours a day; the rest of the time was spent as they pleased.

For the first few days the people were settling in their new environment; every family was given their own living quarters and they were in the process of getting to know their immediate neighbors. After a week into their voyage Governor Flamous called all the officials to gather in his office to discuss the status of Hope. There were: Flamous Oofsis Governor of Hope and Vice Governor Ramiana Thalosis, Lacier Narkanous navigational commander of the vessel, Datherious Formlar Chief of Police, Rhodis Carplero commander of the army and air force, Artia Borgrados in charge of state affairs, and many other officers of lower rank.

The Governor started by invoking the Great Source for help and guidance and then they answered in unison, "Let it be so." He said, "I congratulate all of you on a job well done. Our voyage just started and the journey will be long; it will take many generations until we find our first planet and we most likely will not be there to see it. But we live in a place with all the comforts we had back on earth and we will continue to improve our way of living as we go on. We are the pioneers of this great project and we should be proud that our people entrusted us with such a responsibility.

Then the meeting went on with each official reporting the status of the spaceship and the community. Artia Borgrados was the first one to speak, she said, "Governor, considering all the preparations we had to endure in such a short time I would say that we are doing O.K. for now; but we still have more to do for the people to feel at home. In the next two weeks we promise to prepare a more detailed report." The next one to report was Lacier Narkanous navigational commander of the ship he said, "Our ship is in perfect condition; everything checks out but we will know more about its status after our first evacuation drill which will commence ten days from now."

Somehow Governor Flamous Oofsis wasn't satisfied with Laceir's short report; he wanted to know more about this evacuation drill or E-Vac. He said, "Commander Lacier, what is this drill consists of could you elaborate?" "Sure Governor, an e-vac could be a partial or a full evacuation depending on the circumstances. For instance if we sustain a catastrophic fire we may have to e-vac only part of the population, but if we are hit by a meteor we might have to abandon ship in its entirety until we repair it or build a new ship." "Are you telling me that we have the capability of building a new ship while we are living in pods?" "Yes Governor, in case of a complete abandonment all pods will travel as a convoy for as long as it's needed. We could use whatever material we could salvage from the ship or use new material if we have to. We have everything we will need to rebuild the ship in its entirety." "Thank you Commander Lacier; that should make all of us feel better; we are indeed a power to be reckon with."

Datherious Formlar chief of police was the next to speak, he said, "Governor Oofsis, I am pleased to announce to you that for now all is well in my department. However we anticipate problems in the future especially with our youngsters who may find it difficult to adjust to our new environment. Back on earth we were inundated with all the ecological problems and there was very little attention given to the youth at the time. They were faced with an uncertain future and many of them turned to drugs and into the underworld culture. Inevitably some of these miss guided youths are here with us now and it's only a matter of time before they go back to their old habits. Our new constitution makes it easier for us to act with a specially formulated program to pay the required attention to our children and thus avoid the pitfalls they had back home. So to summarize my report all is well now, and all will be better in the future." "Thank you Chief Formlar, keep up the good work."

Next and last speaker was Rhodis Carplero commander of the army and air force; he said, "Governor our spaceship is a floating fortress. We have the best weapons earth could have given us but while these weapons would have been sufficient on earth; we don't know the enemies that we are going to face in the future. Therefore we have started a newly designed program which will keep our army and air force practicing within the compounds of the ship and outside in space. We will be improving our capabilities all the time and we will be ready for any unforeseen danger out there. Our factories will constantly upgrade our weapons and our space force as we go along." "Thank you Commander Carplero your dedication to your duty makes us feel safe."

The spaceship Hope was sailing silently in the cold dark space carrying within a micro-cosmos of the planet earth along with the fruits of its latest technology, culture, and civilization. Neighbor planets shone in the space and earth still visible wearing its blue and white dress like a bride in friendly skies. People now and then looked back home already with nostalgia and sadness knowing too well that they will never see their birth place again. But for the most part, life went on almost as it was back on earth. Shuttles carried people to their homes and businesses and the citizens of Hope did their best to adapt and acclimate to their new home life.

Danger Looms on Earth

Elder Farow Naromi attended governor Oofsis' meeting with his top officials on a special 3D channel from earth; and he was satisfied with the general status of the spaceship Hope. He congratulated the governor and his staff for all the good work they have done on the ship. He wished them good luck knowing well that as time went on he wouldn't be able to attend too many of these meetings. Farow Naromi was glad that everything went so well with Project Hope and copies of earth's libraries and all the other historical items which for so long were hanging perilously on a string were now safe. His attention now turned to the problems here on earth.

The melding of glaciers, earthquakes, and floods, were almost daily occurrences. All five continents reported great loss of life and materials, and the prognosis was for more of the same. But even under those circumstances the people of earth managed to adapt and live for hundreds of years. However as time went on, their central government stopped to exist and people formed local governments and tried to live as well as they could.

Finally anarchy took over and now people lived in small groups fighting each other for just a mere existence. Some people lived in abandoned government buildings and others in houses that were still standing. Eventually everything fell apart and disappeared covered by water and earth. People lived in natural dwellings, under trees and in caves. For many years there was a rumor of a great civilization that once existed but after a while even that was forgotten. Now people were completely illiterate and only a step ahead of their contemporary animals.

Thousands of years passed; the climatic conditions changed from hot, to cold, many times until eventually the weather slowly became more stable and vegetation and animal life started to recover. There were patches of clear land here and there where animals grazed again, and life began to be easier for all living things.

Better weather brought humans out from caves and the woods; they also took advantage of the improving weather. Thousands of years living under harsh conditions changed them dramatically from what their ancestors used to look like. They became smaller and somewhat stronger but they retained their hairless bodies and used animal furs and pelts to keep warm in the winter months. The average life span was about thirty years. They looked sick and pitiful; and lived in groups of ten to fifteen people. They fought with other humans constantly mainly for better territories and food.

One thing humans didn't lose was the ability to adapt to their environment better than other animals. They had forgotten the language their ancestors spoke a long time ago and now they used a smaller vocabulary modified to their immediate world. Although they didn't know it at the time, they did speak a few words that came from their ancestors like; love, pain, life, death, birth, war, fire food, and water; but they were pronounced a little differently. Other groups of people spoke different languages but they also retained those few words.

As the weather became better and grass and other vegetation was easier to find, more herbivorous and carnivorous animals visited the open fields. However humans who were in smaller groups found it difficult to defend themselves from lions and other predators. And in order to better protect themselves they put their differences aside and joined together to fight their common enemies. It quickly became understood that the bigger the group became, the safer they felt. With more hunters they had more kills and a better diet. For the first time in thousands of years the ecosystem was improving and the animal world including humans was getting better too.

Spaceship Hope

The Vagabonds were leaving behind the ten dwarf planets which were by now a long way from the sun approximately; 5,913,520,000 (Km) a few months earlier they had seen the two dwarf sisters Eris and Ceres and Pluto. Soon they would leave the home solar system and enter the vast uncharted space in search of other solar systems for habitable planets.

The citizens of Hope were alerted to the fact that today would be the last chance to communicate with their friends and relatives back home on earth. After today, reception will become weaker and soon all communications with earth will be cut off. People from both sides were saying their last goodbyes and farewells knowing too well that the thin thread which connected them for the last ten years; will be severed forever. Although the citizens of Hope felt lonely all this time being away from home; they were the lucky ones in comparison. People on earth were entering a time of catastrophic events which would alter their lives for a long time to come.

This would be the second time the citizens of Hope would be called to make changes in their constitution. The last time was five years ago and the people were now overdue for some needed updates. During the last election many officials were replaced with new candidates and among them was Governor Flamous Oofsis. He was replaced with Governor Mooros Kalvian who was one of the teen agers that came aboard. All those who could attend were there for that important occasion.

Governor Kalvian initiated the election procedure by saying, "Citizens of Hope we are gathered here to exercise one of the most important duties as free people. We will proceed with the constitutional changes following our bylaws. Two computer-like boxes were brought-in and they were placed in front of Governor Kalvian, and the rest of the governing officials, including the opposition parties. There were three dimensional pictures in key places so everybody could see and also take part in the process of the change.

The first thing they had to do was to vote for constitutional changes; once that was accomplished all powers from the prime computer moved to the secondary computer. Then the secondary computer was moved away to a secured place. Then all citizens who were of age to vote started voting for removing or introducing new lows to the constitution. This procedure took at least a whole day and sometimes several days. As soon as the new lows were agreed to by the majority of the voters they were accepted by the government and made the new lows obeyed by all. Then the new lows were entered in the prime computer. Next they brought the secondary computer and moved all powers back to the prime computer and entered all the changes to the secondary computer too. From now on the prime computer will be the low and the constitution for all, and the second computer will be kept as a backup. And so the citizens of Hope had a safe government participated in by all, in a democratic way even though they didn't know what democracy actually was.

The ship was like a human body it could protect its self mostly without the crew's interference; in fact there were nanos in every component of the vessel which repaired any sustained damage, inside or outside. Nanotechnology was used back on earth for hundreds of years not only for repairing things but for building too. There were whole cities built by those subatomic particles. They were the most important tool in hospitals and the medical establishment as a whole. In addition to that, the ship used robots for its up-keeping, and humans incorporated them within the army and the police; thereby reducing human participation to the minimum but they always had total control of the structure.

The size of the vessel was like an average city occupied by one hundred thousand people with streets and parks and buildings. However they used mass transportation for the most part and a few magnetos resembling cars; but they both used antimatter for fuelling. The ship had an artificial environment with actually a rotating sun programmed to have four full seasons. Robots were tending the gardens and also raising animals which were used mainly for protein supplement for human diet. All children were implanted with special devices after their fourth year; with all the education they were going to need for life but were frequently upgraded with new information.

The people of Hope were well-nourished and kept healthy in mind and body with continues exercise. There were schools but only for refresher courses and younger kids were kept busy with various programs designed specifically for their wellbeing. There was a strong police force but they seldom needed to interfere with the citizenry. There was an army-air force preparing for any alien enemies and other emergencies. They were composed of younger recruits and when they became older usually they joined the police force.

The spaceship Hope was traveling now for the last twenty years and hadn't seen any planets, let alone habitable ones. The citizens were well organized and although there was some bore-dom especially with the grownups who had seen a more natural life back home; they were happy for the most part. The younger people who were born on the ship were quite content because Hope was the only place they knew. Those citizens who were kept in cryonic state were reanimated in stages and were replaced by other citizens who were picked by a lottery system. That was one of the most unpleasant duty they had to perform; but it was understood by all that it was important for the survival of the community. It was almost like death; because they were kept away from their loved ones for many years at a time.

They were now entering an area with small and large debris; the remains of ancient violent collisions among bigger iced rocks traveling aimlessly with tremendous speed. The structure was protected by a shield that could handle smaller debris but larger ones could completely destroy it. Understandably Commander Narion Dackus and his staff on the bridge were very tense to say the least. Special instruments honed in to detect and avoid the passing junk; buzzed and clattered adding to an already nervous atmosphere.

For the first time in so many years all those evacuation drills finally were put into effect; for this time they were preparing for the real thing. If things were not executed as prescribed; they could lose their ship and home world. People and every living thing were put in pods, everything important such as libraries and other historical items were also put in special pods. The whole spaceship was divided into sections and if needed; they could disengage from the mother ship and navigate on their own like larger pods.

Everything that needed to be done was done and now people waited for possible evacuation. Commander Dackus and his staff put an heroic battle with an unpredictable foe but they were hit by a piece of junk big enough to destroy a portion of their ship. Seconds before they were hit pods were ejected into the open space with their valuable cargo. They quickly formed a convoy following the mother ship and trying to avoid collisions. Although only a small portion of the vessel was destroyed it nevertheless caused much damage to the rest of it. There were fires burning out of control and people were preparing for a second evacuation, but robots and humans were finally able to put out the fires.

Most people were kept in pods until the fire fighters and other emergency crews were able to secure the ship but no second evacuation was needed. Commander Dackus and the bridge staff were shaken but kept what remained of the ship away from new collisions. Finally after a few hours struggle they managed to clear away from that perilous area and once more they found them-selves out of harm's way. All the evacuated pods managed to survive unscathed and they eventually were brought onboard the spaceship.

Rebuild the damaged spaceship

There was a gap the size of a stadium; and except for several pods that abandoned the ship on time; everything else in that area was vacuumed into space. The nanos and robots had already started their arduous work; rebuilding the lost section of the structure. In the meantime humans and robots in special pods searched for salvageable materials that were floating freely in space. One could see the framing of the new structure expanding following the lines of the space vessel like magic. Elsewhere inside the spaceship humans, robots and nanos, were also hard at work repairing the damaged infrastructure.

There were 127 robots lost and many others were damaged; however the biggest loss occurred in the fire and rescue crew where 28 humans were injured and 9 lost their lives. In such a controlled and secured environment it was a big price to pay. If it weren't for the E-Vac survival drills that they had practiced for so many years; it could have been worse. Most of the materials that were found floating in space were brought on board the ship and were used for building the damaged section of the vessel. Eventually with the hard work of the nanos, robots, and humans; Hope was completely repaired and looked good as new again.

A ceremony was held for the 28 injured humans and the nine fallen heroes; it was a very sad moment when Governor Naftal spoke about the fatalities and the big price they paid for helping those in need. A statue was built in the center of town in memory of those killed and was unveiled during the ceremony. And then the crowd dispersed and a page of an unfortunate incident was turned in the long history of the community of Hope. Nine people were reanimated from cryonic state to replace the fallen heroes and slowly people went back to their routine living as best they could and tried to forget that catastrophic event.

Endless Travel

The spaceship Hope had been traveling for ten thousand years and hadn't seen any planets at all; many generations had come and gone in that small community. The ship was rebuilt many times and it was also expanded to accommodate various needs mostly to make room for new hardware such as shuttle and reconnaissance ships. During all this time science in the community of Hope had surpassed the one they left back on earth. The people became even smaller and healthier and lived longer lives; but eyes and their heads became larger. As they became more knowledgeable their brain matter also increased. The ship became not only a floating fortress but an advanced city with many more comforts to accommodate an ever demanding society living in such close quarters.

Navigation commander Dores Lowemare, and exophysicist Thera Pamoua, were on the bridge discussing the upcoming officer's party and the latest gossip about the Governor's affair with Miss beautiful Turala when it happened. It was Thera who saw it first—she said, "This isn't an asteroid are we looking at a planet?" Commander Dores said, "I believe you are right, this is a planet." For a long time now special equipment had been programmed to detect planets and other asteroids and although they had been alerted to asteroids many times; they had never been shown any planets until now.

There were 3-D pictures coming steadily from the monitors

and everybody was excited. Many officials and the governor were on the bridge looking at the pictures which were also shown to the rest of the community. It was in the middle of a busy day but anyone who could stop, and look, did so with great excitement. Everybody in the community had studied galaxies and planets including the legendary Earth but they had never seen one yet. As they were approaching the planet, by now it was recognized as a non habitable-terra it was getting larger; and was about half the size of earth. It was covered with thick ice and huge mountains.

The instruments were spitting out information of all the elements on the planet; the ice was frozen methane, and among the minerals which were buried under the thick sheet of ice were; Copper, Diamond, Opal, and Malachite. They were in great need of methane which they could extract easily from the surface of the planet but the other minerals were too deep underground and it would require too much of their precious energy to get to them. The two most important items they needed were $H2O$ and cadmium but they decided to forgo anymore searching for now. They sent a shuttle crewed with robots and collected some methane and soon after that they left.

They named the planet Thera-Dores for the two people who discovered it. As they were traveling in that area they found more planets and they were named again according to the people who found them. After ten thousand years they finally came to another solar system with many planets smaller and larger but they were all frozen and unfriendly to living things. But the probability of habitable planets increased as they came closer to the sun. They traveled for another year in that solar system and landed on several planets with both humans and robots and extracted a few minerals they needed but so far they hadn't found $H20$.

As they came closer to the sun they found warmer planets with little ice of any kind but no water or atmosphere either. They checked every planet in the area systematically. Finally they found a planet with an atmosphere and some water that was about the same distance as earth was from the sun in the solar system they left behind; the size of the planet was approximately like earth. They sent exo-geologists and other scientists and spent enough time to comb the planet pole to pole until they were satisfied that life was possible there. They left enough scientists and other needed people, and robots, on the newly found planet and they continued searching for the ideal planet to occupy but as they got closer to the sun the planets were too hot and just as inhospitable for life. And so they decided to go back and joined the team they left behind.

They decided to name this planet Hope just as their fore-fathers had named their spaceship because they hoped to make this place their home planet. After many shuttle trips to Hope they brought their spaceship on the planet too. And so after thousands of years they were finally on a planet they could call home. Humans, robots, and nanos started to terra-forming Hope, building their first city and bringing water from underground. Before long they had their first city that was adjacent to the spaceship and life started anew. They found some native lower life but nothing resembling humanoids. The zoologists identified those that could harm humans. Parks were built close to their city and many trees were planted all over the immediate area enriching the atmosphere with more oxygen and making life altogether easier for all living things.

Rebirth of Earth

Earth once more entered a stable period and life started anew; before long humans became farmers domesticated animals and built communities. As time went on they built small countries and adapted to complicated languages all over the world. But their countries were separated for several thousand years until they discovered better transportation. There were rumors of lost civilizations of long time ago, but no one knew or could substantiate anything about it and life went on.

Once more humans used their ingenuity to invent better transportation and traveled through all five continents. They became powerful and now they built their own great civilization but they were never able to match the civilized world their ancestors lost thousands of years ago. Before that world was destroyed by cataclysmic events; they had achieved unimaginable scientific abilities. They lived healthier lives beyond their hundred birthdays, and managed to stop all wars. Unfortunately they over populated the planet and polluted it which hastened their demise.

"If you don't learn from history you are bound to repeat it." The problem was that the second time around people didn't know where they came from. They had no idea of what they had, and lost; so they started from the beginning and it looked like they were going to repeat the same mistake. Humanity has been cursed with wars many wars; they started fighting ever since they were living in caves. They stopped killing each other and got together only when they were about to be eaten up by the wild animals; and they understood that-that was a wise thing to do.

But once they felt secured they were back to their old habit— killing each other again. That went on for eons until the Great War which was to stop all wars but in the meantime millions of people were killed. Twenty years later the Second World War started with the loss of nearly fifty-eight million souls. In the ensuing years and up to the 21st century there were many undeclared wars which created an atmosphere of fear and insecurity all over the globe.

Humans were not the only ones who suffered; the rest of the animal world and the ecology as a whole suffered too. Ever since the Industrial Revolution the environment deteriorated with the use of oil and oil contaminants and other chemicals, pesticides and herbicides. But the worst of all was the use of nuclear energy in industry and in wars. People started to revolt against theocratic and corporate controls followed by instability, anarchy, and fear all over the world.

The corporate establishment especially in the western world managed to secure the biggest portion of the economic "pie" and in order to maintain their hold on power they eased several of the "Check and Balances", which were designed to maintain "Freedom and Democracy." The majority of people especially in Europe didn't take kindly to that and revolted against their governments. The so called, (Ninety-two Percenters) formed alliances with other groups in other countries and fought ferociously against the establishments; in turn they were met with equal brutality. There was a powder keg ready to explode with catastrophic consequences.

In the meantime emerging super powers such as China, India, Russia, and others challenged the established powers creating an uneasy situation. They were building weapons able to destroy their planet many times over; while diverting money from needed people's programs and at the same time making the plutocrats richer. And so it looked as if the second time around human beings were heading even faster than their ancestors towards total destruction.

Planet Hope

The people of Hope followed a program of terra forming their planet as soon as they landed; they planted millions of acres of land with trees thereby improving the atmosphere with more needed oxygen. They built numerous cities all over the planet and as the time went on their population increased and expanded throughout the planet. Thousands of years passed and those few human beings who left a dying earth; managed to make a better life for themselves in their new place. They never forgot why they left earth and continued to be good stewards of their environment.

They built a strong constitution that gave people above all freedom, security, and a peaceful life, and although they never used weapons against each other they kept building powerful weapons to defend their world from any foreign enemies. They used and improve the culture and experience they had brought from earth and as the time went on they traveled to other worlds and made new homes on other planets. They were able to travel much faster than when they left earth and considered themselves one human family. Above all, human beings kept strong commerce and communication throughout their history and forbade wars; all in all they were a peaceful but powerful society.

President Nova Machler, of Hope was also an historian who had studied the human history from the day they left earth thousands of years ago; to present day. From a young age he was fascinated with the legendary Planet Earth. He frequently made use of his implants to learn about the one hundred thousand ancestors who left earth with the libraries and museums well ahead before earth was destroyed. Back then people used the written language and most documents were digitized and actual museum art was micro sized to feed into the spaceship. Now people had implants with the education and most of the information needed for a whole life implanted in their brains at an early age.

At that time the expedition took ten thousand years but now with the use of wormholes spaceships could travel back to earth within a hundred years. The idea of going back to earth was discussed ever since people could travel faster but the authorities for some reason had repeatedly discouraged it. Now President Machler was in a position to find out the reason why. Vise president Novlas was asked to find out as much as possible on the subject and came up with the information. He met the president in his office; Commander Narion Dackus, who was in charge of the spaceships fleet, was with him. The Vise President was the first to talk, he said, "Mr. President I think I know the reason why the idea of going back to earth was discouraged all this time; we all know the reasons why our forefathers left earth. We also know that our ancestors had promised them that at some time in the future we will help them.

For thousands of years we have somewhat kept that promise by sending unmanned ships to scout and report on the progress earth was making. Unfortunately a few hundred years after our ancestors left earth it was completely destroyed and only about ten percent of all animal life including humans survived. And life pretty much started from the beginning. Humans reverted back to living in caves and out in the open like wild animals. They completely lost touch with their previous civilization except for a few words that survived in their poor vocabulary. There is a lot of all the reconnaissance that was made on earth all through the ages. From way back our forefathers had decided not to inform our people about earth until they had some good news to report. Unfortunately the recovery of climatic conditions on earth has taken a long time, and even longer for the animal life to recover.

Our last reconnaissance was done during Europe's so called dark ages in the mid of 1500 A.D. Apparently the Europeans started their calendar from the birth of a messiah called Jesus Christ who was born fifteen hundred years ago on earth in the Middle East in the city of Bethlehem. Many people believe that Christ resurrected himself back to life. According to our records their civilization has gone up and down many times but they have never reached the standard of living our forefathers had on earth before they perished.

Now according to our records earth is once more populated everywhere but they are divided in small countries and speak different languages. They have many wars mainly for religious reasons; but you could have all the information of their history entered in your implants on your next check up. After more than five hundred years we are planning another scouting but this time we are going to send some of our people and try to make contact with their leaders. Mr. President you will be getting more information in the future but I think that I have answered your questions." "Thank you Echou, now I would like to know when this expedition starts and who is in charge." "Commander Narion Dackus is in charge of this project." "We have been preparing for a while for this voyage and now we are in the last stages. If you wish to meet the crew I could arrange that for you sir." "I would like that very much, thank you Commander."

The ship was far superior to the one that had left earth thousands of years ago, but it was smaller with a population of only five thousand. For all of them it will be one way trip; and after one hundred years some of them would still be alive when they reached earth. They were to make contact with the earth people study them and render help as needed. The ship had to be hidden at all times and shuttle to earth in ways that they couldn't be seen. Younger people from the community were to intermarry with earth people and start a program of changing them to the standards of the people of Hope thus fulfilling a promise given by their ancestors before they left a dying earth. President Nova Machler met the crew and wished them good luck but once more the expedition was kept secret from the people of Hope and others, until earth reached a civilization equal to theirs.

"John, look, look, did you see that?" "I sure did, what was it?" "I don't know but it sure looked bright, wasn't it?" "Yah, it looked like a UFO to me but you know? You can never tell these days what you see up there." "Oh well, it could be one of those new U.S. air force planes you Know?" "Yah, you could be right."

In fact people were used to seeing things flying up there sometimes even closer to them since written history and beyond. In the older days people thought that they were gods visiting them; but in the 21st century some people thought otherwise.

The Extraterrestrials

Their ship was kept on the dark side of the moon covered by an invisible shield undetectable from earth. Their shuttle ships to earth were equally invisible. The problem the Hopians had was that they looked different from the local people and they could be spotted right away as extraterrestrials. Ever since they left their dying planet their physiques changed; initially living in spaceship Hope for ten thousand years and then for thousands of years in a dissimilar environment from earth. Their bodies became smaller, their heads larger and with larger eyes and pale skin they looked sickly but in actuality they were stronger and healthier. When they visited earth they always made themselves invisible to the locals because by human standards they looked unattractive and frightening. On the other hand Hopians thought of people on earth as equally unattractive and lacking in health and intelligence.

Few of the old timers that had left the planet Hope were still around, but all of them had a chance to see earth before they died. Those few remaining were treated with respect and some of them were allowed to attend conferences. Governor Theres Ravous had his father Tanio initiate the meeting. He spoke slowly but clearly; he said, "My friends I am approaching the end of my life; and I am lucky to have been born on Hope and lived my early years there, and I am equally lucky to have visited Earth the planet of our origin. A long time ago we started a program to help the people on earth from destroying their planet again. During the last few years we have done a lot towards that goal but we have a long way to go before completing our task.

Remember the people of earth are our ancestors; they helped our forefathers escape a dying planet and in turn our forefathers promised to help them in the future. The reason we are here today is to help them avoid destroying this beautiful planet once more. We have the ability and the knowhow to help them stop the deterioration of earth's climate by introducing them to safer fuels and energies along with new medicines for all living things. We started this project a long time ago; now it's in your hands to continue the process, thank you."

The elder's speech was received with great enthusiasm and appreciation; next one to speak was Governor Ravous, he said,

"Thank you father, without doubt we will do as you say; we will fulfill the promise our forefathers gave to the people of earth." Then the Governor went on to say, "The genetic alteration program is going well; so far we have managed to inoculate millions of citizens of earth with genes that will slowly change their DNA and RNA and eventually will be as healthy as we are. Even though we think they are ugly and we would like them to look like us; we must make sure that they retain their physical appearance as they are and it must also be understood that we will eventually look like them too. The program that we initiated a long time ago was for us to be like them; in essence we are back home to our planet of origin. It is our duty to see that it survives and that we can bring this primitive people to our standards.

The biggest problem they have right now is the use of nuclear energy as fuel and in weaponry; we must stop those weapons from going off intentionally or unintentionally. We have ways of doing that but we must be careful; remember that we are dealing with primitive people able to destroy themselves and their planet sooner than our ancestors did. The change must come slowly there is no sense making them live longer if they can't feed themselves. Information and technology must go at the same slow pace too. The introduction to computer technology and the digital information was a good start for their level of intelligence but it will take hundreds of years before they reach the civilization our ancestors reached before they destroyed earth the first time. It will take much longer before they become like us. All we can do right now is to keep the people and other living things safe and prevent another distraction of the planet."

If there was any doubt that they were not going back home; the governor's speech made it clear enough, they were here to stay. The genetic change was done simultaneously to the extraterrestrials and the local people; the two races were becoming one for the survival of the human species, and the planet as a whole.

Spaceship Hope Two was kept hidden ever since it arrived on the dark side of the moon decades ago. The Hopians saw the baby steps the local people were taking in the space race; undetected from their secured place. It was hard for them not to intervene and speed up the process, but they had to be careful; too much technology to this primitive people could be catastrophic. It was like curing a sick person; giving medicine in small doses would make them well, too much of it and the patients will die. But even though technology was introduced little at the time to the locals, it was beginning to bring results. Many of the altered local people were now in higher positions; in industry, science, medicine, politics, education, media, entertainment, sports and others. People had no idea what was happening to them but they were in the process of becoming physically and mentally superior more than any other time; it was the time of information and the people were learning much more than any other time.

Although it was common to see Altereds living among the Hopians; they were nevertheless ugly and an eyesore to the community. They were made to look exactly like the locals; they were The Inbreeds destined to live on earth and be part of that world for the rest of their lives. It was the fate of the rest of the community to eventually be assimilated with the locals in order to bring the human species to their full potential. It was a promise given to their ancestors thousands of years ago as they were leaving a dying civilization and a collapsing ecosystem.

Mary, and Jack, like many others, were the products of many years of local human and Hopian genetic intermixing that resulted in a new breed of human beings or hybrids. They shared the superior Hopians' health and mental abilities with the local humans' adaptive abilities to earth's climate and their physical appearance. Mary and Jack were a good looking couple healthy and intelligent equipped with P.H.D. diplomas in political science; able to succeed in any endeavor they chose to take. They were in their early twenties and like others; they lived their lives with altered families on earth and with the Hopians hidden on the dark side of the moon. And although they knew that their true ancestry was with the Hopians; nevertheless they felt more comfortable living on earth because of their likeness with the locals.

"Jack, I feel much better living on earth than in this artificial environment and I can hardly wait for us to go back to Seattle; maybe we could visit the San Juan Islands, it's so nice this time of year." "Oh that would be wonderful Mary, but we still have more to do here before we leave this place." "After our last physical check-up we won't have to come back until we are family; and that will be a long time from now, right?" "Yeah, first we have to have our first child and then our children will start the process all over again." "Well it's not that bad, we have the best of two worlds; remember we have friends and relatives here too." "I suppose you are right but I wish I could be here when the change is finally completed and all humans are the same." "I am afraid that would take a few hundred years more before this project is completed."

The End

OUR TIMES

An Essay

It is October 2013in the Year of our Lord, or whatever. This is all about our lives as we live nowadays here in America. Five years ago we elected a Democratic President and for the first time in American history, a black man. So hooray for us, we Americans aren't so bad after all. But now we have a group of forty-seven congressmen and women who decided they were not happy with the "Grand Old Party" and wanted to reinvent themselves. So with the help of deep pockets of those of the right wing persuasion, they reinvented themselves and now they are called the "Tea Party," (no relation to the Tea Act of December 16 1773), those were the real patriots.

Now make no mistake; these forty-seven puppets are doing an excellent job for their bosses. It's Robin Hood in reverse, "Take from the poor and give to the rich." Their aim is to stop most social programs designed to feed malnourished children in public schools, and reduce or stop food stamp help to the poor. It should be mentioned here that many of those who asked for food stamps were working people whose jobs went overseas thanks to the Corporate Elite.

These highway bandits; otherwise known as, "The Two Percenters" have a long reaching arm composed mainly of hospitals, health insurance providers, and other insurance companies, the weapon manufacturing industry, huge corporate farms, large retail markets, and many factories, to mention a few. Their goal has always been to do away with the unions, cut down wages and bring us back to the "good old days" of third world status. They are well on their way to establish their objective.

Oil is another commodity worth mentioning. Ever since it was discovered it has been a blessing and a curse. It's the fuel that has revolutionized industries and transportation all over the world. The Chinese used it extensively in Sichuan, mostly for medicinal uses in 347 AD. When The Arab fleet attacked Constantinople in 673 AD the Greeks burned their fleet using oil or naphtha and it was called "Greek fire." In ancient times oil, in its crude form, was found all over the world, but most people didn't know what to do with it.

The first time it was extracted from the ground with mechanical drilling was from a well in Germany and it was called, "Little Texas" in the 1800s, but others say that it was in the State of Louisiana at about the same time. It was around 1850 that oil was extracted in large quantities in Titusville Pennsylvania. From then on, oil was discovered in other states, and all over the world.

The blessing became a curse when Arab and other smaller countries that had lots of oil, were taken over by England, France, and the U.S.A. These countries used Arab oil and in return they paid them peanuts. The Western countries saw the value of oil early on and made themselves at home in the Middle East. They used the "golden rule," "Divide and Conquer"—and divide they did. They created small kingdoms and made sure the leaders were on their side. Anyone who disagreed did not live long. Oil has caused many wars and millions of deaths; it has destroyed the ecosystem to the point of no return.

Religion has always been used by authorities to achieve their goals even from the ancient times; the hierarchy of that time policed their people better than now; damnation in hell beats the poky anytime. Now people mostly use the, "whip and carrot" formula. Die for our cause and you will be rewarded with seventy-two virgins and all the pilaf you can eat, or damnation in hell for ever. I'll take the virgins; keep the pilaf, thank you very much.

Here in our country we have the televangelists; oh—they are good actors, no question about it. They know how to separate your dollars and sometimes your houses from you. They can easily shed crocodile tears for you in split seconds; some of them even tear their shirts for effect. And it's all for the good of the church; the poor guys work so hard to save your souls they just have to relax a bit in their multimillion dollar villas. Poor things my heart bleeds for them. One of our chosen televangelists, Oral Roberts, said, (and I am paraphrasing here), "Folks, if you do not contribute, God will call me home." Well, thank God; he must have gotten enough contributions because he lived a few years longer before he was called home.

Damnation in hell is very popular here too; on the other hand we can find virgins here on earth; but you do have to look a little harder. We also die for "God and Country." Our God is good to us; he helps us steal your oil and if we have to kill you to accomplish that he is always on our side. Of course we have to behave because he is omnipresent and writes our sins on his lap top.

Most industrialized countries in the world have a medical plan that covers all their citizens with a reasonable single payment premium. We pay twice as much and get half the medical coverage; except those who can't afford it, they have no coverage at all. Treating people like commodities; that's capitalism for you. The so-called, "Obama Care" that was introduced by President

Barak Obama and became law voted mostly by democrats and has been one of the President's best achievements.

It was ill received by the Republican Party as a whole. Never mind the fact that most of their constituents are going to be immensely benefited by this program. All they care is how to please their bosses. It should be mentioned here that most of Democrats were not happy either. They wanted the "Single Premium Payment" like most other civilized countries in the world have had for many years. But if this puny health insurance coverage had a hard time passing through both houses and becoming a bill, it is well understood by all that a "Single Premium Payment" bill would have been impossible becoming a reality. But as long as there are feebleminded people who believe all the lies broadcast from the extreme right wing; the rest of the people have to be on guard. Otherwise the Tea Party Puppets will bring our country to its knees much faster than Terrorism or Communism.

So that you don't think we are one-sided; some of us created the Coffee Party for an antidote to the Tea Party but it didn't stick around for lack of enthusiasm. But then from the heart of the Liberals blossomed the "Ninety-eight Percenters." No deep pockets here, just a group of honest, mostly young people, who saw their lives and future taken over by a mere two percent of the population who stuck with the "Trickle Down" or "Reaganomics" a formula which cuts taxes from the rich and adds more taxes to the middle and poor class. The extra savings from the rich are invested back into new businesses and voila, you have more people working and everything is wonderful. Except the Two Percenters invested their savings overseas; somewhere near the Yellow River and then it wasn't that wonderful here after all.

Now the Ninety-eight Percenters' movement caught on like

wild-fire and this time you had young and old citizens occupying parks and bridges and everything in between from "sea to shining sea." But alas, there was no leadership to lead this massive movement and it was slowed down by an undemocratic well-organized police force; under the auspices of the Corporate Elite.

In writing about China and the Chinese people; I want to emphasize the fact that I don't speak ill about all the country of China or all Chinese. Only for the industrial places and the two Percenters; as a whole I admire the people and the beautiful country they live. The Chinese people have one of the oldest civilizations and many of their inventions enhanced the lives of the rest of the people of the world.

In the meantime 135 million Chinese, out of more than a billion, embraced capitalism as its new toy while retaining Communism for the rest of the Chinese people. So that we don't think that we have a monopoly on a Plutocratic Oligarchy. The Chinese have their own brand of the "Two Percenters" and they are ruthless in maintaining their hegemony on their poor folk. This rich minority runs China; no question about it.

The Chinese people don't have Social Security or Medicare as we know it here; they are on their own as they have been for thousands of years. The people work for starvation wages, and many of them live in some of the dirtiest places of the world with smog from factories poisoning young and old. The same factories dump tons of garbage in the rivers and lakes where people live and work. That's how they can afford to build all the junk they sell to us here, and to the rest of the world.

The Chinese oligarchy has extra money and they do know what to do with it; they buy gold from all over the world and especially from the U.S.A. We are happy to sell it to them-of course at a good price. There was a time when a dollar was affiliated with at least some gold, now it suffices to print on the dollar, "In God we trust" and voila, we don't need gold anymore. I suppose the Atheist must make a special dispensation with it.

And since we are on the subject of gold would it be worthwhile mentioning the 1536 tons of "German Gold?" Well—sort of; you see—during the Second World War Hitler thought it would be a good idea to steal the gold from the European banks just for extra change, and keep it home. But when he lost the war and right before the Soviet Army invaded Germany, the gold was shipped to the U.S.A. For safe keeping of course. The U.S. made good use of it; after all didn't we spend a lot of gold and blood to help defeat them? In 2012 the Germans remembered the mostly stolen gold and wanted it back. But Uncle Sam said, "Not so fast, busters—you have to wait seven years before we even think about sending it back to you." Now that's what I call poetic justice. Actually to be frank I don't think we have too much gold remaining in our country; but we sure have a lot of green paper, of course always with God's blessing on it.

While our bridges and roads and in our whole infrastructure are falling apart, thanks in part to the Bush Dynasty who blessed us with two unnecessary wars for which we are still paying in blood and money. China is investing trillions of dollars in their country; becoming, slowly but surely, the next super power to be reckoned with. And as Walter Cronkite used to say not too long ago, "And that's the way it is." Lately the fabric of American life has changed dramatically from a rich super power, the envy and beacon of justice for all the world, to about to be a third world country in body and spirit.

Sure we still have the best and most weapons in the world; but so did the Soviet Union not too long ago. But look at them now, are we heading that way too? In fact the strength of a country doesn't come only from the barrel of a gun; but from a well-educated, and healthy population. For many years we had both in this country; but then the Corporate Elite had enough with the unions and nearly destroyed them. With the unions decapitated they were now free to manipulate the work force at will.

One of their first tasks was to close some of the biggest factories in this country and move them to China and other third world countries, why pay an American worker $20-25. Per hour when you can pay $1.00 -2.00 to a Chinese worker right? But wait a minute; these supposedly high wages are spent here at home purchasing goods and paying taxes which get the economy going. The Corporate Mafia said at the time, "Outsourcing is good for America; we will purchase cheaper goods from China and other third world countries. We will save a lot of money for the average American; it's a win, win, deal for all of us." Yah, right, as long as people had money to spend, was O.K. but then as the factories and many other businesses moved overseas Americans found themselves without jobs here at home and then it wasn't such a good deal after all.

When people's jobs are gone overseas and they are out of work and money; they become a burdened to themselves, to their families, to the community, and to the State. Their tax money is not there to contribute to the schools, the police force, the fire department and other important community services. This is happening all over our country and slowly but surely we are becoming a third world country. I won't attempt to say that the opposite is happening to the Chinese people. Only a small portion of the population is enjoying the fruits of capitalism; which is their version of the Two Percenters, the rest of the

Chinese people are actually worse now than they were twenty years ago.

If you don't have employment and you don't know when your next dollar is coming, it makes no difference how cheap that pair of shoes made in China is; you can't afford to buy it anyway. Alas, this ingenious American corporate idea of outsourcing caught up with many other countries in the world especially in Europe and now they are in the same mess as we are. And you thought we are exporting only cowboy politics to you ha? In the meantime the Chinese Oligarchy is getting richer, fatter, and sassier, thanks mainly to our international common stupidity. It's well known that "Might makes right" he who has the money pulls the strings and the Chinese, along with several middle eastern countries, are already pulling strings here in America especially at election time. Hooray for our Democracy, "give us your money and we'll make it good for you."

What happened? Well, we Americans are fascinated with movie stars, athletes, and hero personalities, just like many other countries; but unlike others we tend to be so enamored with some that we elect them to public office. And so it was with Ronald Reagan, a mediocre radio, film, and television actor. He was liked by many Americans for his good looks and his pal-like charisma in communicating with the average Joe. And so when he came into politics he simply continued acting as before.

His corporate friends were delighted with Ronny; he was smart enough to play his presidential role and naïve enough in politics to be trusted by his bosses. So Ronny started his ultra-conservative political career under the auspices of the Corporate Elite. In 1966 he became the 33rd Governor of California and again in 1970; then in 1981 he became the 40th president of the United States of America and then again in 1985. All in all he served eight years as Governor of California and eight years as the President of the U.S.A. It should be mentioned here that before Reagan's political career started we were doing reasonably well; that is economically speaking.

At the time we did have a war going on with the Vietnamese people; lest they jump into their canoes and paddle their way to attack our country. Or maybe we wanted to be closer to China just to get to know each other a little better? Whatever the reason was at the time; our corporate friends thought it was a good idea to send our young boys and girls into harm's way and pay a little "Uncle Sam" visit to the Vietnamese. That didn't go well with them and killed about fifty thousand of our soldiers in the process. The Vietnamese lost about ten times that number of their own people.

During the Reagan Presidency and later during the Bush Dynasty the Corporate Mafia became rich beyond all expectations. In effect they were given blank checks and they filled in the amounts they wished. They borrowed tons of money as needed to satisfy their gluttonous appetites thereby putting our nation into a debt crisis. The "drug culture" began in the early seventies. That resulted in another lost generation and the downfall of the Progressive Movement. At the same time we had the genesis of the Neo-Cons. During the eight years of Reagan's administration and while the progressives fell in tatters; the Neo-Cons gained power in federal and state governments. Regardless of the Democratic Presidents and other leaders that followed Reagan; the Conservatives never lost power and are still with us.

It is said that if a large ship sinks, it creates a sink hole and any small boats that happen to be too close; go down with it. So it is with a large and prosperous country like America. When it goes down, little countries follow. Our world has become one big family and when "Daddy" misbehaves the family suffers. The same paradigm exists in other places of the world; there are many "Daddies" misbehaving and our planet is becoming a powder keg ready to explode.

Is there a way out of this mess? Perhaps history will tell us. People have always rebelled against tyrants but seldom managed to defeat them. When they managed to overpower them, they changed history. More than three thousand years ago a small country called Athens, (present day Greece), was run by many tyrants one succeeding the other for many years. Finally there was a tyrant, Hipparchus, (6th century B.C.), who was very cruel and often wrote his orders in blood. When he and later his brother, Hippias, were finally assassinated the people had had enough with oligarchies, tyrants, and dictators, and gave power to the people, (demos). Thus Democracy was born and history was made. People in many other countries have rid themselves of their oppressors only to be taken over by others.

In our time things are a bit complicated in one way and perhaps easier in another. Our world is interconnected and is run mainly by today's tyrants or Corporate Elite. They are the Oligarchs or Two Percenters; they own the big money and our lives. Internet, Facebook, Twitter, U-tube, and other means of communication have made it easier for them to spy on us with every phone call we make or any e-mails we send. On the other hand, hackers sometimes access sensitive information in businesses and governments making their lives difficult to say the least.

Bradley Manning, a U.S. marine, passed thousands of secret files to Julian Assange who in turn, passed at least seventy-five thousand of secret files through his "Wiki Leaks" website, to several news papers and to the world. Edward J Snowden, an

NSA contractor, disclosed many classified top secrets about mass surveillance done by American, British, and Israeli governments. And let's not forget Daniel Ellsberg, Glenn Greenwald, and Sarah Harrison who also spilled the beans to the world at large and to us poor folks.

The way we can achieve real change in our time is through peaceful means as did Mahatma Gandhi in India, and Martin Luther King Jr. in the United States of America. Perhaps with strong leadership the Occupiers will be able to accomplish their goal of peace. A look back in history in any country of the world shows us that revolutions don't usually work and if they do, they are simply replaced by another junta and you are back where you started. When you approach the authorities in a civilized manner, they don't know how handle it. They feel more comfortable with a rough mob so they can clobber them. That's why some times they put their thugs within the protesters to cause troubles so they can use force on peaceful demonstrators.

The Fathers of our Country fought against tyranny and gave us one of the greatest countries in the world. They gave us a constitution with a Bill of Rights that makes us free citizens, but lately our rights have been compromised by a Corporate Elite group which puts money and power above our freedom. Wake up!

REUNION

A Story of Family

As the sun rose in the early morning the train traveled over the frozen tracks on the snow covered prairie. Larry was an early riser and one of the few in the dining car. As he opened his laptop the waiter brought him a steamy hot cup of coffee. Just as the train moved at a steady speed his eye caught the white landscape through the window; and it was hard to concentrate on his writing. When the train made a sharp turn to the right he could clearly see the other side of it and its occupants looking straight at him. People looked through their windows admiring nature at its best. Every now and then there was a farm or a house but for the most part the area was frozen tundra.

Larry Ferguson had received family reunion invitations before but he always found an excuse, not to go. It wasn't that he didn't like socializing with people but within his extended family there were a few people he didn't like. Larry closed his laptop and let his mind wander as he looked at the snow covered country.

Larry was in his forties, the oldest of the four children in his family; his brother Jimmie was two years younger and the twin sisters Leslie and Deborah younger by five years. The twins had gotten along well from childhood but Larry and Jimmie fought all the time and now as they became older, seldom spoke. His parents' were in their late sixties, retired, and remained in their old suburban two story five thousand square foot house with a double garage, and a huge garden. His mother Fiona worked most of her life as an elementary school teacher. His father, John Ferguson, made a killing in the stock market which enabled them to live comfortably. The Ferguson family lived in Oakdale in Washington County in the State of Minnesota.

Larry and Jane married in their early twenties; they were high school sweet hearts and they stayed married long enough to produce their daughter Sue but after a couple of years they split and went their own ways. Sue lived mostly with her mother but often stayed for short periods with her father. Larry kept the apartment in New Your where he worked as an attorney with a well-known firm in Manhattan; Jane moved to Los Angeles California and worked in real estate. Larry had many relationships but didn't marry again; Jane had two more unsuccessful marriages and now she lived alone. Sue joined the navy and she is training to be an F-16 pilot on one of the carriers sailing somewhere overseas.

One of the reasons Larry decided to accept the latest invitation was because his father was dying from prostate cancer. There was a message in his cell phone Sue's picture was on the little screen along with the text; she looked beautiful, the last time he saw her was at her graduation from Washington State University. The text read, "Hi dad I am out on leave for a few days and I will try to be at Grandpas' place by Thanksgiving Day, see you soon; love Sue." Larry wondered if Jane would be there too.

Larry was glad he didn't live with Jane anymore; he really never loved her, they were both young at the time and it was more of a sexual attraction than anything else. After graduation they went to different colleges and they seldom saw each other. Then she move to L.A. and he didn't see her at all until several years later when Jane's father died and he went back to

Minnesota to attend the funeral service. Next day he went back to say goodbye to the rest of the family and then he was scheduled to catch a flight back to New York. Jane was an only child and after her father's passing there was a lot to do with the house and to help her mother with all the necessary legal transactions. And since Larry was an attorney she pleaded with him to help her with the estate legal forms and also help her move some furniture in the house.

Jane had changed a lot since high school graduation; she looked more attractive as a matured woman. Needless to say it wasn't in his plans to stay longer in Minnesota he was obligated to be back in his office by next day at the latest. But because he could see that Jane truly needed his help he decided to stay at his parents' house for an extra day. It was during that emotional time their friendship started all over again. A month later Jane moved to New York and lived in Larry's apartment; she also started to work in real estate. Six months later they got married and moved to a larger apartment because Jane was pregnant with their daughter Sue.

Two years later their marriage was over for lack of real love; once more they were attracted to each other for their good looks; beyond that there was nothing else to keep their marriage going. Jane moved back to L.A. with Little Sue and started working in real estate. She married two more times but her marriages didn't last any longer. Larry kept the apartment and worked as an attorney. He had many relationships but he never got married. The only common thing that remained between the two of them was Sue and it was when he went to get Sue to bring her to New York to stay with him during summers for a few weeks that he had a chance to visit for a short time with Jane. After Sue graduated and went her way he stopped going to L.A. And Larry didn't see Jane for many years until one of his twin sisters Leslie married back 2001. Jane attended the wedding with her second husband Vernon also a real estate agent. Vernon was in his fifties he was; short, overweight, and wore his hair long. During their short visit he kept to himself and said very little. On the other hand Jane was very talkative and she appeared to have a good time visiting with old friends.

Jane talked to Larry as though nothing had happened between the two of them; she told him about her business, her new house, her friends, and her busy life in L.A. Larry forced himself to be polite and listen to Jane. He asked her about Sue and she was more than happy to bring him up to date with Sue's life. Larry knew Sue wasn't happy living with her mother and she never liked the stepfathers and her mother's busy life. During her summer vacations she liked staying with her dad and getting the attention she was missing at home. That was the last time Larry had seen Jane. Whenever Sue called and talked with him she would occasionally mention her mother; that's how he knew that Jane was separated for the third time.

The train stopped with a screeching noise at the St. Paul/ Minneapolis-Midway Station; there Larry rented a car and head-ed east to Oakdale Washington County. As he was approaching his neighborhood he noticed a few new buildings but for the most part things looked pretty much the same as they had always been. Larry arrived at his parents' home late in the afternoon; his mother was at the door to greet him, his father was sitting on the couch, they were both excited to see him, he was the first of the family to arrive home.

His mother had aged a bit but his father looked much older; he had that gray shadow of death due to his progressed prostate cancer. But he managed to put a happier face for Larry, and said,

"Well Larry; (long time no see) how are you doing my child? "I am O.K. dad, how are you doing?" "Well; I am dying but I am not dead yet; actually I feel better than I look; but enough of me, how are you doing out there in New York, how is business O.K.?" "Everything is going fine dad but I am concern about you; why didn't you tell me anything about your illness, I only learn very late about your situation, are you doing anything about relieving your pain?" "Don't worry about me I have enough pain killers to last me all the way to my grave; but enough of that I don't want to talk anymore about me. However since you are the lawyer in the family I'd like you to do a few things for us now that I still have all my faculties intact. But not now maybe tomorrow some time before everybody else arrives." "Sure dad, just let me know when you feel like doing that kind of stuff.

While the father was resting on the couch Larry had a long talk with his mother in the kitchen; she was tired and emotionally distressed. She said, "Your father puts on a brave face but he suffers a lot especially during the nights. I am going to miss him but I hope he dies soon so that he doesn't suffer anymore." "Let s not talk about it now mother; how are you doing?" "Oh I am doing much better than your father but I worry what's going to happen to me after he is gone; I want to make clear to you since you are going to have power of attorney that I don't end up in a nursing home. I have heard horror stories about older people being mistreated and abused in those institutions and not being able to do anything about it." "Don't worry mother I will never put you in a nursing home; when the time comes that you need care you'll have all the help you need here in your own home." "That's all I want to know; now tell me how is Sue doing, is she all right?" "Sue is still in the Service and the last thing I heard from her is that she is learning to be a pilot; she also said that she is going to attend the reunion party." "Oh that would be wonderful; I haven't seen Sue for a long time."

Jimmie hadn't seen his older brother Larry since Lesley's wedding back in2001 thirteen years ago. Jimmie didn't care much for his brother and he knew that the feeling was mutual, but nothing was going to stop him from seeing his father before he passed away. Jimmie was married to Jan and they had two daughters Lorry twenty-three and Terry twenty-one. But that didn't stop him from having affairs soon after he and Jan were married. Jimmie was a broker but unlike his father who made a killing in the stock market Jimmie barely made a living and if it wasn't for Jan who worked in a hospital as a nurse they would not have been able to pay their bills. Jan worked mostly the night shifts and if she had any affairs few people would have blamed her. In their early years the girls were frequently left unattended when Jan worked the night shift and Jimmie came home late. Inevitably the girls got into drugs and a few other problems early on but now they were both clean. Lorry finally finished college and became a nurse and worked in the same hospital with her mother. Terry became a reporter with CNN; both girls were very attractive.

Fiona had a soft heart for Jimmie ever since he was a youngster and he took advantage of it; after college he came back home and he was the last one to leave the nest. Whenever Jimmie was broke even as a married man his mother supplied him with needed money; and for better or worse he was the spoiled child in the Ferguson family. Jimmie was better looking than Larry and he knew it. In high school Jimmie played football and was well liked by the girls Larry played football too, but he was interested more in academics than sports; he had his share of sweet hearts too.

The twins Deborah and Lesley arrived the next day; Lesley

with her husband Jeff, and her ten year old son Denny. Deborah came with her twelve year old daughter Irene. Deborah and her husband Michael had gotten divorced a couple of years earlier and Deborah couldn't have been happier being on her own. Jimmie and family arrived a few hours later and the house started to fill with people. Fiona was delighted to see her children and grand children and especially pleased to see her Jimmie again. Within the day most of the extended family arrived too and stayed in various hotels for the night.

The Thanksgiving Dinner was catered for twenty people at the nearby golf course club all paid by the old man, so there was little to do by the immediate family other than visit among themselves. Most of the family was gathered in the living room where the old man was resting on the couch. John Ferguson had dressed appropriately for the occasion and most of all he had taken enough pain killers to last him well into the night. He asked Jimmie how the stock market was behaving and he was happy to tell his dad. Larry as it was his usual demeanor pulled away from the busy crowd and was checking a book.

The young kids were busy showing to each other their electronic gadgets and playing games; while the young adults tried to mingle with both groups. Mother Fiona was in Seventh -Heaven with her children and grandchildren so close to her. The old man was just as happy discussing the stock market with Jimmie, and a few others that had gathered close to his couch by then. Larry looked outside through a foggy window and saw that the snow had covered everything in the immediate area and wondered if Sue would be able to come to the party. There was a knock on the door and little Denny was the first one to open it. There were a few more members of the extended family shaking the snow from their hats and shoes before stepping in. Among the new arrivals were Jane and Sue; Larry put down the book and promptly looked at them. He thought to himself; Sue must have been staying with Jane these few days.

The minute Sue saw Larry she ran to him and said, "Daddy, how nice to see you." She hugged him and kissed him on the cheek. She wore her navy-pilot uniform and she looked beautiful; everybody turned around to see her. Jane was in a subdued mood she shook hands with Larry and said, "Hello Larry, how are you?" And then without waiting for an answer she moved on shaking hands with the rest of the people in the room. Jane had aged and looked tired; one could see that she didn't feel comfortable being there. If it wasn't perhaps for Sue's insistence to accompany her, Jane would have been happier to stay home.

It was getting to be dinner time and Jimmie made sure everybody was aware of it; he raised his voice loud enough to be heard and said, "Ladies and gentlemen in about half an hour we need to be at the club for drinks and dinner so I hope to see you all there soon." Shortly after Jimmie's announcement everybody left. Jimmie trove his dad and mom in their own car while Jan and the two girls drove the family car. Larry drove with several of the younger kids. There were already more friends and relatives at the club having drinks and now they were all mingled together. They all appeared to be having a good time. Old man Ferguson and mother Fiona were sitting on a couch looking from afar at the crowd and felt genuinely happy to be part of this group.

Dave Ferguson John's younger brother was there with his wife Rosemary, his son Michael, and wife Lisa along with grandsons Jonathan and Tomas. Rosemary sat next to Fiona and Dave by his brother John. The conversation between the older ladies and the two brothers was like day and night. While Rosemary and Fiona were speaking of the latest births and wedding in their families and in general looking at the young folks in the room; the two brothers were immersed in politics. John Ferguson was extremely right wing and Dave was the antithesis; and of the left persuasion so there was always enough room for argument.

As it always happens in larger groups, people tend to gather for the most part with their own contemporaries. Sue was talking to her father Larry and frequently looked at her watch, Larry said, "Why do you keep looking at your watch; do you need to go somewhere?" I am expecting my boyfriend to arrive any minute; but I am worried that he may not make it with the snow storm." "You didn't tell me you had a boy friend." "I didn't have time dad; Fritch and I met at the base about a year ago and we've been friends ever since. He is a good guy and I hope you meet him soon." "Don't worry Sue, he'll make it."

Sue didn't have to wait long; shortly after she had uttered those words a young man appeared in the lobby; he wore his pilot's uniform and walked straight to Sue who was sitting by her dad. The two of them were the best looking couple in the room which caused many people to turn around and look at them with admiration. Sue proceeded to introduce Fritch to Larry and then she pulled him by the hand and introduced him to her friends and cousins who were eager to meet him. Then she went to her grandparents Fiona and John, and said, "Grandma, grandpa this is my friend Fritch, Halverson, we were stationed at the same base at Fort Collins Colorado."

Fiona said, "I am so glad to meet you Fritch, and you my dear Sue, grew up to be such a beautiful woman; I am so happy to see you both." John said, "I concur with your grandma you look beautiful; are you flying those fast planes?" "Not quite yet grandpa but I am almost there; but Fritch is flying now and in a few more months I will be able to fly too." Then Grandpa who was very enthusiastic with these two young people who were serving their country so honorably said to Fritch, "What kind of plane to you fly Fritz?" I fly the latest F-16 –NRC sir." "Well young man and you young lady; I comment you both for your great service to your country, God bless you."

Sue and Fritch introduced themselves to the rest of the old folks Rosemary and Dave and then they went on to talk to their contemporaries. Although Dave admired the young couple and appreciated their effort to serve their country in such way; he nevertheless didn't care much for the higher ranking officers. Dave always had an antipathy for the military establishment; he felt that they always took the biggest slice of the pie and they wasted too much money in unnecessary wars and weapons, that's why he and his older brother John never agreed in politics. While John was making a killing in the stock market, Dave was a busy reporter with several of the biggest news papers reporting from Vietnam and other fronts putting his life in danger and making a living under the worse possible circumstances. He used to say to his brother, "John, you didn't even serve in any wars you just made your money out of them." And John would say, "You try to portray yourself as Mr. Righteous and you never had a pot to pee in."

But tonight both brothers acted their age and were more conciliatory; ever since John became sick with prostate cancer he became mellower not only with his brother but with everybody around him. As he was approaching the last portion of his life he became philosophical about life altogether. For a long time now John wanted to tell his brother that not only did he understand his thinking but he appreciated all he had done in reporting the truth from the front and exposing the misery our troops suffered on all those unjustified wars. But all he could utter was, "Dave you were right; I was wrong." Dave said, "John, we are not going to talk anymore about who is right or wrong; it's all water under the bridge now."

Unlike Jimmie Ferguson who was a "wanna be" broker; Michael Ferguson was a successful airplane graphics engineer working at the Boeing plant in Everett WA. His wife Lisa was an optician in Everett city. Their two boys; Jonathan twenty-six worked at Boeing in the electrical engineering, department and Thomas twenty-four worked for the Microsoft Corporation as a software technician in the word processing department. Finally they all sat down for dinner; the old man didn't spare any expense, the meals were excellent and there was a lot of liquor flowing around. The grandfather wanted to impress his family and friends before he departed. There were many who got up and wish the old man lots of love and good health but they knew too well that the their friend, father, and grandfather, was on his way out.

After dinner Grandfather John and Grandmother Fiona asked to be taken home; both of them were tired but especially John who had passed his bed time by a few hours and felt uncomfortable. Jimmie gave them a ride home; and that was fortunate for him because as soon as he left the club his younger daughter Terry announced to the whole crowd that she was gay and promptly left with her lover who was waiting for her at the door. The younger people were more receptive to the news, several of them even applauded for her but it was harder for the older folk and especially for her mother Jan. She knew for a long time now that Terry was acting differently from other girls and she even suspected that she might be gay; but neither one of them confronted the subject.

Jan walked out the door and caught up with her and said, "That was uncalled for; you didn't have to announce to the whole world that you are gay, and especially on a day like this." "I am sorry mother but I wanted everybody to know it and if they can't accept it it's their problem, not mine. Besides I waited for the old folks to leave first before my announcement." Jan went back inside the club clearly disturbed and tried to avoid looking at the people. Lorry came by her and tried to comfort her she said, "Mother don't feel bad about it; it's happening a lot these days, it's her life and she has to live with herself the best way she can." "I blame myself; I was always busy and away from you just when you needed me most, but I had to work. Your father never brought enough money to keep us going; what was I to do?" "Mom don't blame yourself; you had nothing to do with this, it's a hormonal thing it happens to a lot of people and other animals too; we humans are making a big fuss of it."

Larry put up a brave front with friends and relatives but all he wanted to do was to go back home and be on his own world. But he was glad to see Sue; she grew up to be such a beautiful woman and the young man she was going with looked like a good fellow too. Larry was about to excused himself and go to his parents' place for a much needed sleep when Leslie; one of the twin sisters approached him, she said. "I am sorry about Terry; she didn't have to come out of the closet like that." "What can I say, it happens a lot these days; but I do feel sorry for the girls, they haven't had an easy life." "I'd like to talk to you about dad; he is not going to be around for long, I understand that you are in charge of their will. Have you thought of mom? She shouldn't be left alone after he is gone; what do you think?" "Right now all I can think is; that when dad passes away I am going to have a Skype conference with all of you and take it from there." "That sounds like a good way to handle the situation." She kissed him on the cheek and left promising to see him tomorrow before leaving.

There were a few cousins Larry tried to avoid all night but finally one of them, Sam Hirington caught up with him. Larry had good reasons to avoid him; Sam was a maternal cousin, a very unstable character, a bigot and a racist. He was a member of an extreme right wing Nazi society and Larry wanted nothing to do with him. Sam said, "Hey Larry I understand that you are handling, the Gonzales case in New York; is that right?" "Yeah, that's right; what's to you?" "Well let's say me and my friends ain't happy about it." "Well you and your friends can go fly a kite for all I care." "Well, don't say I didn't warn you cousin." "It's my business to defend people and if you bother me again; I am going to report you to the police, do you understand what I am saying?" "Oh I understand what you are saying; just don't forget what I said."

Arturo Margioro was a Puerto Rican emigrant in his sixties who had lived in New York most of his life and work in a Mexican restaurant as a waiter. One late night on his way home he witnessed a hate crime not too far from the restaurant. He saw several white people beating up what appeared to be a Latino man with crowbars. When they saw him they went after him; he ran to the back door of the restaurant opened it and got in; then quickly locked the door behind him seconds before they arrived. While they were banging on the door Arturo called the police and told them what had happened. Finally when the thugs heard the police coming they disappeared. Arturo knew they were after him and they wouldn't stop until they got him too because he saw their faces. The next day the brutal killing was all over the news with many Latinos and other ethnic minorities demanding justice from the authorities. Arturo quit his job and worked in another restaurant to avoid being seeing; he also helped the police to identify the killers and eventually some of them were caught. The victim was a young Mexican man Petro Gonzales in his twenties who was also going home from work that night. Needless to say the Gonzales case brought Larry Ferguson's name from obscurity to fame in a very short time. Larry was given extra help in the office to help him with the Gonzales case. That's why he was anxious to go back home; but this threat from Sam made him more careful about where he went and the people he talked to. In his long career as a defense attorney Larry had many difficult cases but he had never been threatened for his life and especially from a close relative. Larry made a mental note to himself about being more careful these days.

Sue and Fritz were talking to their contemporaries and as he looked at Sue he couldn't help but admire her and felt proud to be her father. He approached her and said, "Sue I am about ready to go home but I wanted to have a word with you before I leave." "Sure dad." Then she excused herself from the people around her and she moved to the side and said, "What's up dad?" "You know that I am handling the Gonzales case; you know—the young man that was killed by a mob a few months ago?" "Oh yes dad; sorry I meant to talk to you about that, congratulations your name was all over the media, I think that's great." "Thank you Sue; unfortunately sometimes fame comes with some degree of danger and I want you to know that I have arranged for you to be in charge of my estate in case I am in anyway incapacitated or dead." "Oh dad don't talk like that you are scaring me now; who is going to bother you anyway?" "Well let's say that I have been long enough in this business to know the possibility always exists." "Are you going to be staying at the hotel tonight?" "Yes mom and I are staying overnight; and we leave tomorrow morning." "Be good, be careful, and keep me posted; will you?" "I sure will dad." Then Sue kissed him on the cheek and went back to her friends.

Before Larry left he talked to Jane who was with a group of ladies; she seemed to be unusually quiet and talked very little. Larry approached her and said, "Jane you seemed to be rather quiet tonight; that's not like you are you alright?" "I am fine thanks for asking; are you leaving?" "Yes, but I was hoping to visit with you before I left but I never had a chance." "Sorry Larry nothing personal but actually I don't feel like talking to anyone tonight." Larry didn't feel like talking to her either but he didn't want to be rude to her and he made the effort to see her before he left. He turned around and he was about to leave when she said in a rather abrupt way, "Please don't leave; I need to talk to you." Then she pointed to a couple of chairs a few feet away. Larry obediently followed her and sat on one of the chairs; next thing when he saw her face there were tears running down her cheeks. Larry said, "O.K. Jane what's going on, are you alright?" "No Larry I am not alright; I am dying from pancreatic cancer I only have a few months to live if I am lucky." Larry thought to himself —that explains her behavior all during the night—then he said, "I am very sorry Jane is there anything I can do for you? "You can't save me no one can save me it's final, I will die soon; but you can do something else for me."

"Larry all I have left is my house; the cancer is not only eating my body but my savings too. Whatever is left I want it to go to Sue; she is the only person I have left. However my last husband Don Pasmico is contesting the ownership of my house even though he knows I don't have long to live. I should tell you that I had the house before I married him and he had contributed very little to our household while we were together. I don't have the strength or the money to fight him in court. I'll give you power of attorney and you can use what money I have left after I am gone; at this point you are the only person I can trust to see that our daughter gets the house. I am sorry I haven't been a good wife to you Larry; but I have been a good mother to our Sue, Larry will you please help me?" "Of course I will Jane, don't worry I will take care of everything; don't forget Sue is my daughter too. Have you told Sue that you suffer from cancer?" "Yes but she doesn't know the severity of my disease and please don't tell her I don't want her to worry about me; she is working hard to be a pilot and I don't want my illness to interfere with her career." Larry embraced Jane affectionately and as he started to leave Jane said, "I feel much better now that I know you will take care of my problem." "That is the least I can do for you and Sue." And then Larry left Jane behind and along with her a portion of his life during better times long ago.

Sue and Jane left the club and drove to their hotel (North Star) with Fritz following them; Fritz was staying overnight in the same hotel. Although it was still snowing the freeway was reasonably clear so Sue had no problem staying on the road. She tried to engage her mother to talk but Jane kept silent so Sue concentrated on her driving and didn't say another word. They hadn't driven too far on the freeway when she noticed a car on her left side weaving dangerously close to her car. She thought he was a drunk driver and she stepped on the gas to avoid him; but no luck. As the driver of the other car came even closer, she noticed that he wore a black hood over his head. Sue now knew that he wasn't drunk he tried repeatedly to push her off the road. Her father's words came to mind, (Be careful, be good, and keep me posted.) Did he try to warn her for something like this? The next time he came close enough hit the rear left side of the car but she kept driving faster trying to keep some distance between the two cars.

Jane said, "What was that?" It's O.K. mother don't worry it's just that the road is so slippery." "Then don't drive so fast!" "I can't talk right now mother, but I have to drive fast." It didn't take long for Jane to realize what was happening and she said, "I am going to call the police." "Yes, do that mother, call the police." The other driver was getting more brazen by now and Sue knew that it was a matter of time before they will be pushed off the road and into the ditch.

In the meantime Fritz who was driving couple of cars behind could see the same car weaving dangerously onto Sue's car and he also assumed that she was dealing with a drunk driver. Since he could not pass the two cars in front of him from the left lane he passed them from the right lane and over the shoulder having to drive through a pile of snow pushed on the side. He managed to placed his car behind the drunk driver's car and as he came close enough he also saw the driver with the hood over his head and then he realized that Sue's and Jane's lives were in danger. He drove right behind him and hit him on the bumper again and again until he got his attention. The other driver rolled down the window and started shooting at Fritz's car that didn't scare him who drove faster and hit him even harder. By then the cops could be seen with their flashing lights several cars behind.

The hooded man tried one more time unsuccessfully to hit Sue's car and then pulled out on the next exit and disappeared into the night followed by the highway patrol officers who by now were close enough to see what was going on. Fritz called Sue on her cell phone and said, "Sue, are you alright?" "We are a little shaken but we are both fine; and you?" "I am fine too; it looks that the cops want us to pull to the side." "Yeah, I see that too." Both cars pulled off the lane and stopped; soon after that the cops came with guns drown and ordered them to come out of their cars. Jane came out with great difficulty and said, "I am sick and very cold I can't stay out too long." The cops didn't respond and proceeded to search her; after they were satisfied with their search, they asked her to go into one of their cars. Jane felt much better in the cop's car but still unhappy with the whole episode. In a short time the cops knew with what kind of people they were dealing and after they signed some papers they let them go. Jane was helped by one of the officers into Sue's car and soon after that they left for their hotel without anymore incidence.

Next morning Sue and Fritz met at the cafeteria; all three of them had a 6:00 p.m. Flight to LA from Minneapolis MSP International airport. Fritz said, "How is your mother doing?" "Last night's episode was a little much for her and I didn't want to get her up early; I am going to send breakfast to her room later on." "So, do you have any idea who is after you?" "This morning I called my dad and told him what happened; he was worried and upset but he wasn't surprise he said, "Those thugs want to scare me of the case and from what you just told me they are doing a good job.

A few hours later Jane felt better but she was anxious to go home; so without further delays they left for the Minneapolis MSP International Airport where they caught their flight on time. At the LA Airport Fritz and Sue said their goodbyes and while Sue and Jane drove home Fritz caught another flight to San Diego Naval base where he was stationed for now. A few days later Sue also left home and flew to San Diego Naval base where she was temporarily stationed too.

Next Day Larry woke up early as usual; the only other person that was up was his mother. Fiona was an early bird like Larry; for many years when the kids were young she had to make breakfast for everyone and then send them to school. Then she had to be in her class before her students arrive. Now even as an older retired person she still got up early; it had now become a habit with her. Larry walked to the living room sat by the window and opened his laptop. As he started to read his mail Fiona brought him a cup of coffee with a piece of toast; and she sat by him she said, "I hope you have a minute I need to talk to you before everyone is up." "No problem mom; what's going on?" "I don't want to alarm everybody else but I think your father needs to go back to the hospital; last night it was a little bit too much for him at the club with all the people and the commotion that came with it. He suffered all night and the pain killers didn't help him at all; finally I gave him a sedative and now he is asleep. I can't manage anymore; he needs to be in the hospital they know how to help him." "Mother have you heard of hospice? At this point this is where father should be, they will take good care of him until he is gone." "He is stubborn he doesn't want to go anywhere else he wants to die here and I can't see him suffering like that anymore." "I'll talk to him when gets up." "Good that's what I wanted to hear; God knows I have tried to convince him to go back to the hospital but he won't listen to me, but he might listen to you."

Larry worked on his laptop most of the early morning and tried to do as much work as he could but he had to be back in his office by tomorrow; there was no way out of it. Sue called him and told him what had happened the night before and then she said, "Who would want to harm us? We haven't bothered anybody?" Larry said, "It doesn't have anything to do with you they are after me; they want to scare me off the Gonzales' case." "Well I hope you stay there and fight them." "I tend to do just that, what concerns me is your well being." "Oh don't worry about us dad, we will be alright." "I sure hope so Sue; please be careful." "We will dad, we will." Larry didn't want to alarm anybody so he didn't mention the last night's incited to anybody in the family. Fiona called him for breakfast. By now there was more of the family up eating and talking aloud; before Larry joined them in the dining room he went by his father' room; pushed the half open door a bit and peaked in. He heard his shallow irregular breathing; he thought to himself at least he is still asleep I must talk to him when he is up.

The twin sisters Lesley and Deborah were helping their mother Fiona in the kitchen to make breakfast and talking about the last night's party. The rest of the extended family were in the dining room; Larry sat as far away from Jimmie as possible and tried to mingle with the rest of the family although he felt more comfortable talking to the younger kids. While Jimmie and Jan kept mostly quiet, Lorry was talkative with young and old. She sat by Larry and said, "Hi Uncle Larry; did you have a good time last night?" "Yes I did, it was nice to see all of you it's been so long since the last time we met." "I had a long talk with Cousin Sue she seems to be happy in the service and I am sure she will be a pilot soon. When I graduated from nursing school I considered joining the navy but I was scared with all these wars that we have now days and started working at the same hospital with mom. I am pretty happy with my job and the pay is good too; I feel that I am also contributing to a great need in my own way." She avoided to mention her sister's announcement about (coming out) and Larry was happy not to have to talk on the subject too.

As the day went on everybody was anxious to leave for home to avoid another snowstorm that was predicted to hit tonight. Everyone made sure to go and see the old man who was up by now and was sitting on his couch in the living room. Neither John nor Fiona said anything about the difficult time John had had the night before; to them the old man looked as sick as he did the night before. Finally they all said their goodbyes and most of them left; the last ones to leave were Jimmie, Jan, and Lorry. Fiona was heartbroken as always when Jimmie left; Larry said as little as possible to Jimmie and before long they were all gone. Fiona managed to wipe her crying eyes and sat down to have another cup of coffee with Larry. Then out of the blue Fiona said, "Larry Jane didn't look like herself last night, is she alright?" "Didn't they tell you?" "Tell me what?" "Mother, Jane is dying from pancreatic cancer; she is not going to be with us for too long." "Oh no, I am so sorry, poor thing she is so young; I knew she was sick with cancer but so many people who have cancer live long lives now a days. My goodness, does Sue know how sick she is?" "She knows she is sick, but not that she will die soon; and don't you tell her either Jane doesn't want Sue to worry about her." "Oh no darling, of course I won't tell anybody, be sure about that."

After dinner Larry had a long talk with his father and convinced him that he should go to hospice for his own good and Fiona's who worried and cared a lot for him. Larry worked on his laptop until 1:00 a.m. and then went to bed very tired. These last few days had been very emotional for him and he knew that there was more of the same to come. The next morning he drove straight to the airport and flew to JFK airport in New York. This time he used his own car to drive home but he decided to stop at the office to pick up a few things to study at home. Larry ended up staying in his office longer that he had intended. As he drove in the garage he looked at his watch, it was 11:30 p.m. It had been a long day and all he wanted at this time was a hot shower and a good sleep. When he opened the door to his apartment he was in for a shock; many things were scattered in every which way, it looked as if a twister had gone through his apartment and especially in his office.

Larry immediately stepped out the area, closed the door behind him, and called the police; within a short time the police and F.B.I. agents were all over the apartment doing a thorough investigation. Larry had to give a deposition to an F.B.I. agent and then drove back to his office and slept on his couch; he thought under the circumstances that was the only save place for now. Next day Larry's name was all over the media; he was the man of the day. His phones were ringing nonstop all from reporters hungry for more news; Larry had his staff handle the media, but he made a few calls personally to close relatives and especially to his mother and Sue who were both worried about his well being.

The cops chased the hooded man through the city and finally apprehended him. His name was Nihou Pavlovich a man in his fifties with a long record of hate crimes and it was revealed that he was closely affiliated with the same Nazi group that murdered Gonzales. Larry couldn't prove it at the time but he was sure that his first cousin Sam Hirington was implicated with the hooded man. But he had a hard time accepting the fact that Sam a close relative would do such a hateful thing to a couple of innocent women. As much as he hated to implicate his cousin Sam with this episode; in his deposition with the FBI he mentioned the conversation he had with him on Thanksgiving Night. Finally with the arrest of the hooded man the police was able to get deep into the Nazi organization and arrest more members that were implicated with the Gonzales murder.

The ethnic minorities as well as the African Americans were

putting a lot of presser on the local authorities and their representatives asking for quick punishment for those thugs who committed such a heinous crime on an innocent person. On the other hand the extreme right wing went out of their way to help the Nazis while at the same time claiming that they had nothing to do with these kinds of people. Needless to say because Larry's daughter Sue and ex wife Jane almost became victims to this Nazi extremist group; the Gonzales court case became personal to Larry and he was determined to put these thugs in jail for a long time.

In the ensuing several weeks two unpleasant things happened to disturbed his busy work at the office; first his father John Ferguson finally succumbed to his prostate cancer, followed by his ex wife Jane who also died from pancreatic cancer sooner than was expected.

As busy as he was he could not avoid attending those two occasions. However this time he was escorted by personal guards assigned to him by the judge in charge of the Gonzales case. The passing of his father and his ex wife Jane left an indelible pain in his heart and reminded him of his own mortality. He promised himself that after this important case was over; he would take off for a while and travel and perhaps find a more permanent relationship. With the two memorials behind him and Sue back on the carrier somewhere in the pacific as an F-16 pilot he could now concentrate and focus on the coming up important trial.

Larry received a letter from his mother in regards to his cousin Sam who was implicated with the hooded man in the car chase on Thanksgiving Day; she wrote, "Larry my dear child, I just got a letter from my sister Laura who says her son Sam is implicated in that terrible car chase who almost killed Sue and Jane. I can imagine how you must feel to know that your cousin

Sam would want to harm them in such a dreadful way. I feel your pain and I am just as enraged as you are.

But Larry I also speak as a mother who wouldn't want to see my son jailed in such a terrible place. Laura has asked me to talk to you and to ask you to go easy on your cousin Sam; would you please do that for me?"

Since Fiona was not using the computer he sent her a letter, "Mother I received your letter and I understand your concern for Sam and Aunt Laura's worries about him. But you need to understand that Sam conspired with Mr. Nihou Pavlovich (The Hooded Man) to harm or kill Sue and Jane and I find it difficult to go easy on him or forgive him. It's beyond me now anyway; he has committed a crime and he has to answer to the law. The only thing I could do and I have done is to not prosecute him personally and I have assigned his case to another attorney. You may not know Sam as well as I know him but he is a thug, a racist and a bigoted. He belongs to a Nazi group who makes it a practice to harm and kill ethnic minorities and I hope he gets punished for his crime. I should tell you that the main reason they went after Sue and Jane is because they wanted me to drop the Gonzales case but I will never do that; on the contrary I will work even harder to see those thugs that killed Mr. Gonzales in jail where they belong." Two weeks after Larry sent that letter to his mother; all the parties that were implicated in the Gonzales murder were convicted. Several sentenced to life and a few others with a lighter sentence.

During the Gonzales' case Larry was assigned another attorney by the name Mary Seinders; a pleasant woman in her thirties and a very capable person who helped Larry tremendously in the office and in the court with all legal preparatory work. She was married to an Iraq veteran who was killed during the first months of the campaign. Before she was married she worked as a paralegal aid to the same firm Larry worked and occasionally they had met at Christmas parties and other office gatherings. After her husband died she went back to school and she became a lawyer. She worked in another firm for a few years and when her old boss asked her to help Larry in the Gonzales case; she seized the opportunity to be part of such a well known criminal case.

Mary was of Italian descent both of her parents came from the old world and she was a first generation American. Mary lived in Chicago close to many other Italian immigrant families and went to catholic schools. She was an attractive young lady with black curly hair and brown eyes. She saw the need to become a legal aid and worked in several offices including the county volunteering and eventually she was hired in the same office with Larry in New York. Her husband Clouse Seinders was of German descend to a family that went back many generations in this country and he was an electrician by trade. Mary and Clouse were very much in love and when he first announced that he wanted to join the army she tried hard to persuade him not to enlist but he said as a veteran he would qualify to go back to school in electronics with all expenses paid. Mary could see the logic of it but also the danger. After Clouse was killed she was discouraged with all wars and concentrated on becoming a lawyer and help poor people in her own way. As Larry and Mary worked in the Gonzales case they became closer friends. Mary could see that Larry was an honest man and for the first time in many years she allowed herself to fall in love again. Larry who had vowed not to get married again found in Marry a woman who could love and above all a person he could trust.

A few weeks after the trial was over they got married and for their honeymoon they travel throughout Europe. Being together outside the office in a different environment gave them a chance to better know each other.

Although Mary had a happier marriage than Larry; after Clouse's death her married life stopped abruptly. After her father died she moved back home and lived with her mother while she went back to school but after she became an attorney she lived on her own. Like Larry Mary also had a few affairs but she didn't think that she would ever find the right person to marry again. Falling in love with Larry was quiet unexpected and a pleasant surprise to her. Mary and Larry had never traveled extensively abroad but now as a newly married couple they had the best of times enjoying every country they visited. It was for both of them a happy honeymoon. Towards the end of their travels Mary and Larry were on the island of Simi one of the many Greek Aegean Islands. They were sitting on a boulder with their bare feet submerged in the warm water listening to Greek music emanating from a tavern behind them. Mary said, "It's so wonderful, I could stay here all night." "I could too, but I smell Greek cooking; how about dinner?" "Yah, I would love that; I am ready for some lovely Greek food."

The End

SOUL

A Short Story
George Karnikis

Throughout the ages since a caveman saw his face for the first time in a puddle of water and realized that trembling face was his, he started to wonder who he was and what was the meaning of life; which put him apart from the rest of the animal kingdom. From that time on many plain people, leaders, chiefs, clerics, philosophers, and many others have discussed and wondered where this so call soul is? Is it in our brains or is it somewhere else in our bodies. Do other animals have souls or are we the only ones gifted with this superior unexplainable feeling or consciousness?

David White read this paragraph in a religious magazine and wondered if we indeed do have a soul residing within us. David was curious about things since he was a toddler. He asked his parents so many whys that drove them crazy. He was a very smart boy and did well in school and later after he graduated from college he entered seminary and became a Catholic priest. But after a few years preaching in a poor neighborhood in Oakland California gave up priesthood went back to school this time at U.C. Berkeley and got his doctorate in philosophy.

David was a man in his early thirties good looking with curly black hair about six feet tall and light complexion. In an earlier age he put off marriage because he answered to a higher call; to be obedient to god and to help people in need. After a few years as a priest he became discouraged because he discovered that he was unable to serve god and to help people as he had hoped in earlier years. Now teaching philosophy in UC Berkeley was more satisfying and he felt more honest with himself.

It was during the time he spent as a post graduate in U.C. he became interested in metaphysics and he wrote many papers on whether there is a soul within us. At the university he also met Sophie Eastman who was teaching anthropology and sociology and they became close friends. In their free time among other subjects they frequently talked about reincarnation and the existence of soul as a different entity residing within our bodies. It was David who first put out the question about extra terrestrials and if they had anything to do with human beings being different from other animals. Sophie said, "I also wonder sometimes why we are so mentally advanced from our other bipedal cousins; what made the difference? But I have a hard time believing that aliens had anything to do with it. For one thing I have never seen an alien myself; have you?" "No I haven't but many people claim they have." Then David went on to say; one of the main questions in our minds should be where consciousness resides in our bodies and is it functioning simultaneously in different regions of our brain?

The Symposium

David and Sophie were participating in a symposium where a well-known psychiatrist, Dr. Stewart T Magnusson, was scheduled to speak on consciousness versus soul. Dr. Magnuson was a well-known professor of psychology. David and Sophie had heard about him before. They had even read a few of his essays. But this would be the first time they would see him in person.

Dr. Magnuson was a large man, about 6'2", and slender with graying blond hair and blue eyes. He appeared to be in his late sixties and wore thick glasses. He was confident and he spoke well.

"Well, Sophie, what did you think; did you find Dr. Magnusson interesting?" "Yeah, actually he was very good but he didn't say anything I didn't know. "You are hard to please; of course I also knew most of what he had to say but I found the answer he gave to that old guy very interesting, didn't you?" "You mean Mr. Wiseman? I found it a little funny too. However, I liked his theory about the soul being pure energy and that energy doesn't dissipate but changes into something else. I don't know how much validity is in that, but yes, I like to think so too." "I am fixing to ask him to join us for dinner one of these days—what do you think?" "That is a good idea but he is a very busy man, you know." "So are we, but we might be able to find the time." "Dr. Magnusson would be the right man to discuss our ideas." "I think so too." David and Sophie drove to a small Chinese restaurant where they discussed Dr. Magnusson's ideas over dinner.

Metaphysical Society for Human Progress

John Blanchard, as usual, was the first one to arrive at the club; after so many years it had become routine for him to turn on the heater and put on the kettle for tea. The other club members usually brought biscuits to go with the tea. John Blanchard was noted for his punctuality and was one of the oldest members of the "Metaphysical Society for Human progress." He was also the chairman of the Society. The club had been started in 1675 by

Lord Daniel Thompson of Southampton England who was a well-known mathematician. The building had been at 245 Dillinger Street since its founding. And although there had been many attempts to put it down and build new housing in the area; all have failed because of the strong opposition of its members. John Blanchard taught philosophy at Cambridge University for the last thirty-five years. He was recently retired which gave him more time to concentrate on his personal writings. John had been a bachelor all his life and although he had a few affairs, he never wanted to marry. He grew up in Southampton born to a well-to-do family. He was an only child. He loved his mother but hardly knew his father who was away in India for most of his growing up years. His father was employed by Walker's Royal Tea Co. John had traveled to India a few times with his mother when he was young. In later years he was encouraged by his father to stay and work there but he never felt at home in India or with his father's life style. His latest book, "Life Quest" which had to do a lot with Paranormal Phenomena, made him famous around the world and with his colleagues at home. The ten members of the club met religiously every Wednesday at 7:00 p.m. rain or shine. The members of the society, now a mixed group of men and women, were carefully chosen based on their parental history, their education, and their status in upper English society. Although they preferred their members to be independently wealthy, however that wasn't a requirement.

It was a cold night and the members were holding their hot cups of tea keeping warm and chatting before the meeting began. The meeting opened as usual with an entreaty spoken in Elizabethan English. Then John said, "Ladies and Gentlemen, do you find me worthy to conduct our meeting tonight?" They all spoke in unison, "Yes we do." (This is a ritual that began back when the chairman had to always ask for approval of the members before he started the meeting).

They approved last meeting's minutes and after the treasurer's report they started their meeting. John discussed several articles in psychology and parapsychology he had read since their last meeting and then each member discussed what they had read. That took most of their time and then during the balance of their remaining time they discussed new business. John again said, "I have a copy of the speech given by a Dr. Stewart Magnusson at the University of Berkeley in California State of U.S.A. I went over it briefly but I would like each one of us to read portions of it and then let us analyze the message he conveys in his speech."

History of Mankind

Dr. Gurry Liatechov climbed up the steps to the main door of H.M. CEYEHOBA one of the oldest medical University in Moscow. It was a very cold winter day with the snow falling continuously since the night before. As Gurry entered the lobby of this old building he sensed the heat and he felt good. As he entered his office he helped himself to a hot cup of coffee that was made earlier for him by his secretary Marinova. On the desk there was an Apple computer and on the side of it a pile of papers waiting for his attention. His lecture was scheduled for 2:00 p.m. this afternoon and then at 4:00 pm he was scheduled to meet with Dr. Basily Furov and Dr. Lianna Croutsava.

He went through the pile of papers; they had all been checked and Okayed by Marinova except for one letter which was personal and confidential. Gurry signed all the papers and then looked at the envelope. He is eye fell on the Queen's stamp—it was from England. The sender was, Dr. John Blanchard of the

Metaphysical Society for Human Progress. Gurry remembered Dr. Blanchard right away from his latest book "Life Quest" which he had read and liked very much. He opened the letter and started to read. Dear Dr. Liatechov my name is Dr. John Blanchard I am professor of philosophy emeritus and now an active chairman of my club "Metaphysical Society for Human Progress." Two years ago the members of my club and I were fortunate enough to attend the symposium given at the Hilton hotel in Genève Switzerland where you were the main speaker on Phenomena in Parapsychology. At the time we met briefly and if you remember I extended an invitation for you to come and visit us here in London. Recently it came to our attention that you will be one of the scheduled speakers in the coming symposium about Mental Pathology July 16 2015 at the London Holyday Inn. At this time we would like to renew our invitation to you to visit us at our club before going home. Your response to our offer would be much appreciated.

Sincerely
Dr. John Blanchard

Dr. Gurry Liatechov was well known in the medical establishment not only here in Moscow but all over the world. He had written five books in psychology and parapsychology and had been teaching at the University of H.M. DEYHOBA for the last fifteen years. Politics in Russia can be difficult and often deadly so he stayed clear of politics and concentrated instead in his studies as the only avenue to succeed in life. He was born in a farming community and was one of five children of two sisters and two more brothers. Gurry was the youngest of them all and the most different one too. From early on he made it clear to his parents that he wanted nothing to do with farming. He loved to read—for him reading was the only way to escape his local environment. Gurry was a very intelligent boy and he excelled in his studies from early on. Gurry read many books in human behavior and especially in paranormal phenomena. He also believed in U.F.O's although he would not say so; he had personal experience with paranormal phenomena.

It was natural for him that his post-graduate preference would be in Philosophy and psychology. It wasn't easy for a farm boy to gain entrance in a prestigious university of H.M. CEYEHOBA but he did. He excelled in his studies which placed him in one of the best universities in mental pathology. From then on Gurry Liatechov, as Doctor of philosophy and psychology, worked in many hospitals in the country. That eventually qualified him to gain entrance back to the prestigious university from which he had graduated fifteen years earlier. Gurry had also unofficial credentials in Ufology which is only now being recognized. But although this was something he knew a great deal about he could never speak freely of it. It all started back home in the farmhouse when he was thirteen years old. Gurry love to look at the stars, they fascinated and mesmerized him. It was a starlit night in August and he was sitting by his bedroom window as usual. He was looking at the heavens when he noticed something unusual. There was a bright light coming from the east very fast and noiselessly. It stopped above the lake yavrona not too far from his house. It stayed there for a few minutes and then dove into the water and disappeared. Even in his young mind he could tell that it wasn't a falling star. Falling stars don't stop and go; they fall. The light was so close to his house it had to be something else. He had heard many times of UFO's but had never paid attention before.

Ever since that episode Gurry started to pay attention to anything which had to do with UFO's and unexplained phenomena. As he was growing up he talked to other people who had seen the bright light he saw a few years back and they all agreed that the light they saw wasn't a falling star. But what was it? They were all perplexed and unable to explain. As the time went on several of these people young and old formed a group and they met monthly to discuss their experiences with UFOs. As the time went on many other people with their own experiences joined the group which eventually became large enough to have their own place and meet monthly. In time Curry, because of his credentials, and the fact he had so much experience in ufology, was elected the chairman of their clump. Curry's 4:00 pm appointment with Dr. Basily Furov and Dr. Lianna Croutsava had to do with something significant. They had a report that could not wait until their scheduled monthly UFO meeting.

Gurry was now in his late fifties a very successful professor in his own right married to Lianna and with two young adult children a son, Urey, 22 and a daughter, Elena, 19 both in university. Gurry was a very athletic looking man with blond hair and slightly oriental features of Eurasian ancestry. His beloved Liana had suffered with cancer and died five years earlier. Those years after Liana's death were difficult for Gurry who had to deal with the household and two young children. But his Secretary, Marinova Chirtsevits, stepped in and helped with the young family and made life bearable. The children were by now old enough to accept and appreciate Marinova's help. It was well understood by everyone including Urey and Elena that the relationship between Gurry and Marinova was more of a couple than a secretary and her boss. Marinova would have liked to be more of a husband and wife but she could see that would not have been easily accepted in the office.

Gurry went through the notes he had taken at his last UFO meeting; nothing new—there were stories he had heard many times before. Dr. Basily Furov and Dr. Lena Croutsava were members of his clump and Gurry always paid attention to what they had to say. Marinova's voice was heard in the intercom; she said, "Gurry, they are here." He said, "Let them in."

Dr. Basily Furov a man in his fifties about six foot tall light skin with blue eyes and curly hair. Basily was a well known physicist and astronomer who at times had participated in the Russian and international space programs. Dr. Lena Croutsava was in her thirties, 5'9" tall with Mediterranean features olive skin and long black hair she was an astronomer who specialized in exo-zoology and exo-ecology teaching at Lomonosov Moscow State University.

"Coming, coming, how good to see you, please sit down." Marinova came in with hot tea and after they helped themselves to a cup they talked without interruption for an hour or so. Lena was the first to speak, she said, "Gurry, at our last meeting we talked about Dr. Dave White and his coauthor Dr. Sophie J Eastman and about the papers they have published on "Soul Consciousness and Perception" Basily and I read the rest of their papers and found them very interesting. Then Basily talked about Dr. John P Blanchard's latest book "Life Quest" and several of the papers his club had published recently. "He said we found all these relevant to what we are going to discuss at our next meeting and we thought that you should suggest to Dr. John Blanchard to have Dr. White and Dr. Eastman, and also Dr. Magnusson at your meeting in London." Lena said, "It will be very interesting to have all the people together in one place I envy you I wish I could be there with you but it will suffice to read the minutes of your meeting."

After the meeting was over Gurry wrote a quick note to Dr. Blanchard he said, "Dear Dr. Blanchard, I do remember you not only from your books which I have read but also the last time we met in France. I also remember several of your club members although I must admit not by their names. I accept your invitation and will be there with my secretary Marinova Chirtsevits. On the list of the scheduled speakers there are three people namely; Dr. Stewart Magnusson, Dr. Dave White, and Dr. Sophie J Eastman. I have read their books and papers and found them to be most insightful. May I make a suggestion; since they are going to be in London at the same time perhaps they can be invited to participate at our meeting? I can assure you that you will find them interesting? Thank you so much and hope to see you soon.

Sincerely
Dr. Gurry Liatechov

It was a beautiful early spring day at U.C. Berkeley; students were busy going from class to class—one of those typical days. David was in the cafeteria going over his notes before class over a cup of coffee; he was so much absorbed in his subject he didn't notice Sophie who was standing behind him with her notes in hand. "Hello David, can I join you?" He looked at her; she looked exceptionally beautiful this morning. "Hello Sophie; of course sit down you look exquisite this morning." "Well, thank you David it is my birthday today remember?" "Oh yes of course; Happy Birthday darling it all makes sense to me now we are going to dinner right?" "Right; we are eating at the Clare Mount Hotel at 7:00 it's all done." "Thanks Sophie; as you can see I am also dressed to go out." "You look handsome." "Thanks." "Dave did you get in touch with Dr. Magnusson?" "I sent him an e-mail but haven't heard from him yet." "I wonder if you will." "Oh I am sure I will; the guy is busy that's all." "I hope you are right; it would be interesting to have a chat with him." "You know, it would be." Dave and Sophie talked a little longer and then they both did their preparatory work before class.

The faculty had a little gathering for Sophie's Birthday in one of the teachers' offices; just a few of their close friends. Sophie looked beautiful and many of her friends after they wished her Happy Birthday they told her so; she felt genuinely happy. Shortly after her party they drove to The Clare Mount Hotel where they had dinner. After coffee and dessert Dave handed Sophie a little box, she said, "Should I open it now?" "He said please." Sophie opened the little box with trembling hands; she was hopping and yes she was right. She started to tear but they were tears of happiness; she picked up the diamond ring and looked at it for a while then she said, "It's beautiful but Dave is this proposal?" "Yes it is; Sophie you know that I love you but I am not good with words when it comes to proposing marriage but this is the best way I can express my love and appreciation for you; what do you say, will you marry me?" Sophie looked Dave in the eye and said, "Yes of course." Then they raised their glasses and drank to their love and happiness.

It was Saturday morning and Dave was up early; he made coffee and a light breakfast. Sophie was still asleep and Dave tried not to make too much noise so as not to disturb her. He opened up his computer and checked his mail; the usual stuff mostly bills and a few letters. Then he picked up his mail from the floor near the door. He went through it mechanically and found two letters that caught his eye—one from Dr. Magnusson the other from

Dr. Gurry Liatechov from Russia. He opened the one from Russia first and started reading. It was at that moment that Sophie stepped into the kitchen. Dave put down the letter got up and kissed Sophie—he said, "Good morning, would you like some coffee?" "Yes I'd love a cup of coffee." Sophie looked at the foreign envelop and commented, "Is this from Russia?" "Yes it is should I read aloud?" "Yes please do." Dave proceeded to read; Dear Dr. White, My name is Gurry Liatechov and I am in charge of mental pathologies in the University of H.M. CEYEHOBA in Moscow Russia. My colleagues and I have read many of the papers you have published on soul versus consciousness and perception and we are very eager to meet you. We have seen your name on the list of scheduled speakers for the coming Symposium on Mental Pathologies at the Hilton Hotel in London England on July 16 2015. We have sent the same request to your coauthor, Dr. Sophie J Eastman. We have also invited Dr. Stewart T Magnusson and he has accepted. Should you accept our invitation we are to meet at Dr. John P Blanchard's club, "Metaphysical Society for Human Progress?" After the symposium; more details will be sent to you upon your acceptance of our invitation.

While Dave was reading the letter Sophie was looking at the stamped envelope admiring a beautiful ptarmigan. "What do you think Sophie?" "Well I hope you accept the invitation?" "Apparently he sent you an invitation too, right?" "I suppose so but I haven't checked my mail yet." "Now it is my turn to ask; are you going to accept his invitation?" "I think so; after all I am going to be there anyway so I might as well join you at the club. It sounds very interesting to me." "Great, now let's see what Dr. Magnusson has to say." Dave started to read the second letter. "Dear Dr. White thanks you for your invitation. I have not met you or your co author Dr. Eastman but I have read most of your papers and I found them to be very interesting. As you might imagine I am very busy at this time but we could meet sometime in early June, the second or third or July the fifteenth or seventeenth. I am scheduled to speak at a symposium about Mental Pathology that is taking place on July 16 2015 at the London Holyday Inn and I won't be available during that time. However I saw your name as a scheduled speaker at the same place and perhaps we could meet there as well. Please let me know if the days I am available are O.K. with you or perhaps we could meet in London at the 16 of July where I will be along with my wife Sonia. Thank you for your invitation and I hope we can meet one way or another soon.

Sincerely
Dr. Stewart Magnusson

Dave and Sophie answered to all three invitations in the affirmative and after they did some more office work they went out to have lunch and enjoy the rest of their weekend.

Dr. John Blanchard as always was the first at the club and while he was setting the tables he thought how important this meeting was going to be. He had sent invitations to four of the speakers at the coming symposium and during the last month all the club's members had read their books and papers and they were well informed.

Although the weather was a little warmer tonight nevertheless a cup of tea was welcomed by the members and after their usual ceremonial opening they started their meeting in earnest. John said, "Friends I hope you have read all the material I sent you; I know I have, and have found everything very interesting and pertinent to what we are about to talk tonight. As you know I have sent invitations to all our guest and they have accepted. Our July meeting will start on the 17 at our usual time after we finish dinner which will be here. Carol Wiseman is in charge of the dinner and at this time I'd like to ask her to tell us how that is coming along." "All our guests have companions; Dr. Gurry Liatechov will be coming with his secretary Marinova, Dr. Stewart Magnusson will be coming with his wife Sonia, Dr. Dave White and Dr. Sophie Eastman are coming together.

"So we have six guests and ten of us I have arranged dinner for sixteen which will be catered here. We will start with aperitifs followed by the main dish which will be choice of fish or beefsteak, salad or soup, then finally dessert and tea or coffee." "Splendid, wonderful, thank you Carol. Now let's go with our main subject (Soul and Consciousness) which is what we will discuss with our guests."

Mr. Swanson said, "I think we should start with Dr. White and Dr. Eastman and then go round the table. I also think we should not burden our guests with too many questions." "I quite agreed with you."

Each member chose the guests of whom they were going to ask their questions based on the material they had studied and then went on to a different subject. Then John acting as chairman said "I have informed our guests that the theme of our meeting will be on "Soul and Consciousness" so I would assume that they will be prepared with their own questions and answers. Carol said," It is my feeling that as our guests we should take them around London on the seventeen of July before they arrive for dinner of course that is if they wish to participate." I think that is a good idea but let's put it to a vote." They all agreed to that and Carol volunteered to escort the quests at the club's expense. By the time they were through they were all satisfied that they had arranged things in a way their guests should be pleased.

The Symposium

The Holiday Inn was exceptionally busy today with guest speakers from all over the world. They were well known professors, academicians, scientists, and authors of many books in their own particular fields and they were participating along with their companions. The subject was "Mental Pathology" each one of the speakers was expected to speak on the subject in their own field which varied from psychic etiology to somatic pathology. Dr. John Blanchard along with all the members of his club was there too. They were busy taking notes from the speakers and especially their guests. Dr. Gurry Liatechov spoke about the ascent of the human race, psychosomatic illnesses that afflict humans as opposed to other animals and the various psychotherapies used today. Dr. Stewart Magnuson repeated pretty much the same speech he had given at the UC Berkeley; he elaborated a little longer on the history of soul and consciousness. Dr. White spoke about religion and psychology and the important role they have played on humanity. Dr. Eastman spoke about the human needs in sociological terms and she was the only one of the speakers who mentioned the possibility of the human species been planted on earth by Extra Terrestrials. There were many other important speakers who contributed their ideas and all in all it was a very exhilarating experience for all the participants.

Arrival of the guests

The seventeen of July was a beautiful sunny day and all the guests were settled in their hotels. They were glad to have given their speeches yesterday at the symposium and now they were looking forward to their tour in London. Carol drove a comfortable van she had rented for this occasion and in no time she picked up all the guests at their hotels. Carol had lived in London all her life so she was familiar with the area. She started at the Piccadilly Square and drove on to the most important places in and out of London. She treated them to lunch and after four hours tour she delivered them to their hotels. All the guests were satisfied with their tour and they were thankful to Carol. They had a few hours to freshen up and then Carol picked them up again and this time drove them to the club where they had dinner.

The conference

After a delicious dinner with excelled wines and desserts the guests were more than ready for the conference. They met in the library's conference room where Dr. Blanchard welcomed them once more.

Dr. Blanchard opened the meeting by saying, "Ladies and Gentlemen it is our honor to have such distinguished guests visiting our club. As you all know the subject we are going to discuss tonight is about Soul and Consciousness; and how do we define the two of them. Throughout human existence people have tried to understand what makes us be who we are, our feeling of being, the dual expression of thought; that which is said verbally and the one composed subconsciously. I don't wish to interject my own thoughts at this time; I'd like to hear you first. You are so much better qualified in this subject.

The first question came oddly enough, not from the club members, but from one of the guests. It was Dr. White who addressed Dr. Liatechov, he said, "Dr. Liatechov I have read all of your books and many of your essays and I am so glad to finally meet you in person, my question is; have humans always suffered psychosomatic illnesses or is it a recent phenomenon due to our advance civilization?"

"I would say the second; you see humans started just like all the other animals they lived their lives in the simplest way possible. Their main task was to find food, shelter, and procreate. What made the humans different from the other species was the ability to think and memorize far more than the others. Due mostly to the fact that humans lived in groups of ten to thirty which gave them the ability to hunt successfully and shelter. They were able to make tools, and the other important thing was having the knowledge of building a fire. That discouraged carnivorous animals from attacking them in their primitive dwellings. If they were not eaten or killed they lived to about thirty years old and that went on for thousands of years. Because of better nutrition which consisted mainly of meat and grains their brains grew far larger than other species. In time they became good hunter-gatherers which in turn helped them develop languages and better communication. As their language advanced they were able to converse in more esoteric and abstract subjects and that's when they began to have psychosomatic illnesses. For instance the so called (fight or flight) response which served them well for a long time started to change as humans became less depended on hunting or be hunted. Which is to say they grew their food under controlled environment and it didn't necessitate the need for them to hunt or be hunted? That in each self created one of the first anxieties. In our days for the most part the (fight or flight) response doesn't apply as it did before. Nowadays the (fight) has been replaced by the inability for people to pay their bills, or for a salesman not being able to sell enough goods to earn a decent living and so on. The fear becomes anxiety and since he cannot run away from it (flight) accumulates and in time it becomes a psychosomatic illness. I could give you more examples but I think you get the idea."

The next question came from Mr. Swanson addressed to Dr. White, "Dr. White is religion necessary in our times?" "Religion has always been used by humans; it's an innate or intrinsic feeling; and although we will never be able to prove it, religion is used only by humans. From the time our ancestors lived in caves they always looked for something better and stronger than themselves, more powerful than their leaders; an entity they could riley upon for their security and wellbeing. They started by choosing the strongest in their group for protection, but that didn't last long, they chose something they admired perhaps an animal on which they depended for sustenance or it could be a big rock that its shape reminded them of a great leader. But unfortunately their deities were heavy to carry around or they were destroyed by another tribe and then they were forced to believe in another deity.

At some point they realized that their deities were expendable on earth and they placed them in the heavens. That was a good idea because now they could profess that their god or gods were powerful and at the same time untouchable. That was a clever idea and it caught on with the rest of humanity. Of course the gods in time changed to the needs of the people from polytheism to monotheism. Some believed in the sun or the moon; after all there were up there too. And so religion is also used in our days because the need is still there and it will always be there until we reach our potential which is to find god within us.

Next question came from Carol Weisman directed to Dr.

Eastman, "Dr. Eastman do you really believe in Extra Terrestrials?" "Yes I do although it would be difficult to prove their existence at this time. The more we discover additional galaxies, stars, and planets, the more feasible becomes the existence of Extra Terrestrial life. When we see billions upon billions of planets logically and mathematically we can extrapolate indeed that life can exists in various forms." The next question was asked by Dr. Robinson, he said, "Dr. Eastman Do you believe that we may have been planted here on earth by another intelligent species? There are a few theories about that but again it would be very hard to prove it. However I can think of a time in the future where we could create robots with artificial intelligence and place them on a planet where humans cannot live, and work in mines extracting minerals for us. And then imagine again if for some unforeseeable reason we were disconnected and they managed to survive and continue to exist and reproduced themselves; do you see a parallel between us and them?

Then Dr. Blanchard directed the agenda to the main topic which was Soul and Consciousness and the club members asked their questions in an orderly manner. All for guests were found to be very knowledgeable in the subject and that surprised and pleased the club members. Then Dr. Blanchard asked the last question of Dr. Magnuson, "Dr. Magnuson could you tell us how you define Soul?"

He started by saying, "if you were to ask me where the soul resides I wouldn't be able to pin point the exact place of it but I could tell you where we think consciousness maybe found. But let us go back to Athens Greece 2600 years ago where two well-known philosophers; Democritus and Aristotle first speculated about the connection between our senses and our minds perception. At the time only a few Athenians bother to think about the deeper meaning of consciousness and most of them thought it was given to mortars by gods. It was these two philosophers who dare to articulate publicly the possibility of consciousness been acquired from other possible ways than gods. In 400 AD St Augustine of Hippo discussed consciousness in a more detail matter thereby establishing the western thought about soul and the way we perceive it today. He said, "When thus a material thing is seen in the mind's eye, it is no longer a material matter, but the likeness of such an object that actually consciousness involves more than the physical organs."

In the ancient times philosophers divided consciousness into a material body that can sense the environment and the immaterial intelligence or if we want to think of it as soul; that at once can recognize and interpret sensory input. This differentiation was later known in philosophical terminology as the mind and body dualism. During the European Renaissance philosophers began to approach the consciousness —soul predicament differently from their earlier associates. During that period a Dutch physician Andreas Vesalius 1543 AD among others produced a book on detailed drawings in human anatomy. A few decades later he was followed by a French mathematician Rene Descartes 1637 AD who dried to find the seat of the soul as he used to say. He introduced the concept of "dualism." "We sense our environment with our brain but regard it with our minds." Descartes thought the pineal gland as the seat of the soul. In 1690 AD John Locke an English philosopher said that, "Consciousness is formed by acquiring knowledge throughout our lives." Gottfried Wilhelm Leibniz 1700 AD was convinced that mind and brain are separate. Finally an American philosopher William James 1890 AD thought of consciousness scientifically and coined the phrase "stream of consciousness" which has been used until our time.

Dr. Stewart Magnuson went on to say that in our times most of us are liberated from religious constrains and are free to discuss our opinions in more scientific ways. It is thought that animals frequently communicate through E.S.P. (Extra Sensory Perception). Ever since humans discovered (logos) or language to communicate with each other unfortunately lost the ability to talk through E.S.P. Consequently this resulted in a much slower communication. There are a few people that still having the ability to use E.S.P. but they are the exception.

The reason I brought up at this time E.S.P. is because it's my feeling that E.S.P. and the soul travel through the same mental waves. And I also think that subconsciously our soul resides in the same parameters. If we were to accept this theory then we should also accept the fact animals have soul.

Then why are we are so advanced in the process of thinking from the other animals? We both use pretty much the same tools of thinking. If the animals as we think use a faster way of communicating they should be way ahead of us; are they? Perhaps in some ways they are but we have surpassed all of them and without a doubt we are the masters of our planet and soon to have dominium of other planets too. Our nearest animal relative is the chimpanzee; in physical appearance we differ very little yet in his natural environment he spends most of his time foraging while we have the ability to travel through space. To be so closely related to chimpanzee and yet to be so far advance in our brain capabilities should give us cause to stop and think why it is so; and what made us so different or perhaps who? Of course there are many theories from religious point of views to scientific ones and throughout the ages both of them thought they were right.

Then for the next thirty minutes or so there was a Q/A period one of the questions that came from Mr. Robert Green he asked,

"Are there more or less intelligent souls?" "I would dare to guess no for the simple fact that if the soul as we know it to be a separate and an etheric entity then intelligence has no part in it. Intelligence is derived from the brain as a whole and it grows from a lifelong experience although there could be an accumulation of knowledge but that has nothing to do with intelligence." The next question came again from Dr. Blanchard, he said, "Dr. Magnusson, do you think there is life after death?" "Dr. Blanchard, that is a very good question but a difficult one to answer, I will try to answer your question as a scientist not as a clergyman. You see no one has come back from the dead to tell us what's out there; I can only surmise, based on my experience as a psychiatrist. Of course it depends how you define life after death, if you think that we will come back to another corporal life I would say no, but life does go on because life is energy and energy doesn't dissipate it only gets absorb by another energy and becomes something else but at this point we do not know what that something else is. However I would venture to say that perhaps that energy is the soul that joins other souls forming a super spiritual power that unites the living and the dead."

The meeting lasted for three hours and after they were done they were all pleased with what they had accomplished. Dr. Blanchard thanked the quests once more and shortly after that Carol drove them back to their hotels. She was happy that everything had gone well, and happier to have gained six very important friends.

The End

NIKITAS

A BIOGRAPHICAL STORY

"Go fetch me the lime and the brush; we have a lot to do today."
"Yes sir, right away." It was a sunny day on the Island of Simi one
of the (Dodecanese) islands close to Turkey. Nikitas was ten years
old, tall for his age, blue eyes and dark curly hair. He loved his
father and he was happy to work with him whenever he was
home, which wasn't very often.

Nikitas spent his youth on Simi; which is dry like the other
Aegean islands. The few trees that grew on the island were pine,
oak, olive, and fruit trees. However People grew different kinds of
trees on their farms and around their houses to make up for the
lack of public parks. There also were many vegetable and flower
gardens. Simi was noted for its beautiful stone buildings. But
most of all it was the hospitality you got from the local people.
On the other side of the island there was the monastery of
Archangel Michael visited by many tourists every year. The
narrow roads leading to the central square of the city were busy
with peddlers on donkeys going back and forth selling their
goods. In the early eighteen hundreds when Nikitas and Tassos
were growing up; things were bleak and depressing for all islanders. They were proud people living under the Ottoman Empire.

Nikitas' father, Manolis, was captain of his ship "Charavgi"
(dawn) which delivered goods from Piraeus, (the port of Athens),
to other islands and coastal ports. Manolis was in his thirties

black eyes, black hair, taller than the average Greek. He had worked on the ships since his was a little boy. He had worked first as a deckhand with sponge divers, and later, on other ships, small and large. He became a captain and eventually owned his own boat, which had been built on Simi, (one of the best places to build a boat at that time). Manolis married a local girl, Despina, a beautiful twenty years old, the daughter of the captain with whom he worked.

They had two boys Nikitas 10 and Tassos 8; they were entirely different. Nikitas was tall, strong, and outgoing—closer to their father. Tassos a smaller person, good looking with black eyes, black hair; he looked more like his mother. From early on he was interested in religion and both parents encouraged him to proceed with his preference. Tassos was also very intelligent and learned quickly. When Nikitas was out at sea helping his father, Tassos stayed home helping with the chores on their small farm and was a big help to his mother.

The reason father Manolis, Nikitas, and Tasos were painting with lime was in protest to the Turkish authorities occupying many of the Aegean islands at the time. In fact they and many islanders on Simi and other islands were doing the same thing. They were painting crosses on their chimneys with white and blue the color of the Greek flag, to make a point that this is Greece, and the houses and the people are Greek and you have no business here. The Ottoman government allowed different religions to coexist within the Empire and to express their faith with their symbols. But painting crosses on chimneys was something that started recently and the local authorities waited for orders from Constantinople to prosecute those who broke the low. Eventually the order did come and people washed the crosses away. By eighteen ninety the Ottoman Empire was falling apart everywhere and especially in the Balkan Countries. After four hundred years of brutal governing people everywhere were sabotaging the everyday living under the Turkish rule by any means they could get away with.

Manolis wanted Nikitas to get a proper education and then become a captain and eventually take over the business. So the priority for Nikitas was to go to school and then get into his father's business. He didn't worry about Tassos who loved school and from an early age he knew he wanted to study religion. Father Manolis was a very religious man and if one of his sons wanted to go into religious studies or become a priest that would be wonderful. The Turks made it easier for them to go to Turkish schools but the majority of Greek people would have none of that. Nikitas and Tassos helped many other islanders to paint crosses on their chimneys before it was outlawed. In the summers when Nikitas was out of school he went out to sea with his father and learned about navigating the ship, delivering mail, and trading goods.

Nikitas usually did what his father asked him to do, but sometimes he took matters on his own. His father had told him many times to stay clear of the authorities. But Nikitas disobeyed when he joined the Resistance against the occupiers. He, along with other youngsters, sabotaged causing destruction on property and equipment on Simi as well as on other islands in the archipelago. By the eighteen nineties Nikitas was a strong and handsome young man about fifteen years old and he was often the leader of his group.

It was during Easter Holiday when Nikitas was out of school, that he called a few of his contemporaries to meet at their usual secret place to prepare for their next scheduled sabotage. Nikitas spoke first he said, "The supply boat "Yazmer" will arrive at Simi tomorrow at about 10:00 pm and according to the information we have from our friends in Datca this time the boat is coming with soldiers and lots of ammunition. It will stay overnight and tomorrow will sail for Rhodes. As usual it will tie on the buoy and tomorrow morning it will go into port. They are scheduled to leave at midday. We don't have much time to lose; we must act quickly and decisively. After dinner find a good excuse to leave for couple of hours better yet don't say anything just go. But above all say nothing to anybody; we will meet here at 9:00 pm."

A week earlier Nikitas and his friends had stuffed the buoy with powerful explosives, it was floating innocently safely at a good distance from the port. The wick was kept dry and well hidden under the huge chain that held the buoy. It was a moonless night, the sea was calm, and the boys were hard at work. Stelios who was a shepherd had brought four goat's skins and they started to work on them right away. First they tied the four legs with string, and then they carefully put the explosives inside the leather sack. They sewed the neck and finally applied grease all over it. By the time they were done it was completely waterproof. They did the same thing with the other three skins and now they waited for Nikitas to come and get into the water. It was unusual for Nikitas to be late, but they still had enough time so they waited.

Tassos was a member of the group too, but his only task was to be the messenger; he never took part out in the field. Nikitas wanted to make sure his little brother did not get caught by the Turks. Earlier in the day Tassos had gone to visit a friend in town but he was unusually late for dinner. Manolis as usual was out at sea and the three of them always had dinner at 8:00 pm. Now it was well past the time for dinner and Tassos was nowhere to be seen. Despina said, "Nikitas, I worry something bad happened to

Tassos; he never misses dinner and he always comes home on time. Where do you think he might be?" "I don't know mother, but I am going to find out soon." And with that Nikitas got out of the house like a bat out of hell. The first place he checked was Tassos' friend Nikos but he said Tassos had left two hours earlier. Now Nikitas started to worry about his little brother. If the constables knew Tassos was their messenger they would torture him until they got what they were after.

Not only was the life of his brother at stake but the lives of the entire group. Nikitas had to do something—but what? The first thing he did was to go back home and tell his mother that he hadn't found Tassos yet. He said, "Mother, don't worry, I will find him and bring him home just stay here and wait, don't go anywhere, don't say anything to anyone. I'll be back as soon as I can. By now it was pretty close to 9:30 pm he decided to go to the place they were to meet tonight and found the boys busy working on the project. When he told them that Tassos was not home and he most likely was at the police station or in prison everybody realized the enormity of the problem and they were scared. Nikitas said, "If Tassos talks all of us will be hanged." Stelios said, "We have to assume that after he is tortured he will talk and they will be looking for us." It was Panos who said what everybody was thinking and saying nothing about it. He said, "We have to find a way to get him out of there, but how?" Nikitas said, "We have to postpone our 10:00 project for later on or no do it at all. But now we have to think how to get Tassos out of there and the sooner the better. All twelve of them spent a lot of time trying to find a way to get Tassos away from his abductors before he talked.

After Tassos left his friend Nikos he headed for home. As he left town it became darker but he kept going kicking small rocks on the way home. Then all of a sudden two constables appeared on horses. One of them grabbed him and pulled him up on the horse and ran back toward the city. They went into the police station and walked into the back room where they often tortured people. They sat Tassos on a chair and started interrogating him. One of the officers was obese and wore a droopy moustache; his face was red and his eyes looked tired he was in his forties and he couldn't have been much taller than Tassos who only thirteen. The other officer was an older person with a full beard and moustache. They looked scary to Tassos who had never been in the police station before and never been in trouble with anyone much less with the Turkish authorities.

The shorter man dragged a chair close to Tassos, looked him in the eye and said, "Listen you little brat, the last few days we have followed you and we have seen you going from door, to door, talking to people. Now you tell us what you know or we are going to beat the shit out of you, do you hear me?" "I haven't done anything wrong I just visited my friends just as I had visited Nikos a little while ago we talked about home work that's all." The officer hit Tassos across his face hard and said, "You are lying, tell us the truth or you are not going out of here alive and then hit him again this time even harder. Tassos' nose and mouth started to bleed and he tasted the sweetness of his blood in his mouth. For a moment he felt like crying but then he thought of Nikitas, his brother would never cry. He thought to himself I am not going to cry no matter what they do to me, I am not going to.

The older man came and sat on the same chair and said, "Tassos we don't want to hit you anymore just tell us what you know and we will let you go." Tassos kept his mouth close and said nothing. Then the old man said again, "If you don't tell us what you know we will bring your mother, your brother, and your father, when he comes back home, and we will kill them. So for the last time tell us what you know and have it done with." Tassos still didn't say anything. This time the older man lifted his hand and he was about to strike him on the face again. Then Tassos put his hand up to protect himself, and said, "Please don't hit me, I'll tell you all I know" "That's a good boy, now Tassos, tell us everything you know."

Tassos told the biggest lie in his life to his torturers. He said, "It's true I went from door to door to four different people. I was their messenger; my job was to inform the four guys of any changes in their plan." Tassos stopped for a moment to compose himself then continued. But the younger constable asked him abruptly, "Who were they and what were they going to do?" "They are the crew of the fishing boat "Gorgona" and they kidnap Annio because Basilis wants to marry her and all I did was to be the messenger for them. But earlier tonight I was studying with my friend, that's all—I am telling you the truth constables." The two officers stepped out of the room. The older guy said, "I tend to believe the young fellow, these stupid Greeks resort to kidnapping the girl if the parents don't concede to the marriage." "But he could easily be the messenger for those in the Resistance." "Let's keep him in jail for tonight and tomorrow we'll find out if he is lying or not." "OK that sounds good to me." They both left for home but on the way out they told one of the guards to keep the little guy tied for an hour or so and then put him in jail for tonight.

Nikitas and the rest of the group talked for a long time until they came-up with a plan to save Tassos and then put it into effect right away. Many years ago the Islanders had made a deal with the Turks. They had agreed to supply the boats and crews to deliver the mail for the Turks to all twelve islands. In turn the Turks kept only a minimal police force on the island. They let the Islanders run their own government and it had worked well for all those years. So the police force consisted of only about a dozen constables with the real military force being on the largest of the Dodecanese archipelago—the Island of Rhodes which was only an hour away by bout. But lately, with the Resistance causing so much damage on all the islands there were more army and weaponry sent from the Turkish mainland. However for now all they had to deal with was a small constabulary.

Nikitas and his group put their plan into action right away. They were equipped with incendiaries and dressed in black, headed for the police station. Nikitas looked into the infamous back room and saw Tassos tied on a chair and with a bloody nose. He knew right away that Tassos had been tortured. He turned around and said to the guys, "Take your posts, Stelios and Demetris go to the stable; do you have the grain?" "Yes we do." Make sure you don't scare the horses before you start the fire." "Sure thing Nikitas we are on it." They went quietly to the stable with buckets of grain. The horses were a little nervous to begin with but after they ate some grain from their nosebags all four of them quieted down.

Stelios and Demetris gently loosened their ropes and guided them one by one outside the stable and far away from it. Then they started the fire. When the horses smelled the smoke and saw the fire; they ran into the dark night and disappeared. The boys waited for the fire to expand and when it did all six guards went to the stable and tried to put the fire out. Now was Nikitas and Takis turn; they forced open the back window into the room and jumped inside, they quickly cut Tassos' rope and whisked him out of the room. They ran into the dark and out of the way. A few minutes later they met at their usual place; the abduction of Tassos was a success.

Nikitas, Takis, and Tassos left right away for Nikitas' home they found their mother praying and crying. Despina was happy to see both of them safe; but she was so excited at the time she momentarily didn't notice Tassos' bruised face. When she did notice she screamed, "My child who did that to you?" The constables beat me mom, but I swear I didn't say anything to them I didn't I didn't." Oh I believe you my Tassos. May God strike those savages dead for what they have done to you my child."

Nikitas and the boys helped his mother collect all the valuables in the house. Before long they had gathered all they could carry. Then Despina, Tassos, and Takis put as much as they could on the donkey, and left town. By dawn they arrived at Pedi a small costal port where Manolis kept his other boat. They loaded everything they had in the boat then Despina gave Takis some breakfast, put him on the donkey, and sent him back home. Then she and Tassos sailed away for a place to hide for a while.

Nikitas ran back to where the others were waiting for him. As soon as Nikitas arrived at the secret place they began to prepare for the next important task. By now they were three hours late but they felt lucky that Tassos hadn't told the constables of their project. Although they were late it was still dark enough to proceed with the job. The water was cold but they were all young and nothing was going to discourage them. Nikitas was the first one to jump into the cold water then Demetris followed behind. They swam under water and came up only to breathe until they reached the buoy, then they waited behind it anxiously for the others to go to the boat.

Andonis, Spiros, Nikos and Costas jumped simultaneously into the water holding the skin bags with the explosives the others waited behind a big bush. They used the bags as floaters in front of their faces and propelled themselves quietly with their feet. Two of them swam to the starboard side of the boat and the other two to port. They attached securely the explosives on both side of the boat and then again quietly swam to the shore.

Demetris handed one end of a rope to Nikitas and he also swam to the shore carrying the other end of the rope. Next Nikitas lighted the dry wick and then he motion three times with the rope to be pulled. The others pulled him to shore as fast as they could. Then they ran behind a boulder and closed their ears. The buoy went off with a thunderous explosion which in turn caused the explosives on the sides of the boat to go off too. Those in turn caused the ammunition inside the bout to go off. In seconds the boat with everything inside went into smithereens.

The tremendous sound caused an echo which traveled from mountain to mountain prolonging the noise on the island. The huge explosion woke up all the islanders who ran out of their houses not knowing what hit them. All that remained from the big boat was little pieces of wood along with body parts washing up on the beach with each wave. Nikitas and the rest of the guys having succeeded in what they had been preparing for months; disappeared in the early dawn each one of them to their houses. Nikitas walked all the way to Pedi where his father's boat was a few hours earlier and smiled knowing his mother and brother were a way from town.

It didn't take long for the authorities and the rest of the people to know that the Resistance had hit again and now the islanders were once more afraid of what the authorities would do to them as a reprisal for the Resistance' latest attack. Most people didn't even go to work afraid they might be arrested. In the meantime the explosions had damaged many houses and especially houses which were close to the water. There was broken glass everywhere from windows and doors blown out to the streets. There were also a few fires caused by the sudden explosions.

Manolis and crew arrived at the Island of Kalymnos for his last delivery before going back home to Simi. There he got the news about the Resistance' latest attack on the Turkish ship. Manolis also learned that the ship was carrying fifty soldiers, a few cannons, many guns and ammunitions. That had to be a big loss for the Turks and there was no doubt in Manolis' mind that there were going to be reprisals. He further learned that the attack was launched by local fighters. That worried Manolis because he knew Nikitas could be one of them. If that were true he would be arrested the minute he arrived on Simi.

He talked to a friend, fisherman, who sailed daily to Simi, he said, "Pano, I have a favor to ask you." Panos said, "Go right ahead Manolis." "Well, you heard what happen on Simi with that big explosion. I want you to go and check on my house and see if everything is ok with them. If you see Nikitas bring him with you." "Sure, I'll see you tonight; with or without Nikitas." Manolis delivered the last cargo and then he and his crew waited a few agonizing hours for Panos' news. Panos and crew arrived with the fish he caught on the way to Simi and as usual, he sold it in town and bought a few things for home. On the way back to Kalymnos he fished again and then sold his catch in town. That had been his routine for many years. After he was done with all his chores on Simi, he went to Manolis' house but found no one. He asked the neighbors for the whereabouts of the Papanikitas family but all he heard was that the family had disappeared three days previously. On his way back Panos delivered the bad news to Manolis. After that Manolis was really worried about his family.

When Nikitas didn't see their other boat on Pedi he knew his mother and Tassos were in it hiding somewhere. In its place they had left the small skiff; when he looked inside he found a packet with a piece of bread, a piece of cheese, an apple, and a cooler of water. Nikitas thought there were two places they could have gone, either Nimos Island, or Chondros Island. They were both close-by. Nikitas had a hunch they were on Nimos, it was the bigger island of the two and a little closer. Both islands were unpopulated. Nikitas was starving so he helped himself to the food his mother had left. He jumped into the boat and headed for Nimos.

When the constables arrived at Tassos' house they found no one there; the neighbors were not any help either. They went to Tassos' friend Nikos, and asked him to tell them if Tassos was a member of the Resistance. First he said he didn't know anything but when the constables threatened that they were going to take him to the station and beat him; his parents ordered him to tell all he knew about Tassos. It didn't take too long for the constables to find the rest of the boys who had helped to destroy the boat. The boys ranged in age from thirteen to fifteen; too young to be hanged. But the Turks were determined to do just that, because of their big loss; and to scare the rest of the Islanders. They arrested all the males over twelve who were related to the boys, and put them in jail. They were going to hang the boys as soon as reinforcements arrived from the Island of Rhodes.

The real Resistance was made up of grown-ups seasoned and ruthless fighters who had been fighting the Turks all their lives. When they heard that the Turks were going to hang the boys, they moved quickly. They wanted to save the boys before reinforcements arrived on Simi. That night they attacked the station with forty well-equipped fighters. They quickly took over the police station, took the remaining eight constables prisoners, burn the station and the adjacent houses. Before they left they asked the families, who were involved, if they wanted to go with them. All of them agreed to go; staying there would have been suicide.

The Islanders left with only their most valuable items. The boats sailed for the free mainland of Greece where they were settled in temporary housing. Finally the Turkish reinforcement arrived on the Simi; a company of two hundred soldiers and police. They quickly imposed a curfew from 8:00 pm to 7:00 am and started rebuilding the police station and other destroyed houses.

More people came from Simi to Kalymnos with the latest news about the Resistance' attack on the police station liberating the boys and their parents and taking them to the Greek Mainland along with eight captured Turkish constables. Manolis finally heard from relatives and friends where Nikitas went after he and the other boys exploded the Turkish boat. He had a pretty good idea where he might have gone after he left Pedi.

Manolis knew that sooner or later the Turkish authorities would come looking for him too. So he told his crew they were not going back to Simi for a while. They were going to look for his family. He also told them that if they wanted to go back to Simi to their families it was OK by him. A few of the older married people chose to leave but the younger crew decided to stay.

They left Kalymnos during the night bound for Nimos and Chondros because Manolis also thought that's where the family was hiding. They sailed all night arriving before sunrise at Chondros. First they spent some time looking around for the hidden boat but it wasn't there. Then they looked around Nimos but they couldn't find it there either. Manolis thought that maybe he was wrong, maybe they didn't go to Nimos either or maybe The

Turks found them and they were taken back to Simi. They decided to hide during the day and start looking again in the night.

Nikitas grabbed the two oars and started heading towards Nimos, it took him a couple of hours but finally he got there exhausted, but happy to be away from Simi and out of danger for now. He pulled the skiff out to land and put it behind a boulder, then lay down flat on his back and caught his breath. He was perspiring profusely his heart was pounding fast and hard. He stayed there looking at the blue sky; a murder of crows flew by cawing noisily—then quiet. He could still hear his heart beating hard.

After a while he got up and reached for the cooler he was so thirsty that he drank it all in a few gulps. He got up and walked up the hill where he could have a better look at his surroundings. From his vantage point he could see almost half of the island but he couldn't see the boat or its mast anywhere. He put his skiff in the water and jumped into it. He sailed to the other side of the island pulled his skiff out and walked again on the highest hill he could find and looked down again. Now he could see the other side of Nimos but he still couldn't find the boat anywhere. For a moment Nikitas wondered if he was on the wrong island. He kept looking until he saw a shiny thing protruding through a couple of pine trees and realized that was the top of the mast. He kept looking until he saw the mast moving. There was no doubt about it that was the boat. He quickly ran down, and got into the skiff. Once more he started to sail but this time he knew where he was going.

Manolis and crew sailed through the night and by dawn the saw the two islands from afar they turned off the boat's navigation lights and stayed there in the morning fog like a ghost ship.

At daylight they made sure there were no other boats around and they sailed through the Narrows; an area with hazardous rocks. Manolis knew it well and avoided hitting them few other people would dare to come close. Manolis steered the boat to a small lagoon and after they secured it they lowered a skiff and Manolis and Spiros got into it and went ashore. Manolis said to Spiros, "If Nikitas or Despina came to this island they would know how to hide so it may take some time to find them."

Nikitas found the boat. It was where he thought it would be. He wanted to make sure no Turks were around; so he approached the boat carefully. Despina and Tassos had seen movements from far away and both of them were looking in that direction. Despina held a gun ready to shoot any Turks heading her way but at the same time she hoped it would be Nikitas. When Nikitas was close enough to the boat he yelled, "Mother this is Nikitas put your gun down. Are you and Tassos alone?" "Yes, Nikitas, come my child, we are alone." Nikitas told them about the other attack from the Resistance and the rescued boys and their parents. Despina was so happy that Nikitas had escaped unscathed but she was sorry that all those people had to leave their houses. She said, "I know your father is looking for us. We need to help him find us." "I know that he was on Kalymnos yesterday; he must have heard what happened on Simi by now, and if he knows we left home and are hiding he will be looking for us on Nimos too. If they left last night they should be here sometime today." "Let's hope so because we are running out of food, and also we need to get out of here or sooner or later they will find us and then it will be all over." "Don't worry Mother I will be looking for him and if he is around I know how to signal him that we are here."

Nikitas and Tassos prepared the boat to be ready to leave with their father on not; they could not stay there any longer, they had to go. When there was enough daylight Nikitas walked up a hill and looked around. He knew his father well enough to guess that he would go through the Narrows. So he walked towards that direction hoping to meet him half way. He was right. He heard voices coming up his way. He hid behind a bush and waited. Before long he heard his father voice; he waited long enough until he saw his father and Spiros coming up the hill. Nikitas stepped out of the bush and said, "Father I am glad you are here." Manolis and Spiros were equally glad to see him. The three of them embraced for a moment and then started down the hill. Despina was happy to have her family together and to have someone else in charge of the boat.

Nikitas sailed the skiff far enough to signal the boat Charavgi to approach, and when the boat was close enough, Nikitas said, "My father wants you to prepare the boat to sail to Piraeus. He'll be coming on board shortly." Manolis came back with Nikitas and loaded enough provisions including water into the skiff, for the "Panormitis." Then he came back to his larger boat, "Charavgi" with Despina and Tassos. When it became dark enough Manolis and crew sailed Charavgi to the port of Piraeus. Panormitis followed with Nikitas and two of his crew.

Three days later the two boats arrived at Piraeus and in Free Greece where they didn't have to hide any longer. They stayed there for a few days to get more provisions for the trip to Volos. Several of the crew on both boats quit and went back to Simi to their families. Manolis hired a new crew and sailed for Volos which was a coastal port city in Thessaly situated midway on the Greek mainland, about 330 Kilometers north of Athens and 220 Kilometers south of Thessaloniki. It was the capital of the Magnesia regional. It was facing the Pagasitikos Kolpos (gulf). There were many trees in the north many more than the southern side. Agriculture flourished with fruit trees and fields for grains and other products. Volos was a busy port serving Greece and other countries in the Balkans and farther to the north.

After arriving in Volos Manolis found land and a house in the city and settled his family in a more secure and freer place than Simi. Nikitas and Tassos went back to school just as it was before and when summers came along Nikitas went out to sea helping his father. Tassos continued going to high school and then to divinity school. Eventually Tassos became a priest in the Greek Orthodox Church serving a church in Anakasia not too far from Volos. Nikitas finished high school as he had promised his father and became the captain of Panormitis sailing the same islands and coastal ports as his father Manolis.

On the Island of Simi all the niceties of the past were gone and now the people were treated as enemies and in the harshest way. That in turn caused more attacks against the authorities from the locals and others. This was happening in many islands and other areas still held by the Ottoman Empire. That went on until 1905; by then there were fewer and fewer soldiers on Simi. The empire was falling apart and at some point there was an agreement between the Turkish and the Greek authorities in which the Greeks paid taxes to the Turks who kept their flags flying and had official ownership of the Simi but kept themselves within their compounds. In turn the elders of the island governed the population. That went on until 1912 when the Turks left all the Dodecanese Islands. The county seat was established on the Island of Rhode, which started the process of reuniting the Islands with the rest of Greece.

In 1901 Nikitas moved back to the Island of Simi. He was twenty-five, tall for a Greek, handsome, blue eyed, and curly brown hair. There he met Rinio a beautiful girl, with long black hair, and brown eyes. She was one of the two Chavaris girls the other one was Maroulio just as nice looking but younger by two years. The Chavaris family had been on the island for hundreds of years. Rinio was twenty when they fell in love and married on the island. Rinio was a high school teacher.

Even though the Ottoman Empire was still technically in charge in the area; Nikitas and many others worked freely just as they worked on the free side of Greece. Nikitas and Rinio had three girls; Fotiny, Elleny, and Christodula (Popi) Maroulio also got marry to Agapitos a sponge diver who had two daughters Anika and Fotiny, and a boy Michael. They all lived on Simi until 1912. They were planning to live their lives on the island but something unexpected happened. As soon as the Turks left, a few months later the Italians took over all the Dodecanese and many other islands around. The Islanders freedom was too short; once more the Island of Simi was under foreign occupation. At the time the Italians took control of Simi; they tried to be nice to the Islanders but the Greeks were not reciprocating. They were furious that they had to put up with another foreign power after they had tasted freedom. They denounced the new occupiers just as they had denounced the Turks.

Once more the people resorted to painting their houses blue, and white, the color of the Greek flag. The Resistance started all over again just as determined as before. For the last four hundred years the Greeks had been attached to Eastern Orthodoxy. This is the religion that had kept them together during the Turkish occupation. Now their new occupiers introduced Catholicism. That didn't go well with them in fact it made the people of all the occupied Islands more determined to get rid of the Italians.

Nikitas found himself in the new Resistance again but this time he was grown up and a captain of his own boat. He was well equated in the Dodecanese archipelagos and coastal ports. He used his knowledge to the fullest. Nikitas didn't get involved directly in sabotaging the Italians; this time he carried the Resistance fighters from island to islands and coastal to coast always avoiding the authorities. In 1922 the Dodecanese were given officially to Italy along with other islands all the way to Turkey. That treaty disheartened Greeks who had hoped they would be united with Mother Greece after hundreds of years of foreign occupations.

Many of the Islanders move to the free side of Greece rather than be subjects to another occupier. By now the Italians had become more brazen breaking into houses at any time of day or night and arresting the Resistance fighters and collaborators. It was at that time Nikitas decided to move his family away from Simi. When he asked his parents to move with them they refused. Manolis was an old man and sick. He wanted to die on the island where he was born. His boat "Charavgi" was leased to more able people and he and Despina lived on that income until he died in the thirties. Despina moved to Volos and lived with Nikitas family until she died a few years later. After Manolis' death Nikitas inherited his father's boat and now he was using both of the boats.

In her last pregnancy Rinio had given birth to twins a boy and a girl. Nikitas was very happy to finally have a son but a few months later the boy died. It was at that time Nikitas and Rinio adopted a baby boy and gave him the name Manolis after Nikitas' father. "In order for the baby to be properly adopted, Rinio passed him through the right sleeve of her coat thereby symbolizing passage through the birth canal. Baby Manolis was nursed along with his sister Popi. As Manolis grew up he helped his father just as Nikitas had done. After Rinio's sister Maroulio died at a young age her children were moved to the Papanikitas home. Eventually they all moved to Volos and lived in house Manolis had bought earlier. Now that the families were away from Simi and Nikitas' parents were dead he was free to take more chances in helping the Resistance without being afraid of reprisals against his family.

Tassos eventually moved to the Island of Rhodes. It would be hard to prove for certain if he was a member of the Resistance or not. However he contributed far more with his homilies than exploding bridges or breaking windows. He never failed to remind his parishioners how superior Eastern Orthodoxy was to Roman Catholicism. He urged them to resist the Italian authorities. He reminded them that the islands and all the land they occupied belonged to Greece. Many times Tassos urged the Greek people not to pay taxes to the Italian authorities but to give money for the liberation of the islands. Frequently the police put him in jail for days at a time for encouraging the people to rebel. The people protested outside the prison to let him go free.

In secret meetings he blessed those who were about to attack the police or the army and he used to say, "The Greek people depend on you for their freedom God is with you." And the people went out with the will to fight reinforced with what father Tassos had told them.

And so the years went by with Father Tassos helping in his own way, and Nikitas delivering the Resistance fighters ammunitions and weaponry to various places across the occupied islands and the coastal ports.

In the late thirties Benito Mussolini the Italian fascist dictator abolished the parliamentary system and became the leader of Italy and an ally to Hitler. In October 1940 he attacked Greece aided by the Albanian army. That was a surprise to Hitler who wasn't ready to invade the Balkan countries but it wasn't a surprise to the Greeks who were waiting for him.

Even though the Italians came into Greece with superior air power, army and weapons; they were in for a surprise. The Greek General Papagos let them come in to the mountainous area where the Greeks were well hidden and prepared. Benito Mussolini told Hitler that he had gained lots of land and he was on his way to Thessaloniki (second biggest city in Greece) He said, "I told you I was going to give you all the Balkan countries on a platter and I am well on my way." Hitler knew how the Greeks fought and had second thoughts about Mussolini's bravado.

After three weeks on the flat lands of Greece the Italian army prepared to fight the Greeks in the mountains and capture Thessaloniki. But the Greeks counterattacked and pushed the Italian army all the way back to Albania capturing many prisoners Italian and Albanians. The Italian human loss was greater than they had anticipated. The Italians withdrew very quickly but in an orderly manner according to their records. The Italians left material, weapons, and provisions behind, they came in handy for the Greeks.

The Greek victory was not a great loss only for Mussolini but also for Hitler who used his well-trained reserve army stationed In Rumania to capture the Balkan countries including Greece. Instead of sending his troops to the Russian front as he planned to the delay cost him dearly. By the time his army arrived at the Russian front they were confronted with the coldest winter in many years. That delay hastened his defeat in Russia.

The reason Hitler attacked the Balkan countries prematurely is because the Greeks had cleared the area for the English army to come in and deprive Hitler from the Balkan countries.

Nikitas was very busy those days; both of his boats along with many others were commissioned by the Greek Government to carry soldiers and material to the front, where they were fighting the Italians. The "gloves were off"; now the Resistance was fighting along with the Greek army and navy. The fighting went on until the Germans captured Greece in 1941. Germany was the third country to occupy the Dodecanese and all Greece. At that time Nikitas was getting old; he was 66. During his life he had lived under one occupier or another. Now the Resistance was fighting a well-organized and ruthless army but they kept on fighting.

The many years of fighting the different occupiers made the Resistance just as ruthless as the Germans. They had the knowledge of the area and they attacked at will. Any time the Germans executed Greek citizens, they did that frequently, there were repercussions for the Germans as well. Sometimes they woke up in the morning and saw their own soldiers hanging somewhere in town, a bridge blown up, or a blazing fire in their own compound. The Germans were good at fighting a regular army, but were afraid of the "ghost army" of the Resistance because they always delivered. The resistance fighters rarely surrendered; they would kill themselves rather than fall into the hands of the Germans.

One day as Nikitas was preparing to sail for a special trip to Turkey his son Manolis said, "Father haven't you done enough? Isn't it about time to quit? Let me go this time so you can take a few days off." "Not this time Manolis, but I promise you this will be my last sail; when I come back I am going to retire." Manolis knew his father well enough not to argue with him. He picked up his bag and walked with him to the boat. Then he said, "Father next time I am going, O.K.?" "O.K. son." And with that he walked up the gangway and on the boat.

Nikitas didn't know what his mission was until the last moment. It was always hidden in a place he only knew. While his crew prepared the boat for sailing, he went to the secret place and found an envelope with the order. After Nikitas read the note he bit his lips and murmured to himself, "God help us." Stelios asked Nikitas, "Captain where to?" "Turkey." The crew looked at one another; they knew what there were in for.

During the Second World War Turkey stayed neutral, unlike Greece who fought two enemies and paid a big price in human losses and money. In fact Turkey was one of the few countries which came out a winner after the war. A lot of weapons and other material were bought and sold. Espionage took place from the first day to the last in Turkey. Nikitas had gone many times to Turkey to buying food and other everyday items. But there were the times he bought weapons for the Resistance, no questions asked. For the Turks it was business as usual. But this time in addition to buying weapons they would be carrying two English spies to Piraeus, the port of Athens.

Carrying spies on board the ship was very dangerous because enemy spies could easily be spying on the two Englishmen. Nikitas prepared for the worst and hoped for the best. After they loaded the cargo they headed for the open sea and after they had sailed for thirty minutes or so a little boat with three men who appeared to be fishing approached them and asked to talk to the captain. One looked like a Turk but the other two men appeared to be foreigners and they looked very young.

They spoke in broken Greek but enough to be understood. One of them said, "We are in need of petrol could we buy some from you?" Nikitas said, "How much do you need?" "About a gallon would be enough; how is the weather going to be today?" "OK for fishing." At that moment the other Englishman who hadn't said a word so far, said, "Captain Nikitas clad to meet you, I am James Shepherd and this is my friend Robert Summerville." That's was all that needed to be said for both parties to know they were dealing with the right people. The English men came on board and sailed away; the other man turned back home, he didn't need petrol.

After sailing for a couple of hours one of the passengers asked if they could be put out on a small unoccupied island to use their wireless radio. Nikitas stopped on the nearest suitable island and let them out. An hour later one of the deckhands brought them back and they continued homeward. The Englishmen helped with the chores on the ship and everything seemed to be going well but on the third day at about 11:00 pm as they were approaching the Island of Andros there appeared a boat going fast in their direction.

Nikitas asked one of the deckhands to turn off the directional lights. The other boat slowed down for a while but soon they directed two bright lights onto Nikitas' boat. There was no doubt. It was a German Coast Guard vessel. Nikitas knew he couldn't outrun them. The next thing he did was to give an order he had hoped he would never have to give. He said, "Long live Greece!" The crew knew what to do; one of them went down to the engine room. After a few minutes he came up and said, "Captain all done." Nikitas said, take your positions." They all did as they were told. As the smaller boat was coming with German soldiers to their boat; Nikitas asked the two Englishmen to step down to the skiff that was on the port side of Panormitis and said, "Go away from the boat as fast as you can if you want to save your lives!" The Englishmen quickly grabbed their bags, jumped into the skiff, and sailed away; they knew what was going to happen.

The crew gathered around Nikitas and they all prayed to saint Nikolas the protector of Greek seamen, then Nikitas directed the boat towards the German Coast Guard vessel bypassing the smaller boat and went full speed on it. It cut the German boat in two followed by a huge explosion. There was very little left; even the small boat with the soldiers was exploded and sank. The only witnesses to the tragedy were the two Englishmen who lived to tell the story.

The End

Epilogue

Nikitas was my maternal grandfather. When I was about two years old he took time from his busy schedule and came to my house to baptize me at a nearby church. He gave me the name George in honor of his favored Saint. At 6'2" he was taller than the average Greek. I grew up to look very much like him the only difference is that I have brown eyes. My mother used to tell me, "Not only do you look like him, you act like him too." I am glad to know that, because I admired him. He was a good man and died a hero fighting the Nazis to liberate Greece. I saw my grandfather only once when I was two years old and too young to remember. However I do remember him tossing me up in the air and catching me as I came down and I felt my stomach come in my throat.

Because Nikitas drowned I was able to get information about his death from the naval archives in Piraeus and the deposition of the two English spies to the Nazis. The rest of the stories came from several of his friends and relatives. Nikitas kept good records of his legal trips and merchandise but understandably there is not one word written anywhere about his engagements with the Resistance. Only after the wars were over he and his friends talked about their participation in the Resistance.

Since I couldn't substantiate all the details of the events; I have written those stories which compare with those of his contemporaries. I thought it would be better to write his biography as a biographical sketch. In doing so I had the liberty to compare some of the similar documented stories to those I wrote in his biography. While I was writing my grandfather's stories I was looking constantly at his picture and it felt as if I was communicating with him.

George Karnikis and proud to be the grandson of Nikitas Papanikitas.

VISITORS FROM AFAR

A Science Fiction Story

Ha, UFO? I think is a bunch of malarkey Prove it! Now wait a minute Derek; there are many people who have seen something unusual out there and they can't all be wrong, can they? Of course they can; just because there is something unexplainable up there it doesn't mean that it came from outer space. Our government has been experimenting with rockets, missiles, and newer planes for many years and that's what we most likely confuse them; with UFOs.

Paul and Derek have been friends since their early school years. Derek was always the inquisitive one and Paul most of the time had an answer for him. They argued a lot but they managed to keep their friendship going all through the years. After high school they drifted away, they went to different colleges and universities. Derek went into finances, stock market, and other business enterprises and he retired in his early sixties with enough money for a comfortable retirement. Derek married Alice and they had David and Suzy who are now married with their own families. Derek White was a first generation American of English background. Both of his parents were born in London England and came in the States in their twenties they settled in Seattle area and that's where Derek grew up. As a young man he looked handsome about 5'10" tall with blond hair and blue eyes.

Paul McDowell was born in Seattle his was first generation

American. His parents came from Edinburgh Scotland. He graduated from Washington University majored in biology and exo-biology. Paul worked and taught in laboratories of universities and colleges in several states but eventually came back to U.W. where he taught and did experimental work for the last thirty years. He retired in his late sixties but he kept doing experimental work at the main lab a few days a week. Paul was also married to Mary Davison who was also a lab technician at U.W.

Although they were both working they managed to have a son Jim who married Derek's daughter Suzy. That reinforced the friendship of the four families who lived in and out Seattle. Paul was about 5'11" tall black hair brown eyes who looked like his mother. Paul was a nice looking guy who had many girl friends as a single guy. But his lab work took priority in his life. Although he always did experimental work in any lab he worked. After he retired he was able to concentrate more into exo-biology. Paul knew that basically in the primordial period every living thing shared the same DNA. As the time went on life morphed in to different entities which in turn they adapted conditions suitable to their survival. He concentrated his efforts mainly in dead (Petrified) and living cells comparing with one another trying to find the origin of life. Paul would often look up in the sky and wonder if life hitchhiked on those meteorites that occasionally fall on earth. Slowly but surely an idea was forming in his mind but he needed more time to prove it.

After Jim carved the Thanksgiving turkey he wasn't needed in the kitchen anymore so he joined the older folks in the living room who were sipping wine and were deep into an argument about

Ufology. Jim listen for a while not interrupting. He agreed with his father but he didn't want to interject his thoughts at this time. It was Derek who asked him what he thought on the subject. Jim said, "Well—I think that you are both right." Derek said, "Now you are being diplomatic Jim—what do you really think?" "I still think that you are both right; you see, our government does work on secret weaponry planes and so on. There is a place called Area 51 which is in a remote detachment of the Edwards Air Force in Nevada State. They frequently test new weapons and especially new planes and I believe you are right; those maybe are UFOs to us but they know what they are but they are not about to tell us and they shouldn't. Other countries have their own Areas 51 as well; that's not secret. On the other hand my father is right too. People all over the world have seen cylindrical shape objects, ships that are three hundred or four hundred feet long, and many other objects flying noiselessly over big metropolitan cities. Our country doesn't have the capability, the money, or the need to build such huge ships for use in our skies and if we can't build them other countries can't build them either.

With so many billions of planets and galaxies in the cosmos it is feasible that older civilizations could have found a faster way to travel through space and visit us. My feeling is that we see very little of what's happening around us. If we indeed have extra terrestrials around us it makes sense that they will not appear to us before they study us. If we were to go to another planet occupied with living things we would want to know their habits and how dangerous they would be to us too." "So are you telling me that you believe on UFOs?" "All I am telling you is that it could be happening and we are not aware of." Thankfully they were asked to come to the dining room where a cornucopia of food was spread out on the table and they turn their attention to something more pleasant for now.

Jim was a likeable guy pleasant to talk to and very smart especially in his own field. He graduated from Harvard University with high marks in physics, currently working at Boeing Aerospace Company in rocketing division. Unlike his parents who devoted most of their lives teaching and practicing biology; he liked physics, it came easier to him. Since he was a little guy he wanted to know how things work. He was interesting in space, spaceships and the technology that went with it. Jim often said I feel lucky because I do what I like and get paid for it. Jim married Suzy a high school sweetheart who is now teaching at Martin Luther King junior, High School, in Everett Washington Suzy was a good looking girl outspoken and she always knew what she wanted and often got it. Her father wanted her to go into finances, be a stockbroker and work with him but she would have none of that; she liked teaching and didn't care about making a lot of money. They lived in the outskirts of Everett overlooking the Port Gardner Bay and all the ship traffic. A beautiful two story Scandinavian type house most likely built by pioneers who settled in Everett in the early nineteen hundreds; old but well maintained. Jim and Suzy could have gone to other states with better pay and more opportunities but they liked being closer to home and they couldn't have been happier being where they are now. Meeting together every Thanksgiving was an annual event since the time the kids were young. Now that the kids were married and having their own families; each year they celebrated in a different house. This year they were at Jim's and Suzy's house; the dining room was close to a huge picture window. Out in the water one could see the bright lighten boats and ferries sailing in and out the pictures Port of Gardner Bay. David was happy to be celebrating Thanksgiving at his sister house unlike his sister he was an introvert but tonight with the help of some wine he found the courage to get up and say a few words on the occasion. He was on a celebratory mood and he got up, raised his glass, and said, "After my close call with the car accident I had a few months ago I feel lucky to be here among my friends and relatives, Trina my wife and my children. It made me think what our priorities should be in life, so let us enjoy Thanksgiving with good food, good company, and let us drink to our health and happiness." And with that they all raised their glasses.

Dave was a good driver he never had a car accident before it was a drunken driver that hit his car on the free way. The other driver died, Dave sustained some injuries but recovered completely from his wounds. Dave worked in the Microsoft Corporation as a programmer technician for the last ten years. He had contributed to many of the software and he was well respected for. Dave and Martha had two children a boy Douglas 14 and Megan 12; they were the only children in the Party. Douglas was a nice looking and intelligent boy but like most children of his age he was pretty much withdrawn working on his smart phone and said very little. Megan was a beautiful little girl with blond curly hair and very white skin in fact she was pale. Little Megan had an unknown blood disease; it wasn't cancer but that ailment made her often tired. She was also living in her own world communicating with her friends through her smart phone.

Mary and Alice, the two matriarchs, frequently found themselves talking alone especially when the two men had their own conversations. Earlier on the younger women had pretty much taken over the kitchen and they had a minute to talk. Mary asked Alice, "How is little Megan doing?" "Ever since her doctor changed her medicine she seems to be doing better but as you can see she hasn't gain her color back and she still gets tire although not as often." "Is there any hope for curing this disease?" "Not at this time anyway, but she is still young and who knows they may come up with a cure for her ailment one of these days." "Well both Paul and I know many doctors that work hard to find a cure for many new diseases especially cancer and we will keep in touch with you guys." "Thank you Mary; the poor thing is so discouraged, at this point all we can do is pray for her." "And we do too Alice."

Outer Space

In the far side of our galaxy there is a gas giant planet unknown yet to the people of earth. It is about twice the size of Jupiter or 618 times bigger than earth. There are billions of gaseous clouds floating on a charted course continuously around the giant globe. In close proximity to the planet there are twelve satellite planets. They vary in size between earth and mercury. Two of them approximately the size of earth and the farthest away closest to a far away sun have atmosphere with rock crust and frozen oceans. The other ten planets are gaseous without atmosphere. Inside the biggest earth size planet there is animal life in a form of giant worm-like and they live inside the water and out on the ice. Inside each worm-like entity there are trillions upon trillions of microorganism from the size of the common virus and other much smaller germs; the worm and the germs are a symbiotic. The germs live in separate colonies with their own kind, in a jelly-like living thing.

They fiercely protect their colonies. They all eat their jelly-like host which is constantly regenerates itself. It sustains its self by eating micro organisms. Some germs frequently leave their colonies and attack other colonies to supplement their diet. This planetary system is over ten billion years old. The worm-like entities have gained intelligence through their long existence that surpasses the human intelligence by far. The germs within the worms have their own ecosystem and have gained vast knowledge too.

All through the ages the worms have tried repeatedly to break loose from their constrained environment but they could never penetrate the silicon-like crust that entombed them all this time. Throughout the eons they persisted and finally at some point they were able to break through, only to be destroyed in the harsh gaseous environment.

Through time several of them managed to fortify their bodies to survive the outer space. Through billions of years they became space travelers. The visited the neighboring planets and as the time went on they built exo skeletal frames which enabled them to break again out of the gravity of their giant gaseous planet and travel through the universe. As they traveled they gained even more knowledge and became powerful. They discovered worm-holes and other fast means to transport through space. The worms had psychokinetic powers which enabled them to manipulate things at will. They also communicated through extra sensory perception. The worms have used nanotechnology to build huge spaceships and for any other need they might have had. Their diet consisted mainly of minerals and proteins which they replicated in their ships. They regenerated in huge pools of water mixed with a variety of minerals.

The worms are sexless and reproduce by parthenogenesis. Their young are fully equip to function on their own at birth and they do not need parental guidance. They live about three hundred years and when the die their corpses are reduced to basic minerals and then are put back in the water pools where they are re-circulated in the food system. This process is done again by nanotechnology. The worms are about 6" at birth and grow to three feet as grown-ups. They are nomadic in nature traveling from planet to planet in very large spaceships and in fleets of hundred or so at the time. They are powerful and can defend themselves successfully if they need to. However in their long existence they have learned to live peacefully with one another. The worms visit another planet only to resupply materials they need; they come and leave in peace. They have the ability to camouflage themselves and they try not to interfere with the species the visit. They have introduced some of their superb technologies to several civilized species but only if they are at an age they are able to handle it.

The worms almost never leave their secure ships except when they visit the home planet. They send smaller ships with robots to accomplish their needs.

Earth - bound

The worms have never visited earth before it's been one of the most challenging planets they have visited. Earth was farthest away too. As it is customary with the worms before they visited a planet they collect as much information before they arrive. The fleet is their home base and from it individual ships leave their base for long voyages that last many years at the time. Before they arrive at their destinations the worms know a lot about the planet and the life it contains. The mother ship stays in cloaked mode and will blind any foreign ship coming their way and will destroy if it becomes dangerous to their ship. They send autonomous robotized smaller ships with robotic crew with the ability to morph and match the local residence and live as one of them. Help is always available from the mother ship to the robots and help from the fleet to the mother ship no matter how far they are.

The robots have been living on earth among the humans for many years now; they could be their next door neighbors and they wouldn't be able to know they are aliens. The worms have lived on earth for fifty human years. They have gotten the material they came here for, not only from earth but from the neighboring planets too. But what was fascinating to them was the human species as a whole; their culture, and history, through their short life. They could see in humans the potential for greatness and also for mutual distraction.

For the last ten years the Worms have noticed other aliens visiting earth. At first they thought they were humans returning from an interplanetary expedition but these humanoids looked a little different. All though they had the same characteristics their heads were larger and their bodies were at least one third shorter. They had spaceships far superior to the locals capable for interstellar travels and powerful weapons. They also had the ability to cloak their ships and themselves but the Worms were able to see them at all times because they had better technology and they kept close surveillance on the humanoids and so far they found them to be no violent or aggressive and rather helpful to the locals. They deciphered their language and were able to penetrate their library and found out that some time in the past they had lived on earth and left for some reason and now they coming back. As long as the humanoids are helping the locals they pretty much stayed out of the way but the worms always kept an eye on both the locals and the humanoids. The humanoids managed to stay invisible from the local humans but the worms were invisible to both humans and humanoids. The worms had a civilization that was a few billions years older than both of these species and they were far more intelligent.

Now that the Worms had accomplished their mission in this planetary system; they could have left a long time ago but decided to stay longer to help the human species avoid a nuclear catastrophe and save their civilization from complete annihilation. They also decided to help and alleviate the local humans from some of their illnesses. After all the Worms were not only hosts to most of those germs and viruses, they were symbiotic and they knew how to control them if they needed to. They directed their robots on earth to help humans make new drugs that will control or abolish several of the killer diseases.

Pathologies

Paul McDowell and some time his wife Mary worked in their separate labs at UW in Seattle. Although they were both retired they continued to work in their labs as their hobby. They were working on different viruses which caused incurable diseases, such as cancer, Aids and other killer diseases. Paul spent many years trying to find the origin of life and among his many failures he also had a few successes. His various papers on properties and structure of DNA on animal and other living things earned him many awards nationally and internationally. Mary on the hand worked and taught the etiology and pathology on common and uncommon diseases. Lately she has worked on the two most difficult diseases; cancer and aids. Lately Davis's little girl Martha was on their minds as they worked in their labs.

Megan's illness was not only incurable, but hard to diagnose. She had one of those rare illnesses which puzzled even the best pathologists worldwide. For the last few weeks Paul and Mary worked together using their vast knowledge to understand this illness not only on behave of little Megan but for many other people. Little Megan was given about three years to live with this disease and she was on her third year now. If a cure was not found soon she will perish.

Paul's schedule hasn't changed much since he retired; even though he didn't come to his lab as often as before, when he did come he did the same thing he has done all these years. He stopped at the cafeteria and got his steamy cup of coffee on the way to his lab. And so was one morning couple of months ago. He took his rain coat off and hung it on a cloths hook, sat in his chair, turned on his computer and had his first swallow of coffee looking on his e-mails.

He went through his mail mechanically and there was a strange e-mail with numerals and logarithms. There were several unfamiliar chemical patterns that he had never seen before. At first look Paul thought someone was playing some kind of a prank or a joke on him and he was about to delete it and carry on with his program. But when he looked more carefully he noticed that when the chemical patterns were accompanied with logarithms the syntaxes form a synthetic message that was repeated over and over as though someone wanted his attention on this formula. Paul knew he was on something important. He discussed his strange message with Mary who was just as perplexed as he was. They both went over the numerals and the chemical patterns. But they could not arrive in a logical solution no matter how many times they went over. However they noticed something that could be making sense. At the end of the formula there was an unfinished theorem when they used known set of axioms and basic assumptions they could almost come to a logical assumption but the numerals were not all there. What could that mean? Obviously someone wanted them to understand a composition of something. But without all the numerals in the theorem it was like someone wanted them to have only part of the answer. Then Mary said, "Maybe they are telling us there is more to come." "But why they don't send us a complete numerical theorem to the formula so that we have something to work with?" "Either someone wants to play no sense with us, or they don't know how to communicate with us. Maybe they are saying; there is more to come." Mary said, "I have never seen these patterns before, have you?" "No, no, this is foreign to me; at this point it doesn't make sense at all." Paul and Mary were hooked on that puzzle it was a brainteaser for sure and they wanted to figure it out.

The next day they received another e-mail with the rest of the numerals to the theorem and the two of them finally came to a logical assumption. An analysis of a substance that contains unknown properties, but what is this substance? What's made out of? Mary said, "Maybe it's a chemical property unknown to us yet." "So someone is telling us here is a chemical substance which we can build using the patterns they sent us; how?" "At this point we don't know; but we shouldn't jump to a conclusion perhaps they will send us more information and help us work it out." "I sure hope so, because so far we have only gotten half truths."

Pawl and Mary did get more information and they were almost sure that they were dealing with an alien entity. As time went on they became familiar with those strange formulae and started to build new powerful chemical substances and then they used them to make new powerful drugs which they could be used to combat all kind of diseases. But it was kept secret for a long time until it was tested and proven safe. After all could they be trusted? Were those drugs they made safe for humans or were they agents of distraction that would annihilate humanity? And how were they going to introduce those powerful drugs to the scientific world? Another thing which was bothering them was who were those benevolent entities that are helping humanity are they our friends? And would the pharmaceutical companies be as benevolent as the aliens have been. Those were all legitimate questions bothering both of them. The formulae for the drugs were ready and that was as far as Paul and Mary were willing to go. From now on it would have to be the responsibility of the Government and the pharmaceutical companies. But they had to make sure that those drugs had to be given to the sick people at a minimum charge and not make it too profitable for the pharmaceutical companies.

Paul and Mary were relaxing having their usual drink talking about their day's work when they got an urgent call from their son Jim, he said, I thought I should let you know that Suzy and I will not be coming tomorrow for dinner because little Megan is in her last stages of dying at home and we want to be there with her. Mary looked at Paul and said, "Well Paul, are we going to let that child die?" Paul said, "What if drug doesn't work; she will be the first human to try it and we don't know what the consequences will be—Mary we have a great responsibility with these drugs. Remember what could happen if these drugs are not what they are suppose to be." "For god sakes Paul these entities are far superior to us, if they wanted to kill us they wouldn't come to us; they could put in the water spay it up above us. They want to help us and they want to see how responsible we are. The child is going to die anyway." "O.K. let's say that we cure Megan —it's going to be the wonder drug how you are going to stop it from spreading like wild fire? You know the pharmaceutical industry will make it, and all the drugs we have made their own and we may even end up in jail too." "We will tell Dave and Stacy that this is an experimental drug that we made and we cannot by low use it directly on a human being. If they want us to use it on Megan; they must not tell anyone." "Mary we are taking a big chance but if they want us to do it we will and God help us."

Paul asked Dave and Stacy to have a word with them away from the crowd he said, "Listen carefully to what I have to tell you. Mary and I have come up with a drug that may save Megan even at this late stage of her illness. But it has never been tested before and we are not one hundred percent sure that it will work; further more we can get in trouble with the authorities for doing this. However no one has helped her so far and she will die soon any way. We have the drug here and all it takes one injection and within the hour we will know if it will work or not. Now I am going to leave you alone and you decide which way you want to go. What I have told you stays here with the three of us. Please don't discuss it with any one not even your parents; you have to promise that to me." It didn't take long for Dave and Stacy to agree with Paul's demands. They both said please try it and we promise not to say anything to anyone.

Then Paul said to them; find an excuse and get everybody out of Megan's room and I'll take care of it; it won't take but a few minutes and I will tell you when I am done. Paul went into Megan's room and administered the injection on Megan then he waited for the critical first five minutes and when he was satisfied with the results he patted her gently on her forehead and he stepped out. Then he walked straight to Dave and Stacy and told them it's done; then he said now you can go into her room. Stacy almost ran to Megan's room but she composed herself and walked slowly Dave followed right behind her and before long all of them were in Megan's room. Paul looked at Mary and smiled; Mary understood that things were ok for now and relaxed.

People went in and out of Megan's room but there was always at least one person in the room. The critical hour came and went and there were not the dreaded sings Paul was afraid of. The prognosis of Megan's imminent death within hours didn't come to pass; instead of dying Megan fell in deep sleep and when she woke up the next day, she was alert and hungry; a good sign of recovery. Stacy and Dave had tears in their eyes but this time they were tears of happiness. Paul and Mary had good reasons to be happy too but they didn't utter one word.

Later in the day the family doctor came and checked Little Megan and he said, "This child is not dying anymore; she will recover completely. But I'll come and check her tomorrow again just to make sure. I have never seen such quick turnaround and recovering in my professional career and I have been around long enough; whatever god you are praying keep on doing it." Once more Stacy had to control herself from showing her gratitude and appreciation for the miracle Paul and Mary had performed.

Paul once again asked Dave and Stacy to walk with him away for the rest of the family and said, "All indications show Megan will make a quick recovery but things could turn around for the worst too; I just want you to be prepare for any change. Remember the promise you gave me—not- a- word. I think the doctor had the right idea; you can say, "We prayed to god and he saved our Megan." This is as good an answer as any."

The rest of the extended family went home glad to have little Megan back and healthier. Dave and Stacy kept their word and said nothing to anyone; even to several doctors who asked them persistently if they had used some folk medicine or if they had used drugs from overseas. Their answer was always, "We prayed to god and he intervened to save our Megan." The drug Paul administered on Megan was delay release and as the time went on she became healthier, with pink cheeks, and a healthier appetite, acting as a normal girl of her age.

After couple of months Paul and Mary knew the drug had cured Megan and were glad everything worked well. But now they had to decide what to do with the rest of the drug formulae they had developed. Mary said, "The best thing to do will be to give the formulae to one of the pharmaceutical companies and have it done with "And you know what it's going to happen — they are going to ask us to sell them the patent and then they are going to sell the drugs for a very high price. They are going to make a lot of money and the poor people still wouldn't be able to have them." "We don't need the money, we are doing alright we'll holt on the patent and let them use the formulae to make the drugs; after all that's why the aliens gave us the formulae so people get cured from these horrible diseases." "Oh Mary you are naïve these drugs will be very lucrative for them and they will not let go until they get what they want. No I don't trust them we will have to come up with something else this is not going to work out." "Paul at some point we'll have to take a leap of faith and let then have the formulae or the aliens could take them away from us." "You could be right, I never thought of that, but I just got an idea. We will give the formulae to all industrialized countries that can afford to make the drugs free as they were given to us. And we will make sure the drugs are distributed equally to all countries and free to those who can't afford to buy them." Paul and Mary got in touched with an international patent attorney and filled for patent protection. They had to pay the attorney on their own but they thought it was worth it. Another thing they did was to send a reply message to the benefactors saying, "Whoever you are on behalf of all humanity we want to thank you for the formulae of the drugs you sent us. Rest assured that we will distribute them equally to all people."

Jim had always been interested in UFOs but he never discussed it at work; he knew that not everybody would believe him or even been interested in that kind of thing. But Jim had many friends including his father who shared his believes and frequently talked with them about UFOs. So when a month ago NASA asked him to participate on a secret subject having to do as they told him with unexplainable phenomena he was very enthusiastic to say the least.

The person who was in charge of the project Officer Stan Greenfield a retired pilot and specializing in rocketry just like Jim, started the meeting by saying, "At the risk of being taken as one of those UFO enthusiasts; I have to tell you there are a few things that are happing around us which for the first time in my career I can't make sense of them. The best thing we can say at this time is that there are unexplainable phenomena. It would be too much for some of us to say that we are dealing with UFOs. However we are faced with something unusual and we need to get to the bottom of it sooner than later.

I have prepared a video with several of those phenomena so that you can get an idea of what we are dealing with." The video projected what in essence were UFOs all though Officer Greenfield didn't want to admit it. Then he stopped the projector momentarily and said, "Ladies and gentlemen I should tell you that we have checked with all the necessary departments and we have been assured that our government is not aware of any such things. Then he turned on again the projector. Jim had a hard time containing his excitement; there were flying saucers and other UFOs and then there was a specific message sent to SETI

(SETI, the Search for Extraterrestrial Intelligence), In it the message read, "We have come back home to earth from an expedition that started many thousands years ago from an earth and a civilization which perished a long time ago. We are what remained from that world. We have traveled into space at nearly the speed of light and have seen other planets, species, and civilizations, and we have acquired knowledge beyond your comprehension. The time and distance which separated us from when we left caused us to remain physically as we were. But after earth perished you started all over and now you look physically different from us. We are humans from another era but we are from the same species. After a long absence we found a different earth and a people with a civilization in its infancy. We are your brothers and sisters and we will help you fulfill your destiny. We will also help you avoid another nuclear war and the distraction of our planet earth.

This is a message to let you know that we are around and keeping an eye on you; but we will not interfere or be seen by you until you are civilized enough to understand and except us as we are."

After they saw the UFOs and other phenomena and after they read the message from the so called relative humans. They were all dumfounded not knowing what to say. Officer Greenfield was the first one to talk, he said, "Well I told you this is going to be different; now I want to know what do you think about what you have seen so far." Jim said, "Mr. Greenfield firstly we must except the fact that we are dealing with UFOs this is something we can't denied any longer, about the message we should take it as it is. Another scientist by the name Steve Dorland, said, "I have a feeling that these people have already helped us with all the recent electronic discoveries and they keep helping us all along. We should welcome any help they can give us and if they can prevent another catastrophic nuclear war so much the better. After all they know how distractive nuclear wars can be." There were many statements made by other scientists in the room but at the end of their meeting they all agreed that they should not mention what they discussed to the people at large and to keep denying the existence of UFOs for the foreseeable future and until we have a better understanding of the visitors.

The worms having realized that there is another group of humans more advance and peaceful that is willing to help and live with the local humans, decided they were not needed any more and left for the home fleet. A few months later Paul and Derek were once more at Derek place having coffee and discussing animatedly this time politics. Derek was by nature conservative and Paul liberal so as always there was a lot to discuss and argue. Mary and Alice were in the kitchen drinking coffee and having their own conversation. For the last few decades the two couples met frequently for dinner and catching up with the latest happening within the families and around the world.

This time Paul and Derek were deep in politics if there was one thing they didn't agree it had to be politics. Due to Paul's line of work health issues were paramount for him and he believed health insurance should be available to every American at the lowest possible premium. On the other hand Derek believed health insurance was business like everything else and that you had to bargain and pay for the best price. Paul and Derek may have had argued many times but when they were done talking any bad feelings stopped right there and they were friends again. That's how it always was. But this time the health issue was so important to both of them it lasted a little longer.

Paul said, "Look Derek The reason health insurance is so

expensive is because we have a monopoly when it comes to drugs in this country. Other countries buy drugs from other countries and there is competition among them and that brings the prices down it makes sense to me and it should make sense to you too after all you believe in capitalism don't you? Let me bring another example; these latest so call wonder drugs that are given all over the world at a low cost have alleviated pain and has cured a lot of people. That's how we should handle every drug instead of making a lot of profits for so many pharmaceutical companies here and abroad." "Yeah and where is the incentive without profit for the companies to come up with new drugs?" Paul would have loved to tell his fried where those wonder drugs came from but of course he couldn't tell. But he did say that if there was one insurance policy that covered all Americans with a single premium it would have brought the price we paid down to one third of its cost And the pharmaceutical companies still would make would make enough profit.

It was at that moment Dave Stacy and Megan stepped in; they had brought Alice's dress from the Dry Cleaner. All eyes fell on Megan; the last few months she had grown to a pretty young teenager. She was not anymore the weak, pale, and sickly, looking girl; she was full of vitality and she had an air of confidence. Alice said, "My dear Megan you look so beautiful and from what I hear from your parents you have become extremely intelligent and the best student in your class; isn't that wonderful?" Paul and Mary looked at each other with wonderment.

The End

WAR STORY

WWII Intrigue

"Come, come, quick; let's hide behind that tree." "I am coming, oh god my feet are killing me." Seconds later a truck full of soldiers drove by with searching lights. It stopped a hundred yards or so down the road. Jain and Robert were glued to that tree one behind the other moving frequently around it to avoid the lights. Jain could hear her heart pounding; she was scared, Robert had his gun at the ready but he knew it wasn't going to be much help with so many soldiers coming at them. The soldiers jumped off the truck and started to look in the woods. They came dangerously close within a few yards but they didn't see them finally after a while they gave up and drove away. Understandably they were both relived; Jain was so shaken with this close call her knees gave up on her and fell down on the ground sobbing, she said, "Robert I am tired and scared; I don't think I can take this any longer." "Don't worry love everything will be alright, we just need to get out of this area and then things will get better; you'll see."

Robert and Jain were high school sweethearts but after they went to college they drifted away and it was only recently that they met again unfortunately under the worst possible circumstances. Robert worked as an attaché at the American Embassy but his main job was spying. His mother was born in Berlin and taught him German since he was a toddler so Robert spoke German like a native. Jain could speak German too but with a heavy accent but she could translate well and that was pretty much her main job in the embassy. But she was also a spy in the field frequently with Robert. In addition to German Jain spoke French and Russian that's mainly the reason she joined the Department of Foreign affairs as a cultural attaché in the American Embassy in France where she served successfully for couple of years before she was transferred to Germany. Although Robert and Jain had to be discreet with their relationship in the embassy grounds nevertheless their friendship rekindled to a point that they were madly in love for each other.

Robert also spoke Russian which came handy when he shared information with Russian spies in Germany. He was recruited when he was in the air force and now he was flying over sensitive German bases with non air force issued planes. After he was done with his service he reenlisted as an attaché at the American Embassy in Berlin Germany. Robert was now in his early twenties, well built, tallish with red hair and blue eyes. He had had a few affairs every now and then but his true love now and then has always been Jain.

Jain was also a beautiful woman in her early twenties slender but strong. She had beautiful black eyes and black curly wavy hair resembling any south Mediterranean woman, very spongy and clever. Her father Louie Cordelier had immigrated to U.S. in New York after the First World War where he started a successful chain of restaurants. Her mother was an American of Greek descent who taught Jain a few Greek words but she never claimed it as one of her languages.

During the first six months of Jain's arrival around 1938-9 Germany was preparing for war and most of the European countries were very nervous and inevitably they were preparing for war too. So there was a lot of spying everywhere and especially in Germany. Although the Americans were not too enthusiastic to participate in any war at the time; nevertheless they were spying and preparing for the inevitable war.

It was in one of those routine trips that turned out to be anything but routine. Robert and Jain went as close as they could get to a base that was under surveillance for the last month or so not only by the Americans, but British, Russians and others. The base was in Bremen Haven one of the busiest deep sea ports in Germany at the time. Lately there was a lot of traffic in and out of the base that caused the curiosity of many spies. The cargo the Germans brought in and out of the base was always guarded and escorted by double or triple the number of soldiers. Robert and Jain were in their usual hidden place trying to gather as much information as they could manage without getting caught.

Jain said, "Look at that track with all the people around it dressed in white overalls." "Oh yes I have been looking at them for the last few minutes." "What do you think they are protecting?" "I would say some kind of chemicals." "I think that's beyond chemicals, judging from the extra security they have around that truck they could be carrying heavy water; wouldn't you say so?" "Well there is only one way to find out." "Use a Geiger meter?" "Yes, and we have to get closer for it to work." "Then let's do it." "Yes let's do it."

They got out of their hide-out and started moving toward the track ever so carefully, finally the came close to a corner of a near-by building and waited for the track to come closer; when it was close enough Robert turned on the Geiger meter and waited— soon enough the Geiger meter showed the familiar radiation sign followed by the (tick, tick), noise but unfortunately it was loud enough for the guard dogs to hear it and started to bark and sniffing at their side. Robert said, "We got what we needed; let's get the hell out of here." And with that they started to run toward the port. Now the guards and the dogs were after them; some driving on cars and others running behind them. They ran until they came to several huge boxes piled up one over the other. They ran behind the first one and then they were hiding behind one after another and that way they gained distance between them and the guards. It was only a matter of time before they would be caught; they had to come up with something to lose them. It was Jain who saw a track with men unloading sacks of something on a forklift from the track to a near-by boat. The driver was smoking a cigarette away from the track. She pointed; she didn't have to say anything they both knew what they had to do it was the only way out of there. They slowly walked on the other side of the track unseen by the driver or the men who were busy with their load. They got in the track; fortunately the keys were on the switch as they had hoped. They started the track and got out of there like a bat out of hell. Jain looked behind and saw no one on the deck, she said, "We are clear, keep going." Everything happened so fast that it took a few minutes for the guards to put two and two together; by then they were out of the port driving away of the town first on the main road for a while then on a side road leading towards the sea and the woods. Not too far behind them there were two tracks one was going towards the water on the left side of the road the other towards the woods on the right side. When Robert and Jain realized that they were coming closer. They drove the track off the left side of road and then they walked on the right side of the road and into the woods. And now that the soldiers had left they had to find a way out of this area. They rested for a short while and then started to go farther into the woods avoiding the road and pathways they walked for couple of hours and stopped to rest again. Robert got out his hand held compass and tried to find his bearings; earlier when they flew over this part of the forest he saw a small city north from the main road so he turned northward and said, "Let's go." They walked another couple of hours and stopped at the outskirt of the city. Not too far away from them was a farm house. They knew they couldn't ask for help from anybody because the authorities would have alerted the people in the area. The time was 4:15 a.m. Robert said, "Jain we have to find some clothing to look like the local people." Jain said, "You'll have better luck than me but we can try." It was a wintry dark morning they walked carefully toward the fence then to the gate; it was locked from the inside, Robert said, "I am going to lift you to the top of the fence then open the gate but don't jump just climb slowly down." "O.K. got it, give me a lift." Jain managed to go down the fence without making any noise then she unlocked the gate, Robert came in and they walked quietly to the barn. They left the gate open in case there was a dog or they had to leave quickly for any other reason. They stepped inside and started to look around for overalls, raincoats or anything they could use to cover themselves. It was very dark and they were careful not to make any noise. Jain said, "Robert there is moonlight above the clouds if we wait a bit we may see some light between the clouds." "Good idea Jain let's wait for the light." They didn't have to wait too long soon enough there was a sliver of light that lighted the barn they quickly looked around, there was a horse but not dog. Jain patted gently the horse on its head while Robert looked around. He found two raincoats just as the light disappeared behind the clouds. Robert knew farmers keep raingear in the barn no matter what country. He gave the smaller one to Jain and he wore the bigger one himself then walked to and out of the gate closing it as close as possible.

Robert and Jain felt fortunate having the raingear because as soon as they left the farmhouse it started to rain hard. They walked through the small city avoiding the lights. There were looking for a phone booth but so far no luck. Robert told Jain, "I am afraid there are no phones around and dawn is almost here; we have to communicate with our conduct very soon before we get caught." "I am sure they are looking for us by now and I don't think it was a good idea taking those coats because if they discover that they are missing they'll know what to look for." "It will be alright until light breaks out." "I sure hope so." They walked in the dark streets until they came to a little park in the middle of town and in it there was a phone booth but unfortunately there was also a police car parked close to it. Robert didn't have any problems talking to an officer; he looked like an average citizen and he could speak German like a native. He was about to go to the phone booth, but Jain stopped him abruptly saying, "Robert they took a good look at us at the port out there and they must have told everybody how we look by now, do you want to take a chance getting coat?" "Do you have a better idea?" "Yes I do; he is not going to stay there for too long sooner or later he has to drive around block why don't we wait for a while longer." "OK, Jain let's try your way." Soon enough the officer drove a way, as soon as he was out of sight Robert walked to the booth, got in and started to dial his conduct number. A sleepy voice answered from the other side of the receiver, "Hello, Karl, don't forget we are going fishing today." "How can I forget I am almost ready; I'll see you soon Fritch." "You don't need to bring bait I have a lot for both of us." Then Robert started telling Karl a story as to where he found bait; to anyone it would have sounded like a normal chat between two friends going fishing but Karl recognized special meaning of words, letters and numbers. By the time they were done talking Karl knew that the Germans were bringing in the base (Heavy Water). From that point on Karl knew what to do. Robert stepped out of the booth not a minute sooner than the police car was driving back to the little park. "All done Jain, now he knows." "And now what, Robert?" "We have to go back to the ends of the woods and wait; he'll come and get us some time this morning." "Good let's get going." By now it was light and they had to be careful not to be seen. They walked as fast as they could and finally reached the forest. They sat by a large tree and waited. They were tired and hungry; and could hardly wait for Karl to come and rescue them. Finally after three hours or so a black car drove close to where they were about a hundred yards or so away. A man came out of the car bend down and tied his shoelace; that was a signal to them to come out. Robert and Jain came out of their hideout; they were both wet to the bone and got into the car. Karl started the car and drove through the town in the early wintery morning.

It had been an exhausted night for Robert and Jain, but a good breakfast and a few hours of much needed sleep went a long way towards recovering. Karl told them that he had communicated the message to the embassy and that there was twenty-four hour surveillance on that particular truck with its valuable cargo. The next day they flew back to Berlin in the American embassy. Those few hours Robert and Jain lived under extreme stress brought them even closer to each other; they were in love all over again. They spent a few days out in the country swimming and hiking, having a well deserved few days off. They were staying in a friend's house overlooking a beautiful lake not too far from the house. After dinner they sat on a couch holding a cup of coffee. From the picture window they could see several boats moving gently in the lake, the light traffic on the road and houses in close proximity to the lake. Jain moved closer to Robert and said, "This feels so good I could stay here forever. Robert said unfortunately this is not our house or our country for that matter but I know a lake that is just as good or better in Minnesota when the war is over we could build a house by the lake and spent our weekends there." "Who knows what the future holds for us but now we are together you and I in a place all to our selves; let's make the best we can at this time and let the future bring what may and with that they both embraced and made sweet love on the couch. Next day on the breakfast table Jain said, "I wondered when and where our next job would be." Robert said, "I know that we and the English Intelligential sooner or later are going to have to be involved in this case; we are not going to let them get away with it. This is a clear indication The Germans are working on the atomic bomb and if they come up first with the bomb we will lose the war, it's as simple as that. As for our fate? I have no idea what's coming up next."

A few hours later they were on their way back to Berlin soon to report for duty. Robert and Jain felt relaxed and very much in love ready for what their next mission was going to be. Jain turned on the radio searching for some nice music when she noticed in the back of their car another car following them too close she asked Robert if he was aware of it, he said, "Oh yeah there is another one in front of us and two more one on each side of us; they are going to arrest us any time now. Hold on I am going to try to squeeze out of here and with that he stepped on the gas the car jumped abruptly and past the car to the left only a few inches in front of it, Robert stepped hard on the gas and gain some distance between the two cars he kept on changing lanes.

He was aiming for the next exit but it was blocked by police cars he kept on driving but now the traffic was slowing down. It was only a matter of time before they were apprehended. Robert said, "We must not tell them that we have communicated with anybody, I love you and I always think of you." I love you too Robert and I will do the same; then they kissed for one more time." By now the traffic had stopped completely and pretty soon the special police force came with guns pointed at them and were ordered out. Robert said in perfect German, "We are American citizens and working as attaché in the American Embassy and under the Geneva Treaty it is against international low to arrest us." "The officer in charge said, "From now on we have our own lows in Germany then he said, to the others, "Arrest them!" Robert and Jain were put in separate cars; and were driven away. As Jain was driven away she thought to herself god—why did it have to end this way? Then she put in practice all she had learned back home of being a spy.

She turned inside for courage and endurance but outside she wore a cold and forbidden face. She was gathering all her thoughts and practicing how to resist, resist! She was taken to a huge building that looked like a prison and wasn't given any time to relax. The building was kept nice and warm but the room they put her in was very cold. She only wore a dress her coat and purse were confiscated. She walked to a little window and looked out it was snowing she kept looking at the falling snow it had a calming effect on her; ever since she was a young girl she was mesmerized looking at falling snow.

The door opened abruptly and a woman stepped in; she was tall and skinny and had a masculine appearance, she said in broken English "Sit down!" Jain said, "I speak German." (Another language doesn't affect you as bad as it does your own).

She walk slowly to the chair and sat down. The woman spoke in German. My name is Berta and I am going to be your interrogator if you cooperate with me I am going to be nice to you if you don't you will wish that you were never born. I am going to get what I need from you whether you like it or not! Berta was dressed well and she had a hot cup of coffee in her hand, Jain would have loved to have her coat and a hot cup coffee at this time but see knew that this was part of the psychology interrogators use to compromise their victims.

She could easily guess how Berta would proceed today and for the next few days, back home when she took a course in spying at the C.I.A base she was interrogated far worse than that and then she also interrogated other students for practice; she was more than ready for what was coming. The only thing that worried her was the fact the Germans appeared to disregard the Geneva Treaty rules. "State your name." "My name is Jain Cordelier and I work as an attaché in the American Embassy." "Yeah, yeah, I've heard this before do you know what we do with spies like you? We torture them until they are dead so if you want to get out of here alive you must tell me what you know; the sooner you do that the sooner you leave here. Who is your contact in Bremen Haven?" "I have no contacts I am an attaché in the American Embassy and you are breaking international law holding me here." "Those niceties don't exist here, you are my prisoner and you are on my mercy." Jain made contact with Berta's eyes and looked at her with the coldest possible way. Berta said, "You are going to be a tough one, but I can handle it." Then she interrogated Jain for five hours with few interruptions but Jain kept her cool and gave her nothing important. When she finally was taken to her cell she was truly exhausted she lay in her bed and tried to gather her thoughts.

What a day it had been, it all started so good; Robert woke her up with a cup of coffee then he lay next to her and they talked for a while about today driving back to Berlin and about their next possible mission then they made love. When they left for Berlin they were so happy and ready to face whatever came up their way and now this; Spy or not they were traveling with internationally protected credentials. In turn the Germans were putting their spies in danger; their confidence eventually will back fire.

Robert was driven to a different place; the Gestapo Head Quarters unlike Jain he was treated very well he was given a room to himself although he was guarded by a special force unit. And they didn't bother him until next day. Two guards escorted him to a special interrogating room where he met Her Brown who was chief interrogator. As soon as the guards brought Robert in, he motioned the guards to leave then with a wide smile he said in German, good morning Robert did you sleep well, did you like your room?" Robert answered in German too, "It was OK thanks." "Well good, sit down." A soldier came with coffee and Danish pastry on a tray and left it on the desk he then saluted and left the room. Her Brown served coffee for the two of them and pushed the tray towards Robert. He offered a cigar to Robert but he declined, Her Brown lighted his own took a deep swallow and exhaled with satisfaction he waited a few seconds and then he said,"Why a good German like you is spying against your own people?" I am not German I am an American working as an attaché in the American Embassy and you are holding me here illegally."Yes of course so you say; But Robert you are one of us, you come from German parents you belong to our superior race come and join us and you will be one of our Fuehrer's best high officers. You know? We are going to win this coming war because we are powerful and our country is best suited to rule the world why stay with the losers?" "I am an American and proud of it." Robert knew Her brown started with the (carrot and stick) approach later or tomorrow someone else will start with the stick and so on. Just like Jain Robert went through the C.I.A. training program and he was aware of what he was up to from now on. Robert thought to himself; give him a little bit of information to put down on his note book not all at once but piece-meal; hold on the important stuff this is going to be a long process. Robert realized that his and Jain's case was a little different from other captured spies because they had seen the Germans carrying Heavy Water. Now the Germans were very anxious to know if Robert and Jain managed to report their find to their nearest contact, if they did then the Germans were no longer working under the cover of secrecy and they would do almost anything to know the truth from Robert and Jain.

The first day of interrogation went on as Robert had predicted it; Her Brown tried to seduce him with all kinds of promises to get him to go to their side or better yet become a double agent. Robert stubbornly refused to go along and so the first day was done. He wasn't looking forward to tomorrow when things would be far more difficult. In his cell he had time to relax a bit and relive the day's events. He was wondering how the Germans found them they were so careful to stay out of the way and driving back to Berlin should have been a routine drive unless they were on them from the beginning and knew who they were. And what about Karl, his contact, was he caught too? He did sound a little nervous on the phone did he talk under duress by the secret police at the time? If Karl managed to relay the information all these troubles will be worth it, if not God help us. He thought of Jain, he knew she would get a worse treatment from her interrogators but he also knew Jain well she was a gutsy woman she would hold on her secret and survive.

On September 1st 1939 Germany invaded Poland and the war officially started; when Hitler demanded the polish port of Danzig, England said she will protect it and that brought England in the war Followed by France and then it went on, and on with many other European countries jumping into the fray. In the meantime the Soviets invaded Poland from the East which created two obstacles for Hitler; Russia in the East, and England and France in the West. But with all this fray going on in Europe America refused to join in. The Americans were indifferent to the European theater of war for the time being.

Karl transmitted the information he was given by Robert and Jain right away so the US and its allies knew what the Germans were up to. Once the Americans knew the Germans were working on the bomb a bill was introduced to the congress to fund the Manhattan Project in Alamo and they also started working feverishly on building the atomic bomb; the race for the bomb was on.

Even though Robert and Jain were captured by the Germans spying in Germany continued by others and of course the Germans did their own spying and especially in England and the USA. Every now and then there was a spy exchange between the Germans and the allies but not before they extracted enough information from their captured victims; so it was a matter of endurance on the part of the spies on both sides. All though Robert and Jain knew and hoped there was a possibility of them being exchanged in the future they also knew the Germans were desperate to know how much Robert and Jain knew and consequently how much of what they knew they gave a way.

Jain was interrogated daily methodically and tyrannically by her masculine-like woman Berta. She was subjected to sleep deprivation, hunger, and water torture and was kept continually in an unheated room. Any other person would have given up by now to their tormentors but not Jain. She kept looking with cold eyes at Berta saying nothing; but she didn't need to; that look in itself was like saying (You will never get anything from me, bitch)! Somehow Jain found strength she never thought she had perhaps some of the Spartan genes that came from her Greek mother helped her cope with torture.

Robert didn't fare better either; the next day started with a different interrogator he wasn't as nice as Her Brown when the soldier brought the tray with the coffee he helped himself with some coffee and then ordered the soldier to take the tray back. Then he said to Robert, "My name is Hans and you will tell me everything you know or you are in for a very bad trip. Robert told himself, (Here we go with the stick). Hans said, "Your Partner Jain said that you transmitted the information you gathered from our base right away to your contact is that right? Robert thought to himself (Does he think that I am a fool to fall for it?) Robert said, "That's not true; we had no time to see anything we just ran for our lives that's all." "You are lying." "No I am not; I am telling you the truth like it or not." "Shut up you swine; I will get the truth from you sooner or later." Then he called in the guard that was outside the door and said," Take him to block-H." The soldier put the handcuffs back on Robert and escorted him away.

When Robert and Jain failed to come to the embassy it didn't take long for Mr. Nelson in charge of the American spy ring in Germany to find out they were captured by the Germans. It had been the norms that even though you know several of the attaches are spying you don't arrest them unless you catch them in action. Robert and Jain were caught on their way to the embassy. The Germans were changing the rules and if that's how they were going to behave from now on; then their spies are going to be treated likewise too. Mr. Nelson informed the FBI what had happened and to be on the look on German spies in US. The same message was sent to all the allies too.

Robert was subjected to mental and physical torture and after each torture the guard would escort Robert back to Hans for more interrogation but to the frustration of Hans, Robert would never give in to his demands. That went on for weeks which affected Robert's health. He had lost a lot of weight and looked pale; he was dying a slow death but he didn't give the Germans what they wanted. A few months later they sent him to quarry where he worked along with many thousands of other prisoners. The work was hard but it was better than torture; he was gaining his strength and even though they fed them poorly he managed to survive.

Jain went through the same routine just like Robert and she also lost weight and she was very sick. Finally her tormentors realized they were not going to get from her what they needed they gave her a desk job as a translator. She worked with a few other women from different other countries. Because she was very good at what she was doing she was moved in the head quarters of the Gestapo and worked there for many months. Her job consisted of translating German to English and French. However she didn't have the luxury of going back home to a nice warm house as the German women did. She slept in a crowded room with very little privacy but all in all she did better than Robert.

After a few successful years at war the Germans started losing;

the scale bounced the other way. After D-Day the Allies gained the upper hand on the German army. The Americans and the English were hammering the fatherland from sky and land while the Soviets after many loses to the Germans rebounded back and now they were on the outskirts of Berlin. Hitler on a desperate move to save the fatherland sent his youth to the front to fight a well trained ally force with horrible consequences to the kids. Soon after that Hitler committed suicide and his generals started negotiations for surrendering the fatherland. The Germans once more played the superior race card and were crashed by the free people of the world.

During the last few days of the bombing over Berlin, the Gestapo building was hit badly and those who survived ran out on the streets for dear life. One of them was Jain who was saved because she lived among other prisoners in the smaller buildings spared by the attackers. She mingled with all the other Germans on the streets avoiding the bombings and looking for something to eat like most folks. Finally the Russians came in Berlin fighting, stealing, and raping until the last resistance of the German army capitulated. Jain lived on the streets a few days more selling any valuable she had with her to the black market to survive. Eventually she ended up on the west side of Berlin and when the US army entered she was one of the first persons to meet them. She showed them her credentials and was quickly sent back to an army hospital.

Robert worked all this time at the quarry; he was so malnourished he looked like a walking corpse. When the bombing hit the quarry he too escaped along with other prisoners out in the country. He found himself once more in the woods this time alone. Robert used all the training on surviving in the woods he had received in the CIA base. He lived on wild berries, grubs, and at times rabbits and fish. As miserable as his life appeared to be in the woods, he was happy to be free once more. Every once in a while he would climb up a tree and look down on the nearest city for American troops. He was still wearing the prisoners' outfit and was afraid to be seen by German people. Finally after ten days in the woods he saw a line of US army trucks driving down the road he ran to the nearest truck and told them who he was. He was immediately given worm clothing and food and drove with them all the way to the base.

Eventually Both Robert and Jain along with many other ex-prisoners were sent to London England to continue to recuperate in a hospital. When Jain left the hospital she moved to the American embassy in London and stayed there for three days then she was sent back home to Washington D.C. and reported to the special agency affiliated with the CIA for further screening before she was released as a retired employee. All this time Jain didn't know Robert's whereabouts; she assumed he had died either in the prison or during the bombing of Berlin. When she asked at the CIA head quarters about his whereabouts they plainly refused to give her any information about him. And so they couldn't find each other because of bureaucratic rules and regulations. Jain flew to Seattle back to her little apartment and tried to recover emotionally and physically.

It took longer for Robert to recover but after he was out of hospital he too was sent temporarily to the American embassy in London. Robert asked several attaches in the embassy if they had heard of Jain But no one knew for sure because the embassy was busy with so many that came in recently. Finally Robert was sent back home too. The State Department gave him a paid long leave but he was still on the payroll. He flew to his parents' house in Minnesota where he continued his recovery among friends and relatives. Robert never stopped searching for Jain but it was difficult locating her because she was hired by one of the many different agencies affiliated with CIA; this is something Robert didn't know and never discussed with Jain he just assumed she was hired by the same department as he was. And with so many of the staff killed or missing in all those agencies it was hard to pin point exactly her whereabouts.

On September 2 1945 both wars in the Atlantic and the Pacific officially ended; after that America became the super power to be reckoned with, and as a super power had the interest and the ability to help materially and financially the two defeated enemies. America sent many tons of food by plane to a starving Germany who was now threatened by the Soviet Union. After the war Germany was completely ruined and bankrupt it took not only America but most of her enemies in Europe to help her financially to recover. Later on in April 1948 Americans initiated the so-called Marshal Plan, helping not only Germany but the western European countries with approximately 13 billion dollars with current value of 130 billion dollars. Japan didn't fare any better and America helped Japan even more than Germany materially and financially.

After two months absence Robert reported back at the CIA head quarters and this time was sent to Japan working again as an attaché at the American embassy. Robert was happy to be back at work at a non war zone but his happiness wasn't complete without his Jain and no matter how hard he looked to find her he had no lack at all.

Jain settled in her little apartment in Seattle and for a while it was exactly what she needed but after couple of months she realized she was too young at almost thirty to live like that; she had to do something to keep her busy. Although she was encouraged by her last employer to file for a job at the State Department she nevertheless had second thoughts about being an attaché with all the implications of spying and so on. Lately she was depressed, unusually tired, and had severe headaches; her doctor advised her to change environment, he said, "Take a trip somewhere and see if that would help you."

After the war with Japan ended many Americans visited that exotic country. Jain didn't have to think too hard she purchased a ticket and flue to Japan but when she saw all the destroyed cities it reminded her of Germany and that disheartened her a lot. One morning at the breakfast table she met two ladies who were commiserating with her about the destruction of the cities. When Jain asked them how long they were staying in Tokyo they said, "Oh we are not staying in Tokyo too long; we are going out in the country to visit a Buddhist Monastery; won't you come with us?" And so Jain went to the monastery with Mary and Tasha and it was such an experience she was never going to forget it. The monastery was up on a hill with beautiful flower and vegetable gardens. The monks were very receptive and smiled at them all the time. They stayed there for three days and the third day they walked with many other tourists to another hill to see the famous Buddha statue.

Robert was happy to be back at work again; he made many acquaintances but until he was sure that Jain wasn't alive he wasn't going to have a new relationship therefore he was always searching for his beloved Jain. One morning he noticed an advertisement on the wallboard of the embassy's cafeteria about a three-day excursion to a Buddhist monastery out in the country. Robert was not a religious person but he was fascinated with monasteries; he joined the group and went to the monastery. Luck had it so that he would be in the same group Jain was in;

but because neither one of them were looking for each other they did not noticed themselves. It was when Robert asked a question to the monk guide that Jain heard that beloved familiar voice she thought to herself he couldn't possibly be here. He must be someone else but she still wanted to know who that person was. Unfortunately she was way back and had to repeatedly excuse herself and push her way to the front. And then there was her beloved Robert a little changed but very much the same. She went behind him and tapped him on the shoulder and said, "Robert?" He turned around and said, "Jain?" and then they hugged and stayed like that for a long time. The two lady friends who by now came to see her realized this man was Robert who Jain had talked about frequently to them and tears came to their eyes. Then they told the rest of the people what was happening who by now stopped listening to the guide and were looking at the young couple and then they all started clapping.

The End

EPILOGUE

Robert requested to be transferred to Seattle where he worked for the State department and lived temporarily at Jain's apartment. Jain was hired as a translator at the same place. Then when they found out they were expecting their first baby they moved to a larger house. Later they bought a little country house on Orcas Island which they visited frequently and lived happy thereafter.

PERHAPS THERE IS STILL HOPE

A Science Fiction Story

Three million years ago in the Orion Galaxy, in the Blue Belt area there was a planet called Suku among other animals it was occupied by a humanoid species the Sukuans Their civilization had lasted more than a billion earthly years. It was an advance society; they were able to travel through wormholes to other galaxies and planets. They were not good looking people as per our standards their average height was about five feet, large heads, large eyes, and frail looking, but they were healthy and lived long lives. In their travels they met many different species from the tiniest microorganism to huge entities but so far they were the only humanoid species that they knew of. That's why three million years ago when they first visited planet earth and saw the similarity between them and the chimpanzees they chose the most advanced chimpanzees and inoculated them with their own genome so that the human species would live and prosper in another galaxy too.

They knew that this would be a slow process and for many thousands of years they visited earth and checked on their experiment. At first they were happy with the progress the hybrid humans were showing. They shed most of their hair and developed skin that resembled their own; their brains began to get larger but their behavior changed very little. As the time went on the hybrids became more human-like and more intelligent and finally became the superior being over any other animal and took over the planet. But unfortunately their behavior still didn't changed much. They engaged in wars from the time they lived in caves to the time they became powerful in science and weaponry. They were so vicious that they used nuclear weapons on their own species and finally destroyed themselves, the rest of the animal life, and the ecosystem as a whole. They had done that twice in the past and both times they started all over from the beginning and again their behavior change very little from their cousins the chimpanzees. And now they were about to repeat the same destruction. The Sukuans felt responsible for creating a subspecies resulting in the destruction of all animals and the ecosystem of the planet earth. The Sukuan benevolent gene never morphed and never materialized in the experiment. And now this humanoid subspecies are dangerous not only to their own planet but to other planets as well. The Sukuans had a choice to either help them destroy themselves, or help them develop the benevolent gene once and for all; they chose to help because that was in their nature.

It was a cold winter Morning Tom was at the Kitchen table looking out through the steamy picture window; the branches of a nearby tree were moving rhythmically pushed by a cold wind. Up in the sky clouds were rushing westward in a race to cover the remaining little clear space of blue sky. The grass was now recovering from the summer drought wearing its new green panoply for the harsh winter. A few birds were trying to balance their flights against the wind.

Although there were still brown spots on the grass everything was bathed by the fresh rain. The pale sun managed to penetrate through cracks between clouds creating diamond drops on leaves and grass. Chloe, the cat, slept on the chair oblivious to the outside world; every now and then she extended her paws and yawned.

Tom was in his thirties, of average height with Teutonic characteristics. He worked in the stock market most of the time in his home. He was composing a letter to a friend when a buzz on his cell phone alerted him to a phone call, "Hello; oh Loren how good of you to call how are you?" "I am fine Tom I just needed to talk to a trusted friend like you about something I saw this morning. I was cutting a fallen log in my woods because of the last storm and I noticed that the rushing water exposed a hole next to a boulder. Curiosity took over and went inside the hole and discovered that it was the beginning of a dip cave. I used my cell phone for lighting and found something foreign and strange and decided not to go any farther unless I talk to someone; and that's why I called. I'd like the two of us to go close enough to find out what that huge thing is—what to you say?"

"Loren, if I didn't know you any better I would have thought that you have gone crazy but I do know you well. But you have to admit what you are telling me is at the minimum bizarre but yes I will come and see you soon." Loren lived at the outskirts of town on a twenty acre wood land he was also in his thirties but shorter than Tom about 5'11" black hair brown eyes, and because of the work he was doing he was strong. He worked as a deckhand on one of those huge cruise ships that sailed all over the world. He worked for six months straight and six months off; when he was off duty he withdrew to his end of the woods and enjoyed being alone and busy on his land. It was a life he preferred. Occasionally he would go visit friends or have friends visit him but that was pretty much his routine, he was a loner.

Tom arrived in the early afternoon at Loren's place and they walked into the cave carrying this time strong flashlights. They walked about fifty feet until they came to what appeared to be a gray container of some kind only the corners were rounded; they walked as close as they dared and stopped. Tom said, "Wow, that looks foreign; how did it get in here?" "I don't know but it looks extraterrestrial to me." They both stepped closer to it hesitantly; it looked like an average truck container a little wider with smooth round corners its color matched the gray surroundings. When Tom went closer part of that side matched his red coat like a chameleon. Something was drying the condensation that bathed the whole structure; you could see the dryness overtaking the moister. Loren found the courage to walk closer and the two of them circled around it directing their flash lights at it. They looked for a door, a window, or something to indicate that this was some kind of a vehicle or a space ship. Considering the time it might have been there it looked very smooth and shiny.

Then all of a sudden lights lit the whole area emanating not from within it or the walls of the cave but from the thin air. Instinctively both of them ran a few yards away from it but stopped abruptly when they heard a synthesized voice saying, "Do not be alarmed, you will not be harmed; if you wish you may come closer." They looked at each other unsurely then Tom said, "It sounds friendly, I think we should go closer—what do you think?" Loren said, "If it was going to harm us it would have done it by now; let's go." And so they did, but this time when they came close enough an opening appeared on the right side that extended all the way to the ground; again the voice said, "Please come in do not be afraid you will not be harmed." Tom and Loren found the courage to walk in; it felt like they walked on air but once they were in they felt the gravity of the floor.

There was no one to welcome them; they stood there for a few seconds looking around but there was nothing in there except an empty room with bare walls. The hole was still open presumably they could step out any time they wished. They kept waiting for something to happen but nothing did. Then Tom pointed to the wall in front of them and said, "Do you see that flashing light?" "Yes I do; do you suppose it wants us to push it?" "I think it does." And with that Tom walked to it and pushed on it. All of a sudden a cloud of shiny dust in a form of a cone appeared in the air turning like a top and in a few seconds it built two chairs for them to sit. As they sat down the wall turned in to a screen and the hole closed behind them but there was a picture of an open door for someone to push if needed. That made them feel easier; someone was trying to make them feel safe.

A picture of bride stars appeared on the screen and the synthesized voice began to speak again only this time it was very clear and sounded more like a natural human voice. It said, "We come from what you call the Orion Galaxy from the Blue Suku Planet and in that sea of stars there was a small dot flashing indicating where they come from. Many thousand years ago we sent many of these ships all over your planet containing artificial intelligence to help your people. We will ask you to take a simple test and if you pass it we will continue with more information. If not you will be asked to step out and you will not remember any of this. Then there were a few easy questions based on their contemporary life; Tom and Loren had no difficulty answering. One of the questions was, "Do you think the earth is round or flat?" Another was, "Do you believe in God and who is your God?" When the test was over the voice said, "Congratulations both of you passed the test. I should tell you that several of your forbears were not as advanced as you are and had to be excused. The voice continued to speak in a now familiar manner it said, "Your intelligence will be enhanced so that you can understand the complicated program on which you are about to embark. With my help the two of you along with other chosen people will save your people and your planet from an impending catastrophe that awaits all of you in the near future. Should you decide not to participate in this endeavor you are free to step out of here; you will forget instantaneously everything you saw or heard and will go back to your everyday lives. Should you decide to accept this offer you and the other future participants will be obligated to help in this program as long as you live." Tom and Loren didn't have to think too hard to accept the offer; they both answered in the affirmative saying, "We want to do all we can to help our people and our planet."

Immediately after their acceptance the screen in front of them disappeared and they were guided to a larger room. There was no talking anymore they were given directions telepathically they lay on different couches and were bathed by an intense blue light and they felled in to a trance. When they awoke they had no idea how long they had lane there but they both felt energized as though they had awaken from a restful sleep. Their memories were enhanced tremendously they could tap into any subject and remember in details anything they needed to know. Again the wall in front of them moved away and there appeared a person who spoke in the foreign language they had just learned. He was a humanoid entity with anthropomorphic facial characteristics with large eyes and a large head but somewhat smaller body about five feet tall, he was pale and frail. He looked at them with those large shiny black eyes and said, "Greetings we come in peace we come from the planet Suku in the blue belt in the Orion Galaxy. When you receive this message I will be long gone; but we want to help you because your planet and your lives will be in great danger in the near future. Our civilization is over a billion of earthly years old and we have seen many entities such as yours come and go in many different planets and different galaxies. We know that you have destroyed your own planet twice in the past and you are about to destroy it again. We are aware of that because we have the ability to travel in your past and future. We want to help you because our progenitors visited your planet three million years ago. At that time you looked and acted like your distant relatives the chimpanzees you are their direct cousins. We inoculated you with our own genes; it was an experiment that did not succeed to our expectations and we are dreadfully sorry for that. You have inherited the potential to be as intelligent as we are someday in the far future but without our benevolence. Instead you have retained your primitive distractive nature and that makes you a very dangerous entity to yourselves and in the future a danger to other planets. We initiated this program a few thousand years ago and have been waiting until you are able to understand directions to start correcting your behavior and become benevolent. This will take a big afford and time on your part but we hope you will achieve that before you destroy your planet again. We wish you good luck.

Tom and Loren were endowed with many languages as well as the language of the extraterrestrials'. Their brains were like an encyclopedia. They were programmed to help humanity. Then they were told to go home and tell no one they didn't trust of their experiences and that they would be given more directions in the future. Tom and Loren had no idea how long they had been in the space ship but when they walked out it was dark. Loren looked at his cell phone the time was 10:25 p.m.; this experience lasted more than eight hours—they were exhausted. As they walked out of the cave the hole closed behind them, no one will ever know what was hidden in there; Tom and Loren agreed to meet next day at Tom's place.

Tom had a restless night; he relived the whole episode over and over again. Of course he was happy to have so much knowledge about the history of earth and its people that went three million years ago and also the knowledge of the history of the planet Suku. At the same time he was sad to learn of the distraction of earth twice in the past and the possibility of another distraction in the very near future. Loren also had a difficult night thinking of the things that happened and the things that may happen in the future.

The next day they had lunch at Tom's place. Tom made a lot of coffee but ordered lunch from a Chinese place. Tom filled a cup of coffee and gave to Loren, he said, "Well Loren I don't know if I should thank you for asking me to come to your place or if I should curse you." "Oh I am sorry Tom but I couldn't handle it alone." "No, no, actually you did the right thing; I am just kidding you but seriously how are we going to approach it; just the two of us are not going to save our planet. We need to get more people involved; people we can trust. I know I can trust my girlfriend Suzy; she'll think that I am crazy but she'll get the Idea, how about you?" "Well I don't know Tom, Karen thinks that I am already crazy if I let her in on this she'll just walk away from me but yeah I trust her too." "But Loren if I remember well they told us they will let us know what and when will be our next project why don't we just relax for now and let things fall as they may. But there is another thing is bothering me I have a feeling that this is going to keep us busy 24/7 even if we eventually have more people involved with this it will still interfere with our regular jobs." "Well I know when I am working on the ship I won't have time left to do anything else." Tom said, "I have an idea it's not quite "kosher" but for the good of humanity I think we should do it." "Well let's hear it." "I don't know about you but with the powers I have acquired my brain can analyze stocks in a way that I can make a lot of money in the stock market. We could invest all we have for a while and come out with a lot of money so that we don't have to worry about working and devote one hundred percent of our time on this cause what do you think?" "Is this going to be alright with our benefactors?" "I don't know but they should know that on this planet we have to work for a living and as long as we contain this within reason and between ourselves I don't see why not." "Then we won't say anything to the girls, for the time being anyway, "Right?" "Then let's do it, but I hope you know what you are doing because I don't want to lose my life's savings on this scheme." "Don't worry I know what I am doing."

Suzy was a serious young woman in her mid-twenties with brunet hair and brown eyes she had her own beauty parlor in town she wasn't rich by any means but she did earn enough to make a reasonably good living. Tom use to go to her shop and have his hair cut that's how they met and they got to know each other well and became good friends. They had dinners at each other houses but occasionally went out to dinner too. Tom called her a few days later for dinner at his place; nothing unusual except this time he had some interesting news for her. He fixed her usual drink and sat down to visit before dinner. Tom appeared to be a little nervous tonight and Suzy was wondering if he finally would come up with it and say it; but she was in for a surprise. Finally Tom found the courage to tell her what had happened a few days earlier Suzy said, "You have to be kidding is this for real?" "I swear Suzy I am telling you the truth the only other person that knows about it is Loren; in fact he saw it first."

"I don't know what to tell you and why are you telling me all this; what do you want me to do?" "Nothing for now except that you must not tell anyone else at this time." "Of course I won't tell anyone else, they'll think I am crazy."

Karen was in her early twenties too; blond tallish blue eyes beautiful not as serious as Suzy a little superficial but good hearted. She was a lawyer and had her own practice in town. Loren was her client they got to know each other when he asked her to write his will and a few other things about his real estate. They met frequently when he wasn't working at sea which was for only six months. A wedding wasn't on their horizon for the time being but they loved each other. Loren asked her out for dinner in town closer to his place a nice quiet homey kind restaurant that they had visited a few other times in the past. They ordered drinks and soon after that he started to tell her about his experience earlier in the week.

He said, "Karen I need to tell you something; it may sound a little weird but hear me out first before you react your usual way." "Are you in trouble?" "No, no, nothing like that; you see after that stormy weather I was in the woods clearing a few fallen branches. It was there that I noticed a hole in a bank I walked in there and discovered a cave I walked a little farther in and you won't believe what I saw." "Now you have me going what did you see?" I saw something that looked like a container but not quite. It was shiny and looked really different and I couldn't understand how it got in there. So I got spooked and got out of there. Then I called Tom you know him he is a good friend of mine. I told him what I had seen and I asked him if he would go with me so both of us could have a better look at it. First he thought that I was joking but then when he realized that I was serious he did come and both of us walked into the cave. Then

Loren described word by word what happened to them and then he said, "And now you know the whole story; do you believe me?" "You said you went in there with Tom?" "Yes I did." "I know Tom, he is a serious man and because of him I tend to believe you but you have to admit you story sounds ridiculous." "Oh I grant you that but believe me it's the truth; and please, please, don't tell anyone anything until we learn more from them." "Oh I won't, who is going to believe me; anyway remember I am a lawyer I don't want to lose my practice. But why did you tell me all these what do you want from me?" "Karen we need you to help us you are just about the only one we could trust with this." "How many other people know about this?" "Only Suzy Tom's girlfriend; she can be trusted." "I think the four of us need to meet at my office and talk about it; I'll set the appointment and let you know." "O.K. sounds good; now let's eat."

A few days later the four of them met at Karen's office they helped themselves to hot coffee and doughnuts. Karen started by saying, "When I first heard this story I had a hard time believing it but now I do. However neither Suzy nor I have had firsthand experience as you had with the extraterrestrials. Unless you or your friends can come up with some kind of extra ordinary powers to convince the billions of people on this planet and especially those in power to change their ways, there is very little the four of us can do at this time. You said they asked you no to tell of your contact with them to anyone, but you already told Suzy and me. We know you well enough to believe you but you will have a hard time convincing others." Tom said, "We thought of that at the time but we decided to tell you and see how they will react but so far they haven't said anything and so we assumed that it's o.k. with them." "But I still want to know how we can change the world for the better and stop this catastrophe that's about to happen."

It was at that moment a three dimensional person appeared on the middle of the table; it was a different person from the one Tom and Loren had met in the cave. He had the same characteristics as the other one but appeared to be a younger person; he said, "Greetings, my name is Tubo and this is the name I prefer to be addressed to I am an artificial intelligent entity and have been created specifically to help you stop the impending catastrophe that will destroy your planet and all its living things. I will endow you with powers that will help you change the way your leaders think and act. You and those you will choose to help you in the future will be involved in a program specifically created for all humans to start becoming a benevolent species as we are. But that will take a long time and many of your generations, you are only the beginning. Should you need any help you can always call upon me for help and advice you; and now Karen and Suzy I will endow you with the same powers Tom and Loren have. And then the same blue mist bathed Karen and Suzy but this time it only took a few minutes and when they came out of it they had the same powers. Then Tubo said, "You have been changed; you are on your way to become benevolent people like us, in the near future I will visit you again and we will put in affect the program to save humanity. And now carry on with your lives and do not abuse the powers you have been given." Then Tubo disappeared as quickly as he had come. Karen said, "I am so glad to finally understand what you have gone through, now I can feel the same way you feel; now I am a new woman I am invigorated and with these powers invested on me I know I can contribute to this cause and I can hardly wait for us to start helping humanity and our planet." Suzy said, "I feel the same way but I am so busy I don't know where I can find the time to do anything. Loren said, "I think they have studied us for a long, long, time and they know the way we live as well as our difficulties and I trust they will come up with the proper solution to our predicament." Then Tom said, I agree with you but I am still going to invest money in the stock market as we agreed earlier and if they don't like it I am sure the Extraterrestrials will let us know; I have no doubt about it." Then Tom went on to explain to Karen and Suzy what he and Loren had in mind. They both liked the idea and agreed to give Tom their savings. Tom used his superior mind in the stock market and because he was already a broker no one paid any attention to how quickly he became wealthy. Of course the money was distributed back to everyone according to the amount of money they had contributed. As time went on they were earning enough money to spend less time working and more on the program.

They met two or three times a week as they needed to in different houses. It was in one of those meetings they were given new directions. The extraterrestrials always communicated with them telepathically. This time the instructor said, "You are now at a stage when you can ask more people to join in the program. Then he explained step by step how to proceed with their next project. Because Tom was a better P.R. person they chose him to be their leader but they were all equal partners in this great effort.

During the last few months all four of them worked on writing a book on the global climate change and the state of the world. It was a well written book in great part because of their improved superior minds. The book was informative and reveal-ing and gave clear reasons why earth was heading to a full catastrophe. There was so much information in it that it was used in colleges and universities. They were asked to appear to T.V.

shows and radio talk shows and in a very short time they became well known all over the world. People at large were impressed by their etymology and their abilities to recall names, dates, and scientific facts so easily. And that was part of their program; to make them famous so that they could attract people.

Having accomplished that first step now they were having meetings of their own. Finally they open a school they called Lyceum for Human Integrity. It had a huge membership with well known intellectuals, academicians and plain simple people from all strata of society. That very same thing was starting by citizens in other countries with Lyceums becoming places where people could express their concerns about people's well being and the survival of the planet earth. With their own TV and Radio Stations they created a powerful media bypassing the established media that reached most people in the world. People now put a lot of pressure on their leaders and representatives to change to more friendly alternative energies.

At the same time there was another program going on; a human behavioral change of a more benevolent nature. Many selective people were given mental and physical powers to become the leaders in their own groups and so it went on for many years. Slowly but steadily the environment was changing for the better. The humans themselves were becoming a more benevolent people. But they had a long ways to go to accomplish their goal because there was a lot of resistance from the industries and an oligarchy which still had the power to dictate policies to maintain the status quo.

This time the Sukuans had devised a formula that would change the human genome to once and for all abolish the inherited bad gene from their cousin the chimpanzees and be closer to the Sukuans. But that would take a long time. It wasn't something taken by mouth or injected in their bodies it was spread out in the air and people inhaled it. Once it penetrated their bodies it was imbedded in their DNA and it started the long process of morphing humanity closer to the Sukuans. The change did not show right away it started with baby steps and it would take hundreds of years before it becomes a reality. In the meantime people all over the world were meeting and exchanging ideas and learning how to trust each other. They were learning for the first time in their barbarous lives how to live in a world without nuclear weapons and weapons of mass destruction. But that didn't mean that they will be unprotected to any outer space danger instead, they would adopt a defensive policy just like their powerful parent Sukuans.

Many years past since that fateful contact with the Sukuans; Tom and Suzy married and had two children Marty and Ken now married with children of their own. Tom true to his word didn't abuse his powers at the stock market. He made enough money for all four of them to live a comfortable life; after all he was well on to being a benevolent person. Tom and Suzy now retired in the outskirts of Portland Oregon in a large house for the children and grand children to visit. Loren and Karen also married and had three children who also married and had children of their own. After they retied they lived in Vancouver Washington only a few miles from Tom and Suzy. The two families often met during holidays and had a wonderful time and looked forward for their next get together.

There were many families all over the world like Tom's and Loren's who became more benevolent and lived peaceful lives. But for those who weren't personally contacted by the Sukuans had a good start but they had a long ways to go and even longer way for all humanity before they became like their benefactors. In the meantime the aggression and the violence subsided not only in America but all over the world. For the most part people in America and other countries stopped buying and using guns and as the time went on they learned to trust a little more each other. The leaders of the world met more frequently and signed long term treaties for reducing nuclear weapons and other weapons of mass destruction. Coal and other fuels that were so distractive to the environment were replaced with cleaner substitutes. People who had been working in the mines and other industries were given cleaner jobs with adequate compensation. It was a good start for the well being of humanity and all the other animals.

The Sukuans who sent all those spaceships with artificial intelligence to correct the mistake they had made three million years ago when they tried to humanize the chimpanzees would be very happy to know that this time their program of repairing the human genome was well on its way to be a success.

The End

95476497R00150

Made in the USA
Columbia, SC
12 May 2018